Hannah Dennison *PA Rev* but on leaving school landed a job as an obituary writer/ amateur dramatic reviewer for a Devon newspaper. The urge to travel was too strong, however, and she became an air stewardess, first with British Caledonian and then on private planes. Many adventures later she ended up in Los Angeles, where she met her future husband – and still lives there with him and their cat.

www.hannahdennison.com

www.hannahdennison.blogspot.com

@HannahLDennison

Murderous Mayhem at Honeychurch Hall

Hannah Dennison

CONSTABLE · LONDON

CONSTABLE

First published in the United States by Minotaur Books,
an imprint of St Martin's Publishing Group, 2017

This edition published in Great Britain in 2017 by Constable

Copyright © Hannah Dennison, 2017

1 3 5 7 9 10 8 6 4 2

The moral right of the author has been asserted.

A CIP catalogue record for this book
is available from the British Library.

ISBN: 978-1-47212-380-0

Printed and bound in Great Britain by
CPI Group (UK) Ltd, Croydon CR0 4YY

Papers used by Constable are from well-managed forests
and other responsible sources

MIX
Paper from
responsible sources
FSC® C104740

Constable
An imprint of
Little, Brown Book Group
Carmelite House
50 Victoria Embankment
London EC4Y 0DZ

An Hachette UK Company
www.hachette.co.uk

www.littlebrown.co.uk

*To my lovely and most vibrant mum, Brenda Dennison,
whose zest for life remains the inspiration behind
the Honeychurch Hall mysteries*

Acknowledgments

Writing can be a lonely labor of love, which is why treasured company, helpful guidance, selfless encouragement, and endless snacks fed by family and friends makes each book a group effort. But putting a book together requires a cast of dozens.

My heartfelt thanks go to:

My boss, Mark Davis, chairman of Davis Elen Advertising, who still hopes I'll grow weary of my writing "hobby" and focus on my job. Thank you for indulging my passion for storytelling.

My wonderful agent, Dominick Abel, whose candor and no-nonsense approach provide me with valuable counsel—thank you for everything you do.

The publishing team at St. Martin's Press—Marcia Markland, my dream editor; Shailyn Tavella, publicist extraordinaire and fellow chocolate enthusiast; the wonderful Talia Sherer; and the fabulously super-efficient Nettie Finn. You are all a joy to work with.

I'd like to thank the creative talents of David Baldeosingh Rotstein, who designed this exquisite book cover, and Pourio

Lee, my innovative Webmaster and creator of the gorgeous Earl of Grenville crest.

I'm grateful to Trina Lake, my UK publicist and dear friend, who continues to generously bring the UK edition of this series to the attention of British readers in exchange for a glass of wine.

A special thank-you to fellow author Angela Sanders, whose knowledge of every perfume invented since time began is utterly mind-boggling.

I'm indebted to Heather Hirdes of www.PupTalkPetCare .com, dog-whisperer and incredibly gifted animal photographer, who takes our two Vizslas out on all-day adventures to the Oregonian forests and lakes when I need to be pup-free. You are an angel in disguise.

And of course, I speak for all my kindred spirits when I thank YOU, the reader. Without you, this story would never be given life. I deeply appreciate my audience from around the world—especially those who have been with me from the very beginning—in particular, Barbara Ballard—and those who keep in touch. One unexpected gift is hearing from descendants of the Honeychurch clan and from those who have memories to share of the little hamlet of Honeychurch in North Devon.

As always, I couldn't do any of this without the support of my daughter, Sarah, my family, and my talented comrades in the trenches—Elizabeth Duncan, Clare Langley-Hawthorne, Daryl Wood Gerber, Kate Carlisle, and Mark Durel.

And lastly—but always first in my heart—I am grateful to my wonderful husband, Jason, who continues to champion my writing and amaze me with his endless patience, love, and infinite support. You will always be my hero.

Earl of Grenville
Created by Henry V in 1414, the title of Earl of Grenville has been passed down the male Honeychurch line and still exists today.

8TH EARL OF GRENVILLE
Rupert James
Honeychurch
B: 1800 D: 1880

EARL of GRENVILLE

Edward Rupert
9TH EARL OF GREENVILLE
B: 1835 D: 1899
Fought in Crimean War (1853–56). Decorated soldier, brought back mummified hawk.

Gerald James
Married American heiress—moved to New York. *Died in 1912 in the Arctic. He was a Polar explorer.
B: 1840 D: 1912

Elizabeth Edith
B: 1864 D: 1895
Never married. No children. *Fell from horse and broke her neck out hunting.

10TH EARL OF GRENVILLE
Harold Rupert
B: 1865 D: 1912
Fought in the Boer War (1899–1902).
*Died on *Titanic*.

James Rupert
B: 1873 D: 1950
Married showgirl. Ran a Turkish harem in London, fond of Burlesque & ran with Edward VII set.

Cassandra Mary
B: 1872 D: 1965
Never married. Lived in desert with a sheik, drove ambulances in WWI, war office WW2.

11TH EARL OF GRENVILLE
Max James
B: 1887 D: 1916
No children.
*Fighter pilot shot down over France in WWI.

12TH EARL OF GRENVILLE
Harold Edward
Edith's father.
B: 1900 D: 1940
*Died in London Blitz with wife.

Gerald Rupert
B: 1903 D: 1932
Lived in New York. Lost everything in the Wall Street Crash and committed suicide.

Rose Anne
B: 1907 D: 1988
Married German POW at end of war, moved to Germany. Huge scandal! Had 3 children.

13TH EARL OF GRENVILLE
Rupert James
B: 1921 D: 1959
Spitfire pilot WW2.
*Died in duel with Edith's lover Walter Stark.

Dowager Countess Edith Rose
B: 1929
Married Cousin Edward in 1959 to keep hold of title.

14TH EARL OF GRENVILLE
Cousin Edward
B: 1931 D: 1990
Returned from New York to inherit the title and marry Edith.

15TH EARL OF GRENVILLE
Rupert Max
B: 1963
1st wife: Kelly Jones
2nd wife: Lavinia Carew

Harold Rupert Max
B: 2005

Ad perseverate est ad triumphum

EARL *of* GRENVILLE

Chapter One

"Muriel!" I exclaimed. "What a lovely surprise. Come on in."

I gestured for the Little Dipperton postmistress to step inside out of the sun. Even though it wasn't quite ten in the morning, it promised to be another hot day.

Muriel's face was red. She was perspiring heavily in a black cotton dress and clutching a canvas shopping bag.

I spotted an old bicycle propped against the wall outside.

"I hope you didn't cycle in this heat," I said as I let her pass by and into the coolness of the West Gatehouse, the new home of Kat's Collectibles & Valuation Services.

Muriel looked miserable, which was hardly surprising. Her husband of nearly fifty years had died of a heart attack just two weeks before. Like many married couples in the village whose family had lived there for generations, they had known each other from birth.

Muriel took in the interior of the eighteenth-century gate-house. It was one of an identical pair that flanked the main entrance to the Honeychurch Hall estate. The dowager countess,

Lady Edith Honeychurch, had rented both out to me so I could set up my new business.

Cardboard boxes of stock ranging from antique dolls and bears to a variety of enameled boxes and Tunbridgeware, Tiffany lamps and Art Deco decorative objects, were stacked haphazardly along one wall.

"It's smaller than I expected." Muriel wrinkled her nose. "Paint."

"Yes. I just finished decorating."

The gatehouse consisted of one large living area, one and a half stories high with a gabled ceiling and two tiny dormer windows. At one point there had been a mezzanine level with a ladder that led up to a sleeping area, but the floorboards had been rotten and Edith agreed that I could take them out. A modernized galley kitchen and bathroom had been tacked on the rear back in the 1970s—judging by the décor. I planned on redoing both when I could afford it.

The place was light and airy with three bay windows that looked on to the driveway. I loved it. "It's perfect for me."

"Of course, Albert Jones used to live here. He was the gatekeeper before the Great War," Muriel went on. "His brother…" She paused, then frowned. "No, I can't remember his name. He lived in the other one. They were a strange lot. There was this scandal—"

"I'm using the East Gatehouse for storage at the moment," I said, stopping Muriel's notorious penchant for gossip in midflow. "I'm just waiting for shelves and display cabinets to be installed in this gatehouse and then I'll really be in business."

Muriel cocked her head. "You're not going to get many customers coming all the way up here, though, are you? You're a bit off the beaten track."

"I don't expect to," I said. "It's by appointment only." But Muriel had hit a nerve. My original dream of Mum and me owning an antique shop in London had ended the minute she impulsively bought the Carriage House here on the Honeychurch Hall estate. I had moved past all that now and was just determined to make things work in my new life. Besides, I had fallen in love with Honeychurch Hall and the Devonshire countryside and seeing my mother so happy made me happy, too.

Gesturing to a red damask–covered Knole sofa, I said, "Take a seat. I'll make you a cup of tea, unless you'd prefer some of Mrs. Cropper's homemade lemonade?"

Muriel pulled a face. "Peggy makes it too tart. Tea will do nicely."

As I busied myself in the galley kitchen I wondered why Muriel had come—and by bicycle no less. Although the village of Little Dipperton was less than a mile and a half from the Hall, the lanes were narrow, flanked by tall hedge banks and full of hairpin bends—very dangerous to cyclists and pedestrians alike.

I brought tea in on a tray along with a plate of McVitie's chocolate digestive biscuits.

"What is wrong with your car?" I had grown used to seeing Muriel zipping around the country roads in her brand-new canary-yellow Kia.

"It was stolen," she said bluntly.

I was surprised. "From the *village*?"

"No. Dartmouth. In the car park at Tesco's," said Muriel. "Last Friday."

"But that's terrible."

"And what with my Fred being gone…oh, Kat," she wailed. "I don't think I can carry on." She looked so utterly forlorn that I slipped beside her and took her hand in mine.

"It must be so hard to lose Fred," I said gently. "I know I miss my dad. You should talk to my mother about the first few weeks and how difficult it was for her."

She nodded and retrieved a lace handkerchief from a concealed pocket to dab at her eyes.

"Thank you, dear. You're very kind." Muriel gave a heavy sigh. "Forty-nine years married and never a cross word said."

Somehow I doubted that. Many a time I'd heard Muriel complain that Fred spent too much time up at the Hare & Hounds pub and at the Newton Abbot racetrack.

"It probably hasn't sunk in yet," I said. "It must feel surreal."

"It's real enough, but it looks like your father made sure Iris was well provided for, which is more than I can say for Fred. I keep looking out of my bedroom window, expecting to see him working out there in the churchyard. It was the stress of the court case that did him in, you know, but we had to do it."

"It's tough, I know."

"Fred was my life. He was a good husband."

Muriel's comments echoed my mother's about my father. Much as I had adored Dad, he had been very controlling, and yet, as we passed the one-year milestone of his death, he seemed to have evolved into a saint.

"But you should be careful. I've had a bout of shoplifting in the general store—just bits, sweeties and chocolate—that kind of thing," said Muriel, promptly changing the subject. "And what with the upcoming Skirmish and that dangerous criminal on the run—"

"Skirmish?"

"That's what we locals call the re-enactment," said Muriel. "There were a series of skirmishes before the siege at Honeychurch Hall during the English Civil War."

"Ah. I didn't realize," I said.

"The old earl started the tradition—before my time of course. You've got the Roundheads and the Cavaliers—that'll be the Royalists, as we prefer to call them in these parts. They'll be setting up camp right outside your back door. You'll have a lot of strangers milling about for three whole days."

"Maybe I'll get some new customers," I said lightly.

"I hope you've got an alarm." She pointed to the windows. "And curtains. You're very exposed, and with all these strangers—"

"I'll be careful," I said. "Did you want me to value something for you today?" Over the past few weeks, I had had a slew of antique armor and weaponry to value or sell that someone had discovered in a cellar or attic. Most were reproductions.

"Oh no." Muriel opened her canvas bag and handed me a jar. "I brought you some homemade strawberry jam from Fred's last batch."

I was touched. "That's very kind. I love strawberry jam. Thank you."

We fell into an uncomfortable silence. I could sense that Muriel wanted to tell me something by the way she was playing with her lace handkerchief, but she seemed to be reluctant to speak. It also occurred to me that it was a Thursday morning and she should have been manning the post office. "Is everything alright?"

"I wanted to ask a favor, but it must be in confidence," she began. "I don't want anybody else knowing my personal business."

As she was *the* village busybody, I thought Muriel's comment ironic. "Of course not."

"I think his lordship is going to evict me."

"What?" I exclaimed. "Why?"

"A Jarvis has run the post office since 1828. A Jarvis has mown the churchyard since the Gunpowder Plot. A Jarvis has—"

"The post office belongs to the Honeychurch estate?" I knew that most of the cottages in the small village of Little Dipperton were tenant occupied, but I hadn't thought the post office and general store were as well.

"Every cottage with a blue door belongs to the Honeychurches," said Muriel.

"But why would Rupert evict you?" I said again. "Who would run the post office? Are you thinking of retiring?"

"Fred handled all the money," she said. "He died so suddenly and well … he didn't leave a Will. I don't understand things like probate." She started to cry softly into her lace handkerchief.

"Do you have a solicitor?"

Muriel nodded.

"Then don't worry," I said. "Let him sort it out for you."

"But I can't afford to pay his fee or my rent until he does."

"I'm sure Rupert—his lordship—would understand if you talked to him," I said.

"No. You don't know him like I do." Muriel shook her head. "You see him very differently from us in the village."

"What does Violet say?"

Muriel scowled. "We've fallen out."

"I thought you were best friends!"

Muriel snorted with contempt. "I don't want to talk about it. It's enough having to read about it in the papers."

Too late I remembered the sordid details of their disagreement over the "catastrophic pruning" of Violet's climbing roses that had made the front page in the *Dipperton Deal*.

There was another uncomfortable silence. I just didn't know what to say. "You mentioned a favor?"

"I want you to lend me some money," Muriel blurted out. "Not much. Just a little."

My heart sank. Dad had been a tax inspector and I knew exactly what he would have said on the matter. He would quote Polonius from Hamlet, *"Neither a borrower nor lender be,"* and I totally agreed with him.

"It's just for a couple of weeks," Muriel said quickly. "Just to tide me over."

I knew for a fact that probate—especially when there was no Will—often took months.

"We can't have a post office with no electricity," Muriel went on. "Not that we've been cut off. Yet. My niece Bethany is holding the fort whilst I'm here. I'm training her up to take over—unless his lordship kicks me out."

"I know Bethany," I said. "She's smart."

Muriel just sat there wearing a beaten-puppy expression. "I don't know who else to ask."

It was excruciatingly awkward. I hesitated. "How much do you need?"

"A thousand pounds."

"A *thousand* pounds?"

"It's not as if you'd miss it." Muriel gestured to my stock. "Look at all that stuff. Just a limb from one of those dolls would fetch five hundred."

"That's hardly t-t-true," I stammered.

"And you were on the Telly for years," she said. "Everyone knows people on the Telly get paid millions of pounds."

I was so shocked at Muriel's nerve that it took me a minute to speak. "I don't know what gave you that idea," I said, forcing a smile. "I'm sorry. I can't at the moment." Or ever, I wanted to add but held my tongue.

"Oh. Then I'll be living on the streets." Muriel slumped into the sofa. "Even a hundred pounds would help."

I knew I was going to regret it, but I felt completely pushed into a corner. Without saying a word, I went over to my desk and withdrew my checkbook from the drawer. "I am willing to *give* you—not lend you, Muriel—three hundred pounds and that's all I can do."

"That's very kind," Muriel whispered. "I wouldn't ask if I wasn't desperate."

"But there is one condition."

Muriel regarded me with suspicion.

"You must promise to talk to Rupert this afternoon and tell him what you just told me. Is that fair?"

"Alright," she said grudgingly.

I handed Muriel the check feeling a mass of conflicting emotions—mostly resentment. Things with my new venture had been much slower than I had anticipated, and although I did have some savings, I couldn't really afford to throw away three hundred pounds.

Muriel got to her feet. "I'd better be going."

"Did you want me to run you home?" For some reason my resentment made me feel guilty. "We could put your bicycle in the back of my Golf?"

"No, thank you. I really like riding my bicycle," said Muriel. "I hope you enjoy Fred's jam."

As I saw her to the door, Muriel paused. "Dartmouth Antique Emporium is a good idea. You'll get lots of tourists coming through."

And with that, she waved a cheerful good-bye and left.

As I watched her mount her old-fashioned bicycle and put the canvas bag in the pannier, I thought of two things. First of all, that jam was the most expensive jam I had ever bought. And second, how did Muriel know that I'd been looking at renting a temporary space in Dartmouth for the summer? I hadn't even mentioned it to my mother.

At that moment my mobile rang. The caller I.D. read: "Mum."

"Hello. Speak of the devil—"

"You must come quickly!"

"Are you alright?" Not another drama, I thought. "You sound agitated."

"Eric Pugsley and I are in Cromwell Meadows—"

"You're with *Eric*? Willingly?" This was a first. Mum's relationship with her neighbor and his "disgusting" scrapyard had always been rocky. With its pyramid of tires, discarded pieces of farm machinery and the many "end-of-life" vehicles in various stages of decay that littered the far end of the field I couldn't say I blamed her. It really was an eyesore. Fortunately, the view was only noticeable from Mum's upstairs office.

"Now, before you jump to conclusions, Katherine, I want to make it clear that this had nothing to do with me."

A familiar sense of dread began to pool in the pit of my stomach. "Do I have to sit down to hear this?"

"Of course not. It's so exciting," Mum trilled. "Eric's dug up a body."

Chapter Two

"Eric was digging a trench for a sewer line," said Mum. "He came screaming to the back door in a terrible state—quite hysterical. He's gone to fetch his lordship."

"It's not a body; it's a skeleton, Mother," I said as we peered into a muddy hole. All I could see was the metal top of what looked like a lobster-tailed pot helmet and the upper half of a skull protruding from a thick layer of sludge. "You had me worried for a moment."

"Her ladyship wasn't lying when she said that Cromwell Meadows was riddled with the bodies of the fallen," my mother went on. "Did you know that two hundred thousand people died in the English Civil War?"

"No."

"And the whole population of England was only five million at the time."

Suddenly the morning didn't seem so bright. With the smell of summer in the air, hedgerows flush with the frothy white blossoms of hawthorn and blackthorn, purple dog violets, wood sorrel and golden saxifrage it was hard to imagine that we were standing on the site that saw so much death in the battle to save Honeychurch Hall over 350 years ago.

"And to think he might have lain there for a few more centuries if that monstrosity hadn't collapsed." My mother gestured to what was left of Eric's battered old caravan that he had been using as an office. "I'll be glad to see the back of *that*."

For the past three days Eric had been cutting up the old van with an axe and a chainsaw. Now all that remained were the fruits of his labor in an ugly pile and an iron chassis that resembled a beached whale.

"Perhaps now he'll change his mind and stick his new caravan elsewhere. Shouldn't he have to get planning permission?" Mum continued. "You can't just pick a spot and start digging out a foundation."

"Well, there's no danger of that now," I said. "The forensic anthropologist will have to cordon off the area. This place will be teeming with experts before you can blink."

"I hope it's not just a peasant from the village," Mum grumbled. "It would be very exciting if he was a key member of the family. One more for my tree."

As the unofficial historian for the six-hundred-year-old Honeychurch clan, my mother had become increasingly obsessed with its lineage. She was determined to be one hundred percent accurate. At first, the fifteenth Earl of Grenville, Lord Rupert Honeychurch, had found her constant questions irritating. But as the months marched on, Mum's enthusiasm for tracing his ancestors had infected him, too.

"I think that's highly unlikely," I said. "For a start, the Honeychurches were Royalists and fought for King Charles. They wouldn't wear lobster-tailed pot helmets. Roundheads wore those. And secondly, aren't the Honeychurches all buried in the family mausoleum at St. Mary's church?"

"Oh. Good point."

"It might not even be a soldier."

"Why?"

"Because I don't think that is a seventeenth-century helmet."

There was something odd about the smoothness of the crown. The skull of the lobster-tailed pot helmet was often fluted. Generally, they were made in two sections joined by a raised comb that ran from front to back. Although this did have a nasal bar, it was so wide that it would have impaired the wearer's vision.

As I studied the peculiar iron framework I realized I just had to know if my hunch was right.

Eric had conveniently left behind a handful of tools, including a bucket to scoop out the water.

I grabbed it and crouched down at the edge. "Hold on to my hand," I said.

"What on earth are you doing?" Mum exclaimed. "You'll get filthy for your meeting this morning. You're even wearing a skirt for a change."

"I just need to check something."

"You told me not to touch anything," she protested.

"Well, I'm not touching *him*, if that's what you mean," I said. "Humor me."

"I'm always humoring you." But my mother obliged and gripped my hand tightly as I leaned over the grave.

I scooped out three buckets of the rank, brackish liquid until the water level was low enough to reveal the entire skull and part of a twiggy collarbone.

"Katherine!" Mum gasped in horror. "Is that . . . is that—?"

"Oh God," I whispered. "It's not a man, it's a woman, isn't it?"

"And it's not a helmet!" Mum exclaimed. "It's a scold's bridle! How cruel. How absolutely horrible."

Now the headgear was fully exposed, we stared in dismay at the heavy iron hinged framework that encased the skull. The vicious bridle-bit ending in nine sharp iron points left nothing to the imagination.

"That was in her mouth, Mum," I said. "It pressed down on top of her tongue—"

"No!" Mum flapped her arms in alarm. "Don't tell me any more. It's wicked! What an evil thing to do."

"Those contraptions weighed around fourteen pounds," I went on. "The victims used to be paraded through the streets. The bridle was often fastened so tightly that if the poor wretch was whipped, the pain caused the jaw to shatter. It's barbaric!"

"Do you suppose she was a witch?" Mum whispered.

"Possibly," I said. "But scold bridles—or branks, as they were sometimes called—were not just put on witches and heretics or women who gossiped in the village. Sometimes it was a form of corporal punishment. If she was involved in the war, maybe she presented a threat of some kind?"

"Like what?" Mum demanded.

"You're supposed to be the historian, not me," I said. "But I would assume that given the fact that the Honeychurches were Royalists and, literally, just two fields away Lavinia's ancestors—the Carews—were Roundheads, maybe she was a spy?"

"Don't touch anything!" came a familiar shout. "Stay back! Stay back, I say!"

We turned to see Detective Inspector Shawn Cropper hurrying toward us across the grass waving madly. His trademark beige trench coat flapped open as he ran.

"Why is he wearing a coat in this weather?" muttered Mum.

Behind Shawn, but striding far more sedately, came Rupert Honeychurch and then Eric. Rupert looked cool in jeans and an open-necked pale-blue checked shirt with short sleeves. He towered above Eric and his woolen beanie hat and had the walk of a man born to entitlement.

Shawn joined us. He was out of breath. My stomach did an unexpected flip. The thing was that I was still attracted to him with his large brown eyes, impossibly long eyelashes and tousled curly brown hair. I noted food stains on his Thomas the Tank Engine tie. Whether this tie was a nod to Shawn's passion for steam trains or whether it was a gift from his twin boys was anyone's guess. But I had to admit our meeting was awkward.

It was the first time since I'd seen him after our one-and-only dinner date. Halfway through the meal Shawn suddenly came down with a stomach bug. In his race to get me home, and him to his bathroom—Shawn flatly refused to use the restaurant facilities—he was pulled over for speeding by two of his own men. To make matters worse, Shawn had to dart behind a hedge to save further embarrassment. He didn't ask me out again.

We greeted each other with curt nods and brief smiles.

"We've not touched a thing, Officer," said Mum. "We were standing guard, awaiting further instructions."

The three men peered into the grave.

Eric turned to Mum and me with suspicion. "The water level's gone down!"

"It's the heat of the morning," said Mum. "But as you can see, the skeleton is most likely a female. That's a scold's bridle that she's wearing. We think she was a witch or a spy."

"Not one of ours then, Iris," said Rupert with a wink. "How disappointing."

"Unless someone in the twenty-first century decided to try it on his wife," Mum quipped.

"You really are quite witty today, Iris," said Shawn.

Mum smirked. She had been in very good spirits ever since she had turned in *Ravished* a few weeks ago. It was her latest book in the international bestselling Star-Crossed Lovers series that she penned secretly under the pseudonym of Krystalle Storm.

"I know a few gossips in the village that could take a lesson from seeing one of those," Rupert put in with a grin.

"But rest assured, milord," said Mum, "the Honeychurch family tree is coming along exceptionally well. I've almost finished the seventeenth century. Quite a lively bunch."

Shawn pulled out a roll of crime scene tape from one of his voluminous trench coat pockets. "I'm sure this is very interesting," he said. "But until we ascertain what happened here, this area is strictly out-of-bounds. Nothing—and, I repeat, nothing—must be touched."

"Surely you're being a bit overzealous," said Rupert.

"Just following procedure, milord," Shawn said.

"But . . . what about my new office?" Eric whined. "I've got a Portakabin being delivered tomorrow morning."

"Sorry, Eric. The Portakabin will have to wait," said Shawn.

Eric looked crestfallen.

"Or you could put your new office elsewhere," Mum suggested. "How about over there?" She gestured to a giant car crusher machine at the other end of the field. "I always felt your office was too far away from the action."

"Wait a moment—" Rupert took Eric's shovel and, leaning over the grave, gently pushed the tip into one wall. "What's this?"

"Milord," Shawn cried. "I must protest! I must caution you against touching anything in the grave until we have gone through the proper channels."

But Rupert was on a mission. "I'm just going to see what it is!"

Gently he worked at the earth until the sides began to give way to expose a broken lattice of ribs. Lodged between two of them was a dagger crusted with earth.

Mum gasped. "Is that a knife?"

"Milord!" Shawn's protestations met deaf ears as Rupert swiftly retrieved a cotton handkerchief from his pocket, knelt down and pulled the dagger free. It was long—about twelve or thirteen inches.

"It's a dagger alright," he said, grimly presenting it to all of us.

"It looks like a main gauche," I said.

"A what?" Mum demanded.

"A main gauche was a dagger that was used to parry incoming thrusts with one hand whilst the other wielded a rapier," I said.

"So she *was* a soldier," said Mum.

I shook my head. "I doubt it. A man wouldn't be wearing a scold's bridle."

Rupert began to wipe the blade clean. "Do you have your loupe handy, Katherine?"

Given the fact I had neither handbag nor pockets, I wondered where he thought I kept it.

"Sorry, no. I could run and get it."

"No need," said Rupert. "It looks as if there is a crest engraved on the blade."

We all crowded around to take a closer look.

"That's the Honeychurch crest," Mum declared. "I'm certain of it."

"Your eyesight is far better than mine," I said.

"I must protest," Shawn said again.

"I've been staring at the Honeychurch coat of arms or crest or whatever you want to call it for months" said Mum. "I'd recognize it anywhere."

"You're right," said Rupert excitedly. "There are the two hawks flanking our shield. These daggers were made specifically for their owner at great expense. It's most unusual for such a thing to be left behind."

"Unless it was deliberate," said Mum.

"Deliberate?" Rupert regarded my mother with growing incredulity.

"Mum ... the placement of the dagger—"

"But surely you aren't implying—"

"I most certainly am!" Mum exclaimed. "Whoever is lying in that watery grave was murdered."

Chapter Three

"For once, I agree with Iris," Shawn said. "I'm afraid I'm going to have to declare this a crime scene."

Mum laughed. "I would think it highly unlikely we'd catch the culprit *now*, don't you, milord?"

"It's not like we've discovered the remains of Richard the Third," Rupert agreed.

"But taken into consideration the scold's bridle...she was probably tortured before she was murdered."

"That's awful," I whispered. "But who was she? Why go to all that trouble?"

"She was a spy," Mum said again. "Caught in the act and dispatched by whoever owned that dagger."

"And to think I've been above her all these years," whispered Eric. "You know, it's strange, because sometimes I used to feel I was being watched."

Mum rolled her eyes.

"Do you have some stakes, Eric?" Shawn asked.

"She's hardly a vampire," Mum muttered.

Eric nodded.

"Go and get half a dozen, there's a good man."

So Eric did.

"What do you think will happen to her?" I asked.

Rupert shrugged. "I've no idea."

"It doesn't seem right that she should have suffered so much only to end up in an unmarked grave," I said.

"If you ask me," Mum said slowly, "I think there was a bit of jiggery-pokery going on."

"I beg your pardon!" Rupert was stunned. "Jiggery-pokery! What exactly are you suggesting?"

"I'm just saying that the Honeychurch clan are notorious for hushing up scandals." Mum reddened. "I don't know why I said that. It just came out."

"And I'm glad it did, Iris." Shawn chimed in. "Because I agree with you again. That's twice in one day."

"What kind of jiggery-pokery?" exclaimed a voice heavy with adenoids. We turned to greet Rupert's long-suffering wife, Lady Lavinia Honeychurch, plodding toward us.

Mum and I looked at each other and gasped. "Whatever happened to you?"

Lavinia looked awful. Her pale aquiline face was marred by an enormous black eye. Her lip was puffy and swollen.

"Lav, darling!" Rupert exclaimed. "You really should be resting!"

"I'm perfectly alright," she said with a slight lisp that exposed a missing front tooth. Upon spotting the skull in the watery grave, she added, "And obviously much better off than whoever is laying down there!"

Dressed in her usual attire of jodhpurs and short-sleeved polo shirt and with her blond hair crushed beneath a heavy slumber net, Lavinia looked even more disheveled than usual.

"Are you okay?" I asked.

"Came off and then got kicked in the face," she said cheerfully.

"Which horse?" I said.

"Jupiter got stung by a horsefly." Lavinia winced. "Got three cracked ribs—ouch." She bent over in pain.

"Ribs seems to be the *nom du jour*," said Mum.

"The vet strapped me up," Lavinia went on.

"The *vet*?" said Mum.

"Much better than old Bodger our G.P. He's *ab-so-lute-ly* hopeless—ouch!" She winced again. "Golly."

"Lav, darling," said Rupert again. "Please go and lie down. You *must* rest."

It made a change for Rupert to show his concern for her. Usually he seemed so indifferent.

"I've got some Vicodin left," Mum said. "I'll give you a few. They're really good."

"Mum! You mustn't," I said.

"She can't take drugs," Rupert said. "She's allergic."

"They must have expired anyway," I said. "It was ages ago when you broke your hand, Mum."

"Rubbish. Expiry dates are just one way those drug companies make you buy more drugs."

It was then that Lavinia noticed the dagger in Rupert's hands. "Goodness. Is that one of yours . . . or one of ours?"

I thought it amusing that after centuries the Royalist Honeychurches and the Roundhead Carews still seemed to be on opposite sides.

"His lordship found it in the grave," said Mum.

"You must get Daddy to take a look, Rupert—he's an expert at this sort of thing—or my brother."

"I'll certainly confer with Aubrey," said Rupert. "But I'm definitely not involving Piers."

"And who is Aubrey?" Mum asked politely.

"Daddy is a whiz at military history and armor and swords. He's got an even larger collection of weapons than Rupert—"

"Not by that much," said Rupert.

"The Roundheads were much better equipped than the Cavaliers—"

"Royalists," said Rupert. "We prefer to call them Royalists—"

"*And* much better soldiers," Lavinia went on. "That's why we won."

"Only because we had to pay outrageous, crippling fines to Oliver-bloody-Cromwell," snarled Rupert. "*And* your wretched family."

"I thought the Hall was saved by your steward?" Mum put in.

"It was," Rupert said. "But . . . I don't want to talk about it. Let's move on now. Iris? How are the costumes coming along?"

"I'm finished with yours and Master Harry's," said Mum. "I've nearly finished the dowager countess's and Lady Lavinia's." My mother's handiwork with the needle was well known to everyone at the Hall. In fact, I had a steamer trunk full of beautiful costumes she had made in her teenage years for the traveling fair and boxing emporium.

"Good," said Rupert. "You can deliver them all this afternoon."

"*T-t-oday?*" Mum stammered. "Yes. Yes of course."

"Come at three-thirty."

"I'll be taking the dagger, milord, if you don't mind," said Shawn. Rupert handed it over somewhat reluctantly, whereupon Shawn promptly dropped it into one of his ever-ready Ziploc bags.

"And Lav, go and lie down and rest." And with that, Rupert walked off.

"You should do what his lordship advises, milady," said Mum.

"I know." Lavinia stood there but made no attempt to move. She glanced over at Shawn, who was deep in discussion with Eric a few yards away. "I'm frightfully parched, Iris. Aren't you?"

"Not really."

"But you *must* be," Lavinia insisted. "Standing out here in the hot sun. You look fit to drop."

"I've got the costumes to finish—"

"But you *must* be parched," she said again.

"Really I'm not. Or... should I be? Oh. I see." Mum took the hint. "Would you care to come inside for a cup of tea or coffee, milady?"

"Oh. How kind! That would be lovely," said Lavinia. "Thank you. I expect you're too busy to join us, Katherine. And besides, your mother and I will be discussing my costume."

I was amused by Lavinia's blatant attempt to get my mother alone. "As it happens, I *do* have time for a quick cup," I couldn't help but say.

"But aren't you taking Edith to the railway station?"

"Not quite yet."

"I think her ladyship wants to talk to me about her *costume* alone," said Mum.

"Do call me Lavinia, Iris."

And of course, this personal request to drop her title meant that something was afoot. "I know when I'm not wanted," I joked.

"Oh, but you are—" Lavinia seemed embarrassed. "It's just . . . well . . ."

"Private," Mum declared.

"But perhaps . . ." Lavinia hesitated. "I'd quite like Katherine's opinion."

I shot my mother a triumphant look.

We trooped back to the Carriage House and into the kitchen. Lavinia sat down at the table. I headed over to the counter and put the kettle on whilst Mum brought down three of her coveted coronation mugs. Her knowledge of anything remotely to do with the Royal family bordered on the obsessive.

"I think Queen Alexandra for you this morning, Lavinia," said Mum, brandishing a porcelain mug bearing the image of a rather severe Alexandra of Denmark. "She was married to King Edward the Seventh and he was a notorious womanizer, too."

"Mum!" I said, appalled.

Lavinia crumpled and started to sniffle. "It's true. Your mother is right. I think Rupert is having another affair."

Rupert's indiscretions were legendary, but, though I don't mean to sound unkind, Lavinia had to have known what she was letting herself in for. Their initial engagement was called off when he eloped with one of the staff during a New Year's Eve dinner—between courses, no less—and subsequently married her. It was only following his first wife's fatal accident that Rupert agreed to marry Lavinia to avoid being disinherited by his mother, the dowager countess—although whether he was or wasn't remains a mystery.

"Now, what makes you think his lordship is doing such a thing?" Mum asked.

"He's been frightfully kind to me recently. And this morning—you heard him—he told me I should rest three times." Lavinia attempted to blow her nose but cried out in pain.

"Have you found telltale signs like lipstick on his collar?" said Mum. "Or a lingering scent of perfume?"

"I don't need telltale signs," said Lavinia miserably. "I told you. He's just been too nice. When Jupiter kicked me in the face, Rupert even made me a cold compress. Well, he put a flannel under the cold tap, but he was gentle." She began to sniffle again. "Usually he would have said, 'Jolly bad luck, Lav.' What if he leaves me? I think I'd die."

"Now you're being silly," said Mum firmly. "And besides, there's no danger of him ever leaving you. He relies one hundred percent on your money."

"Mother!" I said again. "For heaven's sake!"

Lavinia brightened. "Oh. Yes. Yes, of course he does, but—no." Lavinia bit her lip. "Since Daddy just passed the torch to Piers, it's Piers who is now holding the purse strings."

"And why should this matter?" Mum asked.

Lavinia struggled to compose herself. She swallowed several times. "Piers told me that if Rupert ever strayed again he'd cut me off without a penny."

"Maybe you'd be better off," I said.

"Are you *mad*?" Lavinia exclaimed. "Apart from the fact that divorce would shame the Carew name, what about poor darling Harry? He adores his father and ..." Her eyes glistened with tears. "Besides, I love Rupert. He is my life."

"Can you guess how long this has been going on?" said Mum briskly.

"A few weeks, but recently he's been out an awful lot at night. He says he's shooting rabbits in the Lower Meadows, but I've never heard the sound of a shotgun and I've kept all my windows open because it's been so hot."

"I've not heard any guns at night; have you, Kat?"

"No," I said.

"And he's been playing a lot of music," Lavinia went on. "A lot of Elton John."

"Elton *John*?" Mum exclaimed. "Oh dear. Then it must be serious."

"I think you should confront him," I said.

"I couldn't possibly!"

"You have two choices," I said. "You ask him outright, or you let it go and accept that it's just the way he is."

"Even if your brother threatens to cut you off if you stay with his lordship," Mum went on, "he's still got too much to lose."

"But he doesn't," Lavinia wailed, then yelped in pain. "The Hall will go directly to Harry. Edith never changed her Will. There's no reason for Rupert to stay with me at all."

I felt sorry for Lavinia but, at the same time, alarmed. Was her self-esteem so very low? True, she wasn't the sharpest tool in the proverbial shed, but she was very sweet and kind and there wasn't a mean bone in her body.

"Men always go back to their wives eventually," Mum declared. "Kat can shed some insight into being the other woman because she *has* been the other woman—"

"I have *not* been the other woman," I snapped. "David was already separated when we met. He told me he was getting a divorce and I believed him."

"But how do I know that Rupert hasn't said the same thing to *her*?" said Lavinia.

"Well, never mind all that," Mum said quickly. "Do you know who it is?"

"I think ... I have a feeling it's Jessica—but she likes to be called Jess."

"Who?" Mum and I chorused.

"Daddy's new wife," Lavinia said with disgust. "Didn't you know he married again?"

"Well, we would have known if we'd been invited to the wedding—"

"Why would we have been invited, Mother?" I said. "We've never met Lavinia's father."

"Nobody was invited," said Lavinia. "It was all very sudden. Piers is still livid."

"I didn't realize you lost your mother recently," said Mum. "I'm so sorry."

"Oh God, don't be sorry," said Lavinia. "It was *ab-so-lute-ly* yonks ago. Daddy's been a widower for over twenty years. I mean ... we'd never even heard of *Jess* until Easter Sunday."

"And you think that's when the affair began?" Mum caught my eye and I could see she was thinking the same thing. Lavinia was being paranoid.

"You think his lordship and Jess knew each other before she married your father?" Mum asked.

"No, I don't think so." Lavinia frowned. "I believe she comes from the Midlands or somewhere ghastly. She tries to pretend she's one of us, but she can't hide her accent. Piers is convinced that she's after Daddy's money, but *apparently,* she's got loads of her own."

"That would be pretty low, even for Rupert," said Mum. "Are you sure there isn't anyone else who might fit the bill?"

"Like who?" Lavinia thought for a moment, then brightened. "Do you think Alfred could be persuaded to ... well ... follow Rupert for cash?"

"Alfred? Why would Alfred want to do something like that?" said Mum just a little too heartily.

I shot Mum a warning look. Unbeknown to everyone except my mother and me, Alfred was still on parole. He'd already had a few narrow escapes with the law and we didn't want to tempt fate.

"Alfred mentioned that he'd done some sort of security work in the past," Lavinia went on—which I suppose was one way of calling breaking and entering.

"Mum—"

"But do you really want to know, Lavinia?" said Mum in earnest. "And once you do know, what are you planning on doing with the information? I thought you didn't want to confront his lordship."

"I suppose I just want to know before Piers finds out."

"But I thought you said Piers would cut you off without a penny if he found out?" Mum looked at me with exasperation. "I do feel you should really think this through."

"Oh."

Poor Lavinia.

"Well, let's just take one step at a time," said Mum. "I'll talk to Alfred—"

"You can't tell him *anything*!" Lavinia squeaked.

"Just the bare bones. I know."

Lavinia brightened again. "Good. That's sorted. Can we talk about my costume now?"

"Yes, dear."

"You must promise to make me look spectacular. I must look beautiful for Rupert."

"Well, let's hope your bruise has gone down by then, and you really need to get that front tooth capped," said Mum. "But meanwhile, come upstairs with me. I have something for you."

"Not the Vicodin?" I said. "You know it's addictive."

"What's addictive?" The dowager countess, Lady Edith Honeychurch, entered the kitchen accompanied by Mr. Chips, her tan-and-white Jack Russell terrier, who proceeded to tear around the room greeting everyone with excited barks.

Edith was carrying a monogrammed overnight suitcase of pale-brown leather that I guessed was circa 1950. She was wearing a tailored suit of pale apricot with a white ruffled shirt, American tan-colored tights and light-brown lace-up shoes. Her hair carried the chemical aroma of the newly permed.

"Goodness, Edith," Lavinia remarked. "You'll boil to death wearing that in London."

I gestured to the suitcase. "I would have come and picked you up at the Hall."

"Nonsense," said Edith. "I may be the wrong side of eighty-five, but I'm not in the grave yet. It's as light as a feather, and since I'm going to be stuck in a stuffy conference room all weekend, I need all the exercise I can get."

Mum cleared her throat. "Lavinia—her ladyship, I mean— mentioned that you ... well ... you might actually be speaking to HRH The Princess Royal."

"Anne is the Royal Patron of the Pony Club," said Edith, "so yes. She's a personal friend. Why?"

Mum's jaw dropped. "You say she's a *personal* friend."

"Did you want me to give her a message, Iris?" I detected a twinkle in Edith's eye, although she kept a straight face.

Mum turned pink. "Can you find out if she will be the mysterious Royal who will be attending the Skirmish next weekend?"

"Anne? Here?" Edith seemed surprised. "Attending the *re-enactment*? What on earth gave you that idea?"

"Muriel at the post office told me that every year a member of the Royal family is the guest of honor," said Mum. "We don't want Emma Bunton."

"Who is Emma Bunton?" Edith demanded.

"She's one of the Spice Girls," said Lavinia, adding, "You know, 'Tell me what you want, what you really, really want.' It was top of the charts for ages."

"Ah yes." Edith nodded. "I wonder if she still doesn't know what he wants."

"Emma is one hundred and third in line to the throne," said Mum helpfully. "I mean, beggars can't be choosers and if we get Emma *c'est la vie,* but I'd much prefer to snag Anne."

"Quite," said Edith, giving me a wink.

Glancing at the clock, I said, "What time is your train?"

"Eleven-o-five," said Edith.

"We must go!" I exclaimed.

I picked up Edith's suitcase—it weighed a ton—and staggered to my waiting car.

Chapter Four

"I'm glad we left when we did, Edith," I said.

We'd been parked along the main drive for the past ten minutes waiting for an enormous marquee rental truck to navigate a narrow five-bar gate into the field in front of the Hall. There was a hive of activity as a team of men in white overalls scurried around erecting an assortment of tents. Nearby, a flat-bed lorry was unloading a row of Portaloos and lining them up along the fence.

Preparations for the Skirmish had begun.

"Should I turn around and take the service road instead?" I said anxiously. We'd had to drop Mr. Chips back at the stables where Alfred would be caring for him in Edith's absence and were already cutting it fine.

"He'll be through in a moment," said Edith. "I told Rupert to use the gate along Cavalier Lane, but he wouldn't listen."

There was an ugly crack of splintering wood as the truck clipped the gatepost and bore it away attached to the bumper along with copious bits of hedge, brambles and earth.

Edith gave a heavy sigh. "There. I knew it. This whole thing is a nightmare, and if the weather breaks the park will resemble the Western Front."

"I heard that the re-enactment is an annual tradition," I said as we were finally able to continue our journey. I took in the beauty of the mile-long drive that was lined with rhododendrons, azaleas and camellias bursting in a rainbow of colors. "The village has talked of nothing else for weeks."

"Oh yes, my grandfather started it when he came back from the Boer War in 1902," Edith said. "And of course Rupert acts like a little boy. Any excuse to show off his skills with the rapier— Oh how *infuriating*!"

Eric's tractor was parked and partially blocking the entrance between the gatehouses. A small trailer held a ladder and colored bunting. As we squeezed through the gap I saw he was putting the finishing touches to a large billboard in front of the West Gatehouse.

THE ROUNDHEADS ARE COMING TO HONEYCHURCH HALL!

MAY 22–23

IT'S 1643 AND THE SECOND YEAR OF THE BITTER ENGLISH

CIVIL WAR

COME AND SEE THE CONFLICT UNFOLD, WITH PIKE, MUSKET,

CANNON AND HORSE

HOG ROAST 6:30 P.M. IN HONEYCHURCH PARK (£7.50 PER HEAD)

BILLETING (£5 PER TENT)

PARKING (£10)

SPONSORED BY: LORD & LADY HONEYCHURCH

LIKE US ON FACEBOOK AND FOLLOW US ON TWITTER!

As we turned into Cavalier Lane *another* flatbed delivery van—this time jammed with chairs and trestle tables—turned up and we had to stop again to let it pass.

Edith pointed to Jazzbo Jenkins, my vintage Merrythought Jerry mouse and lucky mascot who always sat on my dashboard. "Well, he's not doing us any good today, is he?"

Perhaps it "wasn't my place"—to quote my mother, who remained in awe of the gentry, as she insisted on calling the dowager countess and her ilk—but I just had to ask. "It must cost a fortune to host the re-enactment." I knew for a fact that it was a constant struggle to keep the vast estate and the little village going.

"It *does* cost a fortune," Edith agreed. "And because of the government enforcing all these new health and safety insurance requirements, this could be our last year—unless we make a profit or at the very least break even."

"I'm sorry to hear that."

"Of course, our local English Civil War society holds fundraisers throughout the year, but most of the money comes from people who, for some extraordinary reason, love to dress up and play 'let's pretend.'"

We threaded our way through the narrow country lanes toward Little Dipperton, following the stream down through a leafy tunnel of overarching trees and skirting Coffin Mire.

I always got the creeps at the bottom of the hill where the burned-out shell that used to be Bridge Cottage sat dank, neglected and forlorn. The cottage was one of the few that no longer belonged to the estate. It had been on the market for months, but the location was so depressing, there had been very little interest.

Parked in an adjacent bridleway stood Rupert's black Range Rover.

"Now what's he doing here?" Edith mused.

"Perhaps he's thinking about buying Bridge Cottage?" I said. "Wouldn't it give you some of your land back? Even if you never rebuilt the house."

Edith looked surprised. "Ah, I see the Honeychurch charm has worked its magic."

I smiled. "How can you not love it here!"

As if to echo my sentiments, we crested the stone bridge and entered a typical chocolate-box Devonshire village with one narrow through road that snaked around the village green and past the Norman church of St. Mary's with a plethora of ancient yew and cedar trees. A series of whitewashed cottages in dire need of re-thatching and a coat of paint formed a crescent around the church. None had front gardens. Their doors opened directly on to the road that overlooked the churchyard that was encompassed by a low stone wall. One of the last working red telephone boxes stood under the shade of a horse chestnut tree.

As Muriel had remarked earlier, the properties that were owned by the Honeychurch estate had their doors and windows painted a distinctive blue—including an abandoned forge, a tiny greengrocer, Muriel's post office, which doubled up as a general store, and Violet Green's tearoom.

In preparation for the re-enactment, the village looked particularly cheerful. Window boxes were filled with red, white and pink geraniums; colored bunting hung from rooftops and, on every available surface, flyers announcing the Skirmish ensured that no one passing through could be in any doubt that next weekend was going to be one of the most important events in Devon.

But today the tranquility of this normally peaceful village was broken by Violet Green and her dark-green Morris Minor Traveller. Not only was she blocking the street; she also had stopped outside her own tearoom with her hand firmly on the horn making a terrible racket.

"Oh, for heaven's sake, now what!" Edith exclaimed.

"I'll see what's going on." I stopped behind the car and got out. I had a soft spot for poor old Violet. Her sister, Lavender, had died of pneumonia months ago and Violet was completely alone. Village gossip claimed that the pair had lost fiancés in the Korean War and thus had never married.

Violet was sitting in the front seat and looked visibly distressed. I tapped on the glass. The moment she saw me she came off the horn and opened the window.

I took in her usual attire of a neat skirt and matching cardigan. Behind Violet's bottle-top glasses that had been heavily repaired with sellotape, her eyes flashed with fury.

"Whatever's the matter?" I said.

"That…that *trollop* has taken my parking spot!" Violet declared. She jabbed a finger at a white Vauxhall Astra that was parked on a patch of hardened mud sandwiched between her tearoom and the adjacent Honeysuckle Cottage. A hand-painted sign said: RESERVED FOR ROSE COTTAGE in red lettering.

Given the narrowness of the lane that ran through Little Dipperton, it was almost impossible to park in the street. There was one spot in front of the post office, a handful of spaces at the Hare & Hounds pub farther along and a few in the church car park, but that was about it.

"I always park there," said Violet. "His lordship told me it was mine."

I suddenly knew whose car it was—Harry's friend Max Carmichael's mother. "Do you mean Pippa?"

"Whatever her name is," Violet spat.

"I'm sure she didn't realize it's your spot. She doesn't live here."

"Oh yes she does!" Violet declared. "She just moved in and, what's more, she's trying to steal my customers!"

This really surprised me. I'd only spoken to Pippa outside the school a week ago when I'd gone to pick up Harry and she had not mentioned anything about moving into the village.

Edith hit my horn, startling Violet so much she screamed.

"I'm sorry, Violet, you'll have to move out of the way," I said. "I'm taking the dowager countess to Totnes railway station and she cannot miss her train."

Violet's eyes widened to saucers. "Lady Edith is in your car?" If I'd mentioned I was carrying the Queen of England she couldn't be more astonished—or worried. "Of course. I'm sorry. Please tell her I'm sorry. If her ladyship misses her train and it's my fault—"

Violet promptly thrust her Morris Minor into the wrong gear and kangarooed down the street at five miles an hour. As we followed her, twice Edith leant over and hit the horn, and twice Violet stalled the car.

"God help us," murmured Edith.

Finally, Violet pulled into a farm entrance on the far side of the churchyard. She waved as we passed on by.

I caught a glimpse of scaffolding surrounding the skeletal frame of a large stone barn.

I looked to Edith in surprise. "What's happening there?"

"That's the Carew boundary," said Edith. "Their land stretches for five miles north from here."

The reality of neighbor fighting against neighbor during the English Civil War struck home for the first time. "I had no idea you lived so close together."

"In fact, we're going to be even closer," Edith went on. "That pile of rubble will soon be Aubrey's new abode for his fresh young bride."

Of course, Lavinia had mentioned her father had remarried.

As we sped toward Totnes Edith seem to relish giving me the details of Lavinia's family.

"Personally, I quite like Aubrey," she said. "He's our Justice of the Peace, which has come in handy on quite a few occasions. How he gave birth to Lavinia—who is as thick as two short planks—and that twit son of his, Piers, is beyond my comprehension. But what possessed Aubrey to get married again at his age and move into a barn is embarrassing. He's obviously having an end-of-life crisis of sorts."

"Aubrey is giving up Carew Court?"

"Piers has been running it for a number of years—Rupert can't stand him—but it seems this new wife of his prefers an unostentatious life."

We turned into Totnes railway station with five minutes to spare. Flyers for the Skirmish were posted at the ticket office and along the platform railings.

Fortunately, Edith had her railway ticket. She refused help with her suitcase. "Frightfully good of you to run me here."

"It was no problem," I said. "I've got a valuation in Staverton at noon—an antique doll and a nice change from swords and helmets that have been dug out of the attic."

"Or dug out of the ground according to Rupert," said Edith. "Extraordinary that the main gauche discovered in that grave this morning bore the Honeychurch crest." Edith frowned. "It would have been such a valuable weapon, and one not easily discarded."

"I thought the same."

Edith shrugged. "I suppose we'll never know who the woman was and I suspect it was no one of any importance."

"You sound so sure," I said.

"We can account for all our ancestors, Katherine," said Edith with pride. "They're buried in the family mausoleum in St. Mary's church and recorded in the Parish registers."

"Parish registers?"

"The Devon and Cornwall Parish registers have recorded every birth, marriage and death since 1538. Quite remarkable."

"Are they still inside the church?" I knew Mum would love to take a look for her research.

Edith shrugged. "If they were, they'd be in the Parish chest in the vestry. Since the vicar died back in 2000 we rarely use the church—other than for funerals. God knows who will mow the churchyard now that Fred Jarvis has gone."

I wondered whether to mention Muriel's financial situation, but the Penzance to Paddington train was announced over the loudspeaker and the moment had gone.

"I'll pick you up on Sunday evening," I said. "Let me know if anything changes."

And with that, Edith headed for the platform carrying her

case as if it weighed ounces and not pounds and I set off for my rendezvous at the Sea Trout Inn in Staverton.

I'd never visited Staverton before. It was tucked out of the way down tiny winding roads. Its main claim to fame was the South Devon Railway that ran a steam train from Totnes to Buckfastleigh—mostly along the left bank of the spectacular River Dart—and a medieval bridge that was built in 1413. It was supposedly one of the best examples of medieval bridges in the country. The more I explored the South Hams, the more gems I kept finding. My London life seemed so far away, but I found I didn't regret the move one bit.

The only blot on the horizon was that my new business was taking far too long to get going. I'd arrogantly assumed that my mini-celebrity status as former host of *Fakes & Treasures* would have had people flooding to my door, but that had not been the case at all. Muriel was right. No one knew where to find me.

But the phone call I had received yesterday about valuing an antique French doll sounded very promising.

Something told me that today my luck was going to change.

Chapter Five

"Oh no, Mr. Brown, this is a genuine Jumeau Triste Bébé.
A child doll." I was thrilled for him. I had lost count of the
number of fake French dolls that had been manufactured in
the 1960s and had crossed my path over the years. This doll
was exquisite and the outfit she was wearing was the original
nineteenth-century cream dress and bonnet, in near-mint condition.

At this point in the proceedings, the client would usually
demand to know how much the doll was worth, but Mr. Brown
just sat there, fingering his tumbler of whiskey. Judging by
his threadbare herringbone sports jacket and tattered beige
corduroy trousers, I suspected he needed the money.

"I can't believe the Jumeau has been hiding in your cupboard for so many years," I went on.

Mr. Brown nodded but continued to stare into his glass—
obviously the doll must have meant a great deal to his wife, who
I assumed had just passed away.

Despite his untidy appearance, Mr. Brown was a very
handsome man in his early seventies with a mane of silver hair

that swept naturally off his high forehead. His horn-rimmed spectacles gave him an almost scholarly appearance.

"Are you familiar with antique dolls?" When Mr. Brown didn't answer, I plunged on. "She's French and was made around 1880 by Pierre Jumeau." I traced my fingers over the bisque head. "Do you see the delicately shaded cheeks and eyelids and the blue paperweight eyes and closed mouth? A closed-mouth bisque-head doll can be twice as valuable as comparable open-mouth dolls." I looked up to see his reaction, but still, he said nothing. "Her wig is mohair—a tiny bit matted, but that is far more desirable to a collector than a replacement wig." I turned the doll over. "See here? At the nape of the neck is the *Depose Tete Jumeau*, the blue stamp that says 'Jumeau Medaille D'or Paris.'" I beamed. "She's stunning."

But again, there was no reaction from Mr. Brown.

I brought out my iPhone, opened the camera app and snapped a quick photo.

"What are you doing?" he said sharply.

"I always take a photograph to include in my valuation." Gently, I laid the Jumeau onto the white fluffy hand towel and put her back into the Black & Decker power drill box—rather a bizarre choice of packaging, but I'd seen worse.

"You might want to store her a bit more carefully," I said. "A lot of collectors wrap the head in a baby diaper to protect it."

We lapsed into an awkward silence. I took a sip of Perrier water and, as I waited for Mr. Brown to comment, took in my surroundings.

The lounge at the Sea Trout Inn was unusually quiet for a Thursday lunchtime. We were alone in the farthest corner of the bar sitting in one of the eighteenth-century high-backed church settles.

Other than a battered old gray Volvo and a brand-new red BMW convertible, the car park had been empty. I assumed the Volvo belonged to Mr. Brown because the only other people in the bar were a middle-aged couple who looked as if they might be having an illicit tryst in the corner. She was crying.

Claimed to date back to the fifteenth century, the décor was typical of a Devonshire pub with its low, black roof beams and enormous inglenook fireplaces. Dotted about were the usual prints of dead game, horse brasses and gin traps.

One thing I had noticed since I started my mobile valuation service was the number of farmers and local fishermen wanting to sell furniture—some of it really good antiques— paintings and other items that had been passed down from generation to generation to subsidize their income. It made me sad.

It was hard enough seeing huge country estates gradually fade away, but farming was at the heart of the rural communities. Even in the nine months since I had moved from London to the West Country, I'd seen an increase in farmers selling off herds of cows because they just weren't making any money. The empty byres and cowsheds were then snapped up by city folk—like myself—to convert into second homes or holiday cottages. This, in turn, sent house prices up, often making it almost impossible for first-time buyers to purchase a home in the village where they had grown up. Even worse, those very villages were losing their soul, because half the year the second homes and holiday cottages stood empty.

Mr. Brown cleared his throat and finally spoke. "And you

are absolutely certain this French doll is genuine and not just a very good reproduction?"

"I'm one hundred percent positive. I would put a value of at least ten thousand pounds—"

"Ten *thousand* pounds!"

"More, if you have the original box at home somewhere—"

"Did you want to order lunch?" A young woman dressed in black trousers and a black sweater handed us two menus. Her nametag said: *Jen*.

Jen glanced into the open Black & Decker box. "What a pretty doll."

Mr. Brown swept the box off the table with such speed that it nearly overturned. He put it at the end of the settle. "No. No lunch," he said rudely.

"I'm sorry. Did I do something wrong?" Jen looked mortified. "It's my first day."

"Not at all." I smiled and took a menu. "I'd love to order. Why don't you come back in a minute?"

Jen gave me a grateful smile and left.

Mr. Brown got to his feet. "I must go."

"Where would you like me to send the valuation and invoice?"

"What?"

"An address? Unless you prefer to receive it via e-mail?"

"I don't want one," he snapped. "I don't need one."

His mood change was so extreme I was completely taken aback. "If you change your mind—"

"No, I won't." He seemed to find his manners. "I mean, no thank you—here—" Mr. Brown plunged his hand into his jacket pocket and tossed some crumpled notes onto the table, "For your time," and turned away to leave.

"Wait!" I exclaimed. "Don't forget the doll!"

With a grunt, he snatched the box up and hurried out of the bar, leaving me more than a little bewildered. I picked up the banknotes and felt miffed.

Twenty pounds! What a cheek!

"Excuse me, but aren't you Kat Stanford?" Jen materialized by my side. "It's your hair. I've always wanted hair like yours." She gave a shy smile.

My long, curly hair earned me the nickname Rapunzel and I suppose it was a trademark of sorts.

"My mum use to love *Fakes & Treasures*," Jen went on. "She doesn't like the new host at all. We read in the local paper that you were living in Little Dipperton. She's always talked about getting my great-grandmother's armoire valued. She said it was Victorian."

I retrieved a business card and handed it to her. "I'd be delighted. Just ask her to call me and tell her that we met."

Jen turned pink with pleasure. "Have you decided what to eat?"

Despite my resolution to have a salad, I ordered a Ploughman's lunch. I'd been consciously trying to lose the ten pounds I'd gained since moving to Devon, but today I just couldn't resist the homemade crusty bread or the homemade apple chutney. And who could possibly refuse the local Elmhirst cheese from Sharpham Vineyard?

As I waited for my order, I couldn't stop thinking about my strange encounter with Mr. Brown.

I ate my lunch in silence, scanning the daily newspapers that were scattered about for customers to read. The news was full of sensationalism—awful bombings in the Middle East, cyber-hacking, political corruption, domestic violence, an escaped prisoner who masterminded an intricate car theft ring on the run, an advertisement from the adult online dating site, Ashley Madison: "Life is short! Have an affair!" All the ugliness and sordidness of life was in these pages.

I much preferred the local weekly newspaper the *Dipperton Deal* with its earnest stories of village gossip, shoplifting and other petty crimes, amateur dramatics, obituaries and golden wedding anniversaries. My personal favorite was Dog-of-the-Week. But most of this edition was full of the upcoming Skirmish.

A one-page ad made me laugh out loud.

WANTED!
DEAD BODIES FOR THE SKIRMISH!
MISSED OUT ON PLAYING A ZOMBIE FOR
THE WALKING DEAD?
HERE IS YOUR CHANCE TO GET NOTICED.
(GROANING IS OPTIONAL.)
CALL PIERS CAREW ON 0787 2340172.

Piers Carew was Lavinia's brother. What had Edith called him? A twit. He certainly seemed to have a sense of humor.

My old life in London seemed to belong to another person. If someone had told me a year ago that I would be single again and living in a cottage on a country estate in rural Devon, I would have laughed. Mum always told me that no one knows what's around the corner—and she was right. Life can change in a heartbeat.

I checked my watch. I'd promised my mother that I would help her with the costumes this afternoon but hoped there would still be time to squeeze in a ride on Duchess, a dapple-gray mare that Edith had told me I could ride "anytime" and one I had come to regard as my own. Thanking Jen and giving her a generous tip, I headed for home.

It was when I was rounding a hairpin bend just a mile from the neighboring village of East Chiveley that I came across the accident.

An old gray Volvo had ploughed headfirst into a hawthorn hedge. I was certain it was Mr. Brown's, but I couldn't see if he was trapped because the entire front of the Volvo had been swallowed up by vegetation.

I jumped out.

"Mr. Brown!" I shouted, but there was no answering cry. I skirted along the hedge hunting for the five-bar gate that would give me access into the field beyond. Scrambling over—with great difficulty in my skirt—I managed to find my way back to the front of his car.

But when I got there, the Volvo was empty.

Mr. Brown had vanished.

Chapter Six

The field was deserted. There wasn't even a cow in sight.
I scanned the horizon, but other than a large country house
perched on the top of a hill in the distance, there was no sign
of Mr. Brown.

Looking on the bright side, he obviously hadn't been hurt
and was most likely making his way on foot for help. I pulled
out my mobile. There was no signal—no surprises there.

I looked at the Volvo. The front headlight was smashed and
there was a nasty scrape of green paint all down one side. The
narrow lanes in Devon were notorious for close encounters—
made all the more hair-raising by the speed at which the locals
drove because they knew every inch of the countryside.

It was only when I happened to glimpse inside the passenger seat that I noticed the Black & Decker box. I couldn't
believe it! Mr. Brown had completely forgotten to take the
doll—and, even more alarming, the car was unlocked! There
was no way I was going to leave her there. Grabbing the box, I
returned to my car.

I had no idea where Mr. Brown lived, but at least I had his

phone number logged into my mobile. I made it a habit to always keep a record of all new clients. Mr. Brown had called from a landline, not a mobile. My hunch that he must have walked to East Chiveley for help was probably correct. It was unlikely that I'd catch up with him, but even so, as I set off again, I kept my eyes peeled.

Finally, I got a signal at the top of the next hill and pulled into yet another gateway.

After five rings, an answering machine picked up. It was a woman's cheerful voice that threw me slightly.

I was in a bit of a dilemma. Mr. Brown had acted so strangely I didn't feel I should mention the doll on the answer machine.

"This is Kat Stanford," I said. "I have something of Mr. Brown's that he left in his car. Please can he call me so we can make arrangements to return it? Thank you."

Satisfied, I disconnected the line, confident that if I didn't see him walking along the road he would call me.

As I rounded another bend, I thought I saw him. A man was walking slowly along the road with a donkey jacket slung over his shoulders. He pressed himself against the hedge to allow me to pass.

Perhaps he'd seen Mr. Brown. I slowed down and opened my window.

The man didn't look very well. He was sweating and his complexion had a sickly grayish tinge. Large dark circles surrounded bloodshot eyes. Close-cropped hair was at odds with salt-and-pepper stubble.

"Excuse me," I began.

"No thanks. I appreciate it," he said curtly. "I like the walk."

I hadn't planned on giving him a lift—in fact, it had been

engrained into me since childhood never to accept a lift with a stranger or even consider offering one. I detected a brummie accent. Edith had mentioned that the Skirmish would attract a variety of people from all over the country. It would seem that she was right.

"I just wondered if you happened to see a man in his seventies on foot?" I pointed vaguely in the direction I had come. "There was an accident a mile or so back there and I wanted to make sure he was okay."

The man nodded. "Yeah. I wondered what the noise was. I heard a car horn and then a crash."

"Did you see anything?"

"I was on the other side of the valley." He started to cough. It was a wretched, hacking cough.

He really shouldn't be walking in this heat, but I didn't want him in my car, either. Even so, I heard myself say, "Are you sure you're okay?"

"Yeah. Never better." And with that, he touched his forelock and I drove on.

I spent the next half an hour combing the country lanes, but there was no sign of Mr. Brown—and finally circled back to the Volvo. It was still there with its nose stuck in the hedge.

There was not much else I could do except wait for Mr. Brown to call me and pick up the doll.

I passed the scruffy man with the cough once more on the outskirts of Little Dipperton. He was climbing over a wooden stile. I'd walked that way myself many a time. The public footpath ran along the boundary of a cow field and came out at the rear of the Hare & Hounds.

I had a thought. Perhaps Mr. Brown had decided to cut across the fields and had not walked the lanes at all.

Checking my watch, I realized I had left it far too late to go riding now, so I headed straight to Mum's.

As I swung into the cobbled courtyard I was struck at how pretty the Carriage House looked now. When I'd first seen her new home I'd been horrified. Although the two-story redbrick building had been covered in swathes of wisteria and Virginia creeper, it couldn't hide the crumbling brickwork, cracked and broken windows and a slate roof full of gaping holes.

Thanks to my mother's vast royalty checks that came in regularly, only to be squirreled away in an offshore account in Jersey—the details of which I really did not want to know about—Mum had enlisted her stepbrother, Alfred, to help smarten it up.

Windows had been replaced and the roof and skylight that ran the length of the old carriageway had been repaired and cleaned. Alfred had painted the arched double carriageway that spanned both stories, all the trim and even the timber cupola beneath the ogee dome a pale blue. He'd also removed the old horse weather vane and burnished it until it shone once more. Now the sunshine caught the trusty steed as it gently swung in circles to catch the afternoon breeze.

Knee-high weeds dotted with buttercups, thistles and rag-wort had been replaced with red, pink and white geraniums flowering in the window boxes. Wooden planters filled with roses sat on the steps of the stone mounting block. Wild hon-eysuckle wrapped around the wishing well and wisteria tum-bled over the walls of the semi-derelict outbuildings that ranged around the courtyard.

The only thing that marred the scenery was the rear entrance to Eric Pugsley's scrapyard. Even though the corrugated iron gate topped with razor wire was partially shrouded by unruly elderflower bushes, the ominous warning TRESPASSERS WILL BE PROSECUTED: POACHERS WILL BE SHOT spray-painted in crimson lowered the tone—at least that's what Mum was always grumbling about. I can't say I blamed her.

I drove through the double doors and into the carriageway beyond. It was easy to imagine what this place would have been like in its heyday when there was room for four horse-drawn carriages.

All the original fixtures remained. A row of stalls stood on either side accessed through redbrick arches bearing the family crest of arms and motto, *ad perseverate est ad triumphum*—To Endure Is to Triumph. Judging by what I'd learned of the history of the family, they'd certainly endured.

Alfred had made a start on clearing up the interior as well. Just stripping the invasive ivy that had crept under the rafters had taken him two whole weeks. I wasn't sure of my mother's long-term plans, but there had been talk about using the stalls again and having some of Edith's horses here.

They had discussed leaving the iron railings, newel posts and dividers—and the original bite and hoof marks—alone. Also the triangular water troughs and iron hayracks. Only the metal name plaques attached to each stall door would be replaced by ones with the names of the new residents. The old ones would be moved to the tack room along with the ancient saddles and bridles that Edith insisted on hanging on to out of sentimental value. Sometimes I wondered what would happen to them when she passed on. Would her successor honor Edith's wishes?

The entrance to the living area was rarely locked. I trooped upstairs to Mum's office and rapped smartly on her door.

"I'm busy!" came the terse reply.

"Did you eat lunch?"

"No. And don't slice the cheese so thick. And don't bring that dog in here!"

"We left Mr. Chips with Alfred," I said, and returned to the kitchen to rustle up a quick cheese and pickle sandwich for my mother.

Moments later I was in her office, tray in hand. "Whatever happened in here?"

Mum's office was in complete disarray. There were piles of fabric on every available surface. A bolt of blue velvet was draped over the wing back chair. A mound of lace was heaped on the floor. Costume reference books that she had taken out of the library were open on her roll-top desk. Saucers of pins and reels of cotton were lined up on the windowsill.

Mum was sitting at her sewing machine that she had set up on a collapsible table that Dad had used to eat his "TV dinners."

"Oh—Dad's table," I said, feeling an unexpected pang of nostalgia, but Mum didn't seem to hear me. "Did you volunteer to make costumes for the entire Royalist army?"

"I did not volunteer," she said haughtily. "I am being paid, thank you very much."

"What's this?" I spotted a dark-green doublet hanging from the standard lamp. It had lace cuffs and braided buttons. The stitching was exquisite and barely visible. "This is beautiful."

Mum smirked. "That's for his lordship. Lavinia's gown is behind the door."

I turned to see an elaborate creation in deep burgundy. It was still in the pinned-up stage, but I could see it was going to be stunning. "She'll be happy with that."

"I've just got to finish the hats and red sashes—and all by three-thirty."

"Why red?"

"The Royalists wore mostly red and the Roundheads a rather ghastly tawny orange to match their leather tunics."

"And this stuff here?" I pointed to bolts of brown, cream and beige cloth that stood in the corner.

"Camp followers," said Mum. "I agreed to do Muriel, Violet and Doris from the pub, but that's about it. The rest of them can wear sacks for all I care."

"What about your old friend Peggy Cropper?"

"Over my dead body." It would appear that my mother had still not forgiven the cook for that other business in February.

Mum presented me with a miniature version of Rupert's outfit. "For Harry."

"It's adorable!" I said. "You *are* clever. And what about us?"

Mum looked blank. "Us?"

"Well, aren't we going to have to wear something? Get into the spirit of the thing?"

"I suppose so," Mum said grudgingly. She gave a heavy sigh.

"What's the matter?"

"I can't understand why I haven't heard from my new editor about *Ravished*."

"I thought you had," I said. "I thought that was why you have been so cheerful."

"I've been putting on a brave front," said Mum. "Clara St. James called me a high-maintenance author."

"You?" I laughed. "High-maintenance? Whatever next!"

"She wants me to do personal appearances, and of course I can't. I wish Graham hadn't died."

"Why don't you call her?" I suggested. "Isn't *Ravished* supposed to be out in time for Christmas? That's in six months!"

"I know and I haven't even got the notes back yet. She also threw out my idea for the next in the series," Mum grumbled. "She said there were too many Viking stories on the market."

I drifted over to the window that looked out over Cromwell Meadows. The chassis of Eric's caravan remained where it had been felled surrounded by pieces of plywood and metal sidings. A white tent and a white screen had been erected over and around the grave.

"Do we refer to the skeleton as a body or remains or what?" I wondered aloud.

Mum joined me at the window. "Who was she?"

"Edith said something interesting." I went on to relay my conversation with the dowager countess on our way to the railway station.

"No one of importance!" Mum scoffed. "I'm sure she had a family that thought she was important."

"Apparently all the Honeychurch ancestors are accounted for and are in the family mausoleum at St. Mary's church. But she did say that the Parish registers might still be in the Parish chest."

"I wish I had known about those," said Mum. "It would have saved me a lot of work, not to mention all the hours I've been spending in the library and with the Devon History Society."

I thought for a moment. "But Edith did think the presence of the dagger—if it really is a Honeychurch dagger—was unusual."

"Maybe we should get Alfred on the case," said Mum. "Ask him to do a bit of channeling."

I groaned.

"Groan all you like, but Alfred has been extremely successful."

"Won't he be too busy tailing Rupert?" I said drily.

Mum picked up a long brown serge skirt and settled back at the sewing machine. "Talk to me whilst I hem."

"You won't be able to hear me above the noise of the machine," I said, but moved a pile of fabric and sat in the wingback armchair all the same.

"Then you'll have to shout."

"I did a really strange valuation today," I said loudly, and went on to fill my mother in on the details of my meeting with Mr. Brown. "Far from being thrilled, he was freaked out. Rude, in fact."

Mum paused and spoke through a mouthful of pins. "In what way?"

"In the end he didn't even want the valuation. Just threw twenty pounds at me, 'for my time'—"

"Twenty pounds! How insulting!"

"I know. And he couldn't get out of the pub fast enough. He didn't even eat lunch."

"Skipping lunch won't hurt you and it definitely won't hurt your figure."

I could feel myself bristling.

Mum eyed me shrewdly. "I suppose I could put in an elasticated waist—"

"If you are going to talk about my weight again, I'm going to leave."

Mum grinned. She knew exactly how to push my buttons.

"Sounds like your Mr. Brown has a guilty conscience," she went on. "I bet the doll wasn't his. Maybe it fell off the back of a lorry."

I shook my head. "I don't think so. I assumed it belonged to his late wife." I then told my mother all about finding Mr. Brown's Volvo nose first in a hedge. "If he had stolen it he would hardly have left it in the footwell of his car."

"Where is the doll now?"

"In mine."

"How much is this doll worth?"

I shrugged. "At least ten thousand pounds."

"Does he know you have it?"

"Not exactly. I left a message on his answer machine asking him to call me. It was a woman's voice on the recording, so I didn't get into the specifics."

"Why didn't you say so?"

"He was so secretive, Mum. I just thought being vague was better."

"Oh dear," said Mum. "Women can be funny things. She might think he's having an affair."

"You've got affairs on the brain!" I exclaimed. "Anyway, he was in his seventies."

Mum shrugged again. "Look at Michael Douglas and Catherine Zeta-Jones!"

"What about them?"

"There are twenty-five years between them and we know how much you prefer older men."

"I do not prefer older men. David just happened to be older."

"That poor policeman didn't even get a look in."

I got to my feet. "Okay. Enough. I refuse to discuss my non-existent love life with you. And for your information, poor Shawn is not interested in me any longer. We're just friends."

Fortunately, the telephone rang and stopped all further conversation.

"Pick it up, dear," said Mum.

So I did. "Hello?" I answered. "Let me find out." Then, covering the mouthpiece, I hissed, "Quickly. It's your editor asking for Krystalle Storm."

Mum spat out the pins, threw the skirt aside and leapt to her feet. She snatched up the phone. "Hello? It's Krystalle here. How are you, Ms. St. James?"

Slowly, the color drained out of my mother's face. She could hardly speak. Words just didn't seem to come out at all. Even I could hear the tone of Clara St. James from Goldfinch Publishing on the other end of the line, and it was not friendly.

Finally, Mum managed to say, "Of course there must be a mishap somewhere. What about your mailroom?" Ms. St. James chirped an answer. "Yes. Yes. I will find out straightaway. Thank you. Yes. Good-bye." Mum replaced the phone and looked at me as if her entire world had come to an end.

"Didn't she like the manuscript?" I said.

"She never had a chance to like it," Mum whispered. "The manuscript never arrived. My career is ruined!"

Chapter Seven

"**What do you mean, it never arrived?**" I said. "Why on earth didn't they call until now?"

"Apparently, shortly before Graham died he told Ms. St. James that I didn't work very well under pressure—"

"That's true—"

"And it wasn't a good idea to call me and that she wasn't to worry, because even though I was often late I always turned in excellent work."

"So that's a good thing."

"Oh, Kat!" Mum wailed. "What on earth am I going to do?"

"Now calm down—"

"Calm? I can't be calm. I'll never be calm again."

"All you need to do is send them another copy of *Ravished*. We can send it overnight. I'll go into Dartmouth right now."

There was a deathly silence.

"Oh no," I cried. "You don't have a copy, do you? Oh, *Mum*."

"And don't say 'I told you so!'"

"I don't need to." Since my mother refused to use a computer, I had lost count of the times that I had insisted that if she was not going to type with a carbon copy, at the very least she should photocopy everything. The original manuscript really *was* the original—and only—manuscript.

"Let's work backwards," I said. "You posted it in Dartmouth, yes?"

"No. Little Dipperton. I know you told me to go to the main post office, but I was in a rush." She regarded me with defiance. "But how can that have happened!" Her voice shot up an octave. "I paid for it registered post."

"Good," I said. "So that means you have a tracking number."

"Of course I have a tracking number."

"Great. Give it to me and I'll see what happened."

With one sweep, Mum had cleared the desk. Fabric, pencils, books and what remained of her sandwich tumbled onto the floor. She rummaged through the dozens of pigeonholes, all stuffed with scraps of paper—bills, envelopes and Post-it notes. "Oh! I'll never find it in all this mess!"

"Calm down," I said again. "Let me look."

"No. I don't want you poking through all my personal things. I put it somewhere safe."

"Good."

Mum wrenched open one of the smaller drawers. "Ah. I thought so. Here we are," she said triumphantly. "I told you I had it."

I inspected the date. "You posted it—good heavens, on April the seventeenth."

"So where is it?" Mum demanded. "What happened to it?"

"Leave this with me," I said. "I'll go up to the gatehouse and check online."

Honeychurch Hall still didn't have access to any Internet. Little Dipperton was supposed to have broadband installed at some point, but I was able to use a British Telecom Wi-Fi hotspot at the top of the drive.

"I'm coming with you."

"Walk or car?" I said.

"Whichever is the fastest."

Mum clambered into the passenger seat of my Golf and put the Black & Decker box onto her lap.

I reversed out of the carriageway and we sped away.

Mum took a peep inside the box and gave a shudder. "Personally, I've never seen the appeal. Ever since your father made me watch *Chucky,* I've never been able to look at a doll in quite the same way."

"You went to see *Chucky?*"

"Oh yes. Your father always enjoyed a good horror film. He said they made him laugh. It used to scare me half to death."

"I never knew that."

Mum's eyes suddenly filled with tears. "There was a lot you didn't know about him, Katherine."

"And a lot he didn't know about you," I retorted.

Given my mother's insistence that my parents had had a wonderful marriage, I still couldn't figure out why she had felt the need to keep her writing accomplishments secret. I was certain he would have been proud of her. I was.

"And don't look at me like that," said Mum.

"I just don't understand why you didn't tell him," I said. "When I get married, I want to be able to share everything."

"Sometimes, it doesn't work like that no matter how much you want it to," said Mum darkly.

"I disagree." I knew I was sounding self-righteous, but that's what I truly believed. "Honesty is everything."

"Alright, alright," said Mum dramatically. "I'll tell you why, but you might not like what you hear."

"I'm bracing myself."

"When I first left the traveling fair and boxing emporium, my people—"

"Your troupe—"

"Yes. My troupe! We were one big happy family," said Mum. "I can't expect you to understand how lonely I was. I found it hard to adjust to life in a semi-detached house in Tooting."

"Go on," I said.

"I missed life on the road. I missed sleeping under the stars. I missed the sound of the fairground at night, the excitement of the boxing ring." She shrugged. "I adored your father, but . . . my *troupe* never forgave me for what I did."

I could tell the memory still upset her. "I know that, Mum," I said gently. "But you can't help who you fall in love with."

In fact, my mother had met my father when he was representing HM Revenue & Customs. Dad was investigating Bushman's Traveling Fairground and Boxing Emporium for suspected tax evasion. As it turned out, he was right. There was quite a lot of creative accounting going on in the ticket booth. Naturally, when Mum and Dad fell in love and eloped her troupe viewed her decision as the ultimate betrayal.

"I was very unhappy to start with—not because of Frank, never because of Frank," said Mum. "But I missed my kin." She gave me a sheepish smile. "You have no idea how much it means to have Alfred living here."

Alfred. Hmm. I was still on the fence about whether having Alfred around was a good or a bad thing. It was Alfred who had suggested that my mother funnel all her earnings into the offshore account in Jersey and it was Alfred who occasionally disappeared overnight with an empty suitcase and a forged passport only to return the next day with a lot of cash.

"But I don't see what that has to do with the fact you didn't tell Dad about your writing," I persisted.

"Writing was a way for me to escape," said Mum. "I could get lost in my imagination."

"Lost in your fake migraines," I reminded her. "If you knew how worried Dad and I were. We kept thinking you had a brain tumor."

"I know and I'm sorry." She thought for a moment. "You know, I never expected to finish writing a book, let alone write one that would sell. I suppose I felt silly, so I didn't say anything until it was too late."

"It's never too late—"

"Once I started with the tiny lies, they just got . . . bigger and bigger."

"You're telling me, they got bigger," I said. "I'm not judging. I just know that one day it will all come out."

Mum stiffened. "Don't worry about my life, worry about yours."

"I can't help but worry about yours!"

My mother's website claimed that not only had my father been an international diplomat who had died in a plane crash, but also she owned a villa on the Amalfi coast and a Devon manor house. One of her publicity headshots showed her holding a Pekinese called Truly Scrumptious.

"And where did you get the Pekinese? At least tell me that."

Fortunately, we arrived at the gatehouses before we could dissolve into one of our childish squabbles.

"Thank God we're here," she muttered. "That was the longest five minutes in history."

"I'll get it out of you eventually."

We got out of the Golf with Mum carrying Chucky, as she insisted on calling the Jumeau.

Mum turned to look over at the parkland beyond where the activity seemed to have tripled since this morning. "Oh," she said wistfully. "Seeing all those tents takes me back years. We used to set up in that very same spot, too."

Pointing to a row of blue Portaloos that stood along the hedge, she added, "Toilets. How flash."

"I bet you didn't have those in the 1950s."

I let us into the West Gatehouse.

"It still smells of paint," said Mum.

"I don't mind it," I said.

She started roaming around with a critical air. "You've not done much unpacking."

"I'm waiting for Alfred to put in shelves," I said as I ramped up my computer. "There's no rush, though. It's not as if I'm going to get any foot traffic up here."

"Nonsense. You'll get lots of people walking by next weekend. There is going to be a entire camp of Royalists and Roundheads right outside your back door."

"You think they'll be in the mood to buy bears?" I said.

Mum gave an exasperated sigh. "I know you wanted a little antique shop in Brick Lane. I know I ruined your plans, but you didn't have to move—"

"I'm here now," I said firmly. "And I am happy in Devon. Okay? Anyway, I'm looking at an additional space at Dartmouth Antique Emporium this weekend. Just for the summer."

"Oh good," Mum enthused. "It will get you out a bit. I worry about you living like a hermit."

"Ah—success," I said as the Royal Mail website came up. "Finally."

Mum handed me the registered post slip. I typed in the tracking number.

"Did you know that it was King Henry the Eighth who founded the Royal Mail in 1516?" said Mum. "You'd think he wouldn't have had the time what with juggling all those wives."

I frowned. "There must be some mistake." I re-entered the tracking number—then again. "Oh dear."

Mum peered over my shoulder. "What am I supposed to be looking at?"

I tapped the screen. "It says the package is still in Little Dipperton."

"What?" Mum shrieked. "What do you mean it's *still* in Little Dipperton? I don't understand."

"I told you to go to the post office in Dartmouth," I said. "Obviously Muriel must have registered it and...maybe she put it to one side and forgot to post it."

"She *forgot*!" Mum shrieked again. "How can she forget? She's the postmistress!"

"I think that was around the time her husband had just died." I thought back to the check for three hundred pounds that I had written her just this morning. I decided not to mention this to my mother. "I expect she got distracted."

"I don't care! And I can tell you right now King Henry

would have had her head off for a lot less. I'm going down there right this minute."

"Not for Muriel's head, I hope," I said. "Let me go."

"I'm so upset—"

"We don't know for sure," I said. "Let's not jump to conclusions. Let me find out what happened. You've got to finish sewing the costumes, remember?"

Mum's shoulders slumped in defeat. "You're right. I do."

"I'll be back within the hour," I promised. "And look on the bright side. The manuscript is most likely still there. It won't have been lost at all."

Chapter Eight

Ten minutes later I parked my Golf behind St. Mary's and took the shortcut through the churchyard to the post office. From this perspective, I had a good view of the crescent of cottages beyond the low moss-covered stone wall that embraced the churchyard boundary—and they had a good view of me.

The churchyard was lined with lichen-covered headstones and raised tombs. Some were enclosed by wrought-iron railings and watched over by stone angels. Most of the graves were family plots. There were about a dozen surnames that I recognized from those who lived and worked on the Honeychurch estate or were still tenants living in the village.

I thought again of the dead woman who had lain forgotten in Cromwell Meadows for so many years. Someone had to have known who she was and how she met with such a violent end.

As I picked my way through the graves, I spotted the imposing Honeychurch mausoleum in the corner framed by two ancient yew trees. The Honeychurch motto was carved above heavy bronze doors that were framed by a pair of hawks in flight. The style was very much in keeping with the architecture of the Hall only in miniature.

Although the grass surrounding the mausoleum was neatly mown, most of the churchyard was ankle deep in thistles, clover, buttercups and daisies.

Only Fred Jarvis's brand-new headstone stood out. Built of granite and etched in gold, it looked expensive. A fresh vase of roses sat beneath the inscription that brought a smile to my lips. My dad used to say the exact same thing to my mother.

YOU'LL MISS ME WHEN I'M GONE

FREDERICK JARVIS

AUGUST 8, 1942–MAY 3, 2017

ALWAYS TOGETHER

It was also hard to miss the wheelbarrow that was blocking the grassy path. It still contained Fred's gardening implements—a hoe, fork and shovel—that he had been using on that fateful day.

According to Mrs. Cropper, the cook, Muriel forbade anyone to move the "barrow of death" for mysterious reasons of her own, but with St. Mary's church holding a "living history" exhibition as part of the re-enactment next weekend someone was going to have to.

I paused at the lych-gate where directly opposite Violet's dark-green Morris Minor Traveller had reclaimed its rightful space between Rose Cottage and Honeysuckle Cottage, Pippa's new abode.

Violet might have had a point about Pippa trying to steal her customers.

An elaborate sign embellished with curlicues peeped between frothy lace curtains in Pippa's front window.

DEVONSHIRE CREAM TEAS IN MY SECRET GARDEN

£7.50

REAL CLOTTED CREAM AND LOCAL JAM

HOMEMADE SCONES AND CAKES FRESHLY MADE TODAY

I had to admit Pippa's cream teas seemed far more enticing than poor Violet's efforts. Pippa's cottage was covered in fragrant honeysuckle climbing either side of the front door and over the pitched porch. Violet's cottage looked positively bald without her signature climbing roses that had covered the flaking whitewashed bricks that were now a dirty gray. No wonder she had been upset. Even worse, the victims of Fred's zealous secateurs still pooled in pathetic dead piles under the front windows and around the side footpath between her cottage and the post office. Since there was no one who was likely to clear it up, I decided to come back over the weekend and volunteer.

Pippa had also undercut Violet's price for a traditional Devonshire cream tea and a pot for two by three whole pounds. Although I had to admit you could fell an elephant with one of Violet's fruit scones.

I wondered if Pippa realized that she was alienating the locals who always seemed to regard any outsider—and I was speaking from experience—with caution bordering on hostility. I suppose someone would have to tell her and that someone was probably me.

The door to the post office and general store stood open. I

stepped down into the gloom. No matter how sunny it was outside, the place always seemed claustrophobic. The low-beamed ceiling didn't help.

The store was jammed to the gunnels with items ranging from tiny sewing kits to fly-spray killer. Shelves were haphazardly stacked with pliers, tinned goods, jigsaw puzzles and hemorrhoid cream. A revolving wire display stand offered picturesque postcards of Devon for sale.

I always felt like I had stepped back in time here. On the counter sat an old-fashioned cash register and brass bell. In front stood a low bench spread with a selection of trashy magazines, national newspapers, the local *Dipperton Deal* and the dreaded *Star Stalkers*. Along the back wall were shelves filled with large glass jars containing old-fashioned sweets that I tended to buy just too often these days—Sherbet Pips, Fruit Chews and Black Jacks.

In one corner a Plexiglas window encased a small cubbyhole that bore the sign POST OFFICE. On the notice board the usual flyers and handwritten cards that offered a variety of services and local events had been overshadowed by the upcoming Skirmish. Piers Carew's bloodthirsty appeal for dead bodies was tacked alongside a heavily embossed invitation from the Master of Weapons inviting anyone in need of practice with "pike, musket or rapier" to "muster" in the grounds of Carew Court on Saturday at nine a.m.

I half-expected to see Muriel's niece manning the fort, but she wasn't there—nor was Muriel. I rang the brass bell.

Moments later Muriel emerged from the door behind the counter. I noticed that her black cotton dress had a splotch of red just below the neckline.

When Muriel saw it was me she smiled. "Oh, Katherine. I can't thank you enough for your kindness," she said. "You haven't told anyone, have you? I'm so embarrassed."

"No, I haven't said a word."

"Not even to Iris?" said Muriel. "I know you are close."

"Not even to my mother." Although I had been tempted to. I just hoped that Muriel wasn't going to ask for money again.

"Did you want to buy some stamps?" Muriel said brightly.

"Not today." I pointed to her dress. "You've got something on your—" I leaned in closer. "Is that—I think it's jam?"

"It's Fred's," she said, and wiped it off on her sleeve. Her eyes filled with tears. "Eating his jam makes me feel closer to him, somehow." She gave a heavy sigh. "I've still got twelve jars of gooseberry, but it's the strawberry that was his best."

"And I'm looking forward to eating his jam, too." I thought for a moment. "Any news on your car?"

Muriel looked blank. "Car?"

"The car that was stolen from the car park in Tesco?"

"Oh, that," said Muriel, settling onto a stool behind the counter. "No. Not yet." She retrieved a copy of last Saturday's *Dipperton Deal* from under the counter. It was folded to page 4. Muriel had circled a tiny paragraph in the sidebar. The piece was so small I hadn't even noticed it earlier in the day at the Sea Trout Inn. "But thefts are on the rise. Take a look at that."

I read: *A china Dalmatian dog and a tin tea caddy were stolen from an Oxfam charity shop in Dartmouth last Friday.*

It was hardly in the same league as her car, but I said, "Well, just make sure you keep your door locked."

"And you, too. Did you say you wanted stamps?" Muriel asked.

"Actually—" I plunged in. "I need to talk to you about a parcel that my mother registered a few weeks ago."

A tide of red raced up Muriel's neck and flooded her face. She couldn't have looked guiltier if she tried. "A parcel, you say?"

"I have the tracking slip," I said, and gave it to her.

Muriel got to her feet and unlatched the half door that separated the post office from the general store. She sank onto another stool behind the Plexiglas divider.

Muriel glanced at the receipt. "It left here on April seventeenth. That's what it says. You see?" She drew a circle around the postmark and slid it back under the glass looking defiant.

"I know," I said gently. "But I went online and I was able to track it. It says the parcel never left the post office."

"Well, that's wrong," she declared. "It did."

"I know you've had a lot going on what with losing Fred—"

"Not to mention Violet," Muriel put in. "She refuses to pay me despite what the judge said. She had another accident, you know. She really shouldn't be driving with her eyesight—"

"Would you mind looking in your sorting room or wherever you keep things before they're picked up?" I said. "Maybe it's still there?"

"Of course it won't still be there," said Muriel with scorn.

"Do you mind if I take a quick peep?"

"You're wasting your time, but alright then." She gave a heavy sigh and lifted the countertop. I followed her into a small windowless room painted lime green that jarred with a pair of shocking pink Crocs that she was wearing. On top Muriel might well be in mourning, but her footwear certainly held a spark of life.

The sorting room was highly organized, with three large canvas bins for incoming and outgoing mail and one for parcels. There was an entire wall of pigeonholes with the names and addresses of every resident in the village, all neatly labeled in black ink. I felt an odd thrill at seeing mine—MS. KATHERINE STANFORD/JANE'S COTTAGE.

I peered into the outgoing mail bin. It was empty. The incoming bin only had a handful of letters, too. I imagined what the village post office would have been like before e-mail.

"People don't write letters so much anymore," said Muriel as if reading my thoughts. "I remember when sorting the post was my Fred's full-time job and he didn't have to beg for work."

"You're very organized," I said. "I'm impressed."

"Nothing gets past me," said Muriel with a hint of pride.

And it also went a long way to explain why Muriel knew everything that was going on in the village.

I noticed a brand-new label—CAREW/THE OLD BARN. "Is that the barn conversion behind St. Mary's?"

"That's the one," said Muriel. "Lady Lavinia's father and his new wife."

"Oh." I continued to scan the room for any sign of my mother's parcel, very conscious of Muriel's eyes boring into the back of my skull.

"And she's already getting packages," Muriel went on. "Set herself up a nice little mailbox, as they say in America. Why she wants it sent there instead of Carew Court is beyond me. The barn won't be ready for months. Have you seen it? It's a shell."

"How many times a day does the post get picked up?"

"Once," said Muriel. "Used to be three posts a day when I

was a little girl, but now—" She shrugged. "Bill-the-post picks up at ten in the morning. The letters and parcels are put on the train to Exeter and then go on up to London."

"You're right," I said, defeated. "Mum's parcel isn't here."

We returned to the post office and general store. Muriel settled back behind the counter again. I saw a half-eaten piece of toast on a plate and a jar of Fred's famous strawberry jam.

"How important was the parcel?" Muriel said suddenly.

"Very important."

"Oh dear," said Muriel. "So what happens if it never turns up?"

"Let's hope that doesn't happen."

"What was it?"

"I don't know," I lied, "but it means a lot to my mother."

Muriel frowned. "Let me think a moment." She nodded slowly. "I seem to remember a package being addressed to Goldfinch Publishing? Would that be right?"

"I don't remember," I lied again.

"I thought to myself, Goldfinch Publishing in London. Now, that rings a bell." Muriel cocked her head. "I even thought for a minute that maybe Iris fancied herself as the next Krystalle Storm." Muriel laughed, showing all her teeth. "Fancy that."

"Krystalle who?" I said, feigning innocence.

"She publishes the Star-Crossed Lover series." To make her point, Muriel retrieved a dog-eared copy of *Forbidden*, Mum's last book, from under the counter and showed me the spine. "You see here?" She jabbed a finger. "That's their logo. A goldfinch." Muriel regarded me keenly. "As I said, not much gets past me. It's part of my job to be vigilant."

How infuriating. I hated being put in such an awkward position, but there was no question of me confirming her suspicions. I felt a rush of annoyance at my mother and her ridiculous obsession with secrecy.

"It would make sense, though," Muriel persisted. "I mean, what does Iris do up at the Carriage House all day?"

"At the moment, she's sewing costumes for Lord and Lady Honeychurch and you," I said drily.

"Well, all I'm saying is that my niece Bethany has the Internet and she told me that on Krystalle Storm's website it says she has a manor house in Devon and a villa on the Amalfi coast—"

"And a Pekinese called Truly Scrumptious," I said. "My mother doesn't have a dog."

"I thought you hadn't heard of Krystalle Storm," Muriel said suspiciously. "Anyway, Bethany said the dog looked stuffed."

I stifled the urge to laugh. "Perhaps Krystalle Storm lives in Italy most of the time."

"Say what you like. I've got a feeling in my water."

"Why would you think it was my mother anyway?" I couldn't help but say. "There are other people who are new to the area."

Muriel sat up straight. "You're right. There are. Pippa whatever her name is has moved into Honeysuckle Cottage with that naughty little boy Max—he's a bad influence on Master Harry. I've seen them stealing sweeties right under my nose. No, perhaps... Have you met her ladyship's new stepmother?"

I was beginning to feel quite tired from hearing all of Muriel's observations. "No."

"Likes to be called Jess, so I'm told." Muriel leaned in conspiratorially. "Had plastic surgery, if you know what I mean—and she's young enough to be his daughter. The old earl has got to be decades her senior, but the Carews have money, you see."

"There you are," I said. "Maybe Jess has a villa on the Amalfi coast and it's where she writes her racy novels."

"Yes. She looks the type. A proper gold digger."

"Am I the type?" We both looked over to see an elegantly dressed woman wearing a pale-blue leather jacket and white Capris. She was pretty, with an elfin face and a blond pixie cut. The minute she saw me she gave a gasp of pleasure. "Oh! I don't believe it! You're Kat Stanford from *Fakes & Treasures*. I'm your biggest fan . . . but who on earth is Krystalle Storm?"

Chapter Nine

To say I was embarrassed was putting it mildly. I had never thought of myself as a gossip, and even though I had been trying to steer the subject of Krystalle Storm away from my mother, it didn't make it right to start a rumor—however innocuous—with someone like Muriel Jarvis.

I suspected Jess and I were about the same age. Recalling Muriel's catty remark about plastic surgery, I had to admit she could be right. Jess's breasts seemed completely out of proportion to her slender frame. On her shoulder she carried an oversized white leather Tory Burch tassel handbag. A silver bangle and simple platinum wedding band were her only jewelry.

"Well, I'm sorry to disappoint you both," Jess said pleasantly. "But I am neither a gold digger nor do I write racy novels." She smiled to reveal a set of perfectly capped teeth that she pointed to with one of her perfectly manicured fingers. "Although I do have veneers, I have never had plastic surgery. Not so much as a chemical peel."

"Do y-y-ou want to buy some s-s-tamps?" Muriel stammered.

"You should have seen my teeth when I was a teenager," Jess went on. "They used to call me Buck Rabbit at school."

The fact that Jess had dealt so graciously with our insults made me feel even more embarrassed.

"Mine was Rapunzel," I said.

"I know. And I'm so jealous. I'd do anything to have hair likes yours. Mine is so thin." She offered her hand. "I'm Jessica Carew, but all my friends call me Jess."

"Do you want to buy some stamps?" said Muriel again.

"Not today, thanks, Mrs. Jarvis."

"Call me Muriel."

"Do you carry Lemsip?" Jess asked. "I think I'm coming down with a cold."

Muriel pointed to the far corner of the general store. "Top shelf," she said. "Out of reach of the kiddies, but if you want my opinion, the only way to knock a cold on the head is to have a glass of port and brandy and go straight to bed."

Whilst Muriel rang up Jess's purchase, Jess said, "Are you visiting or here for that silly Skirmish—such a funny name."

"No. I live in the area now."

Jess's eyes widened. "Really? *Here?* In Little Dipperton?"

"Yes. On the Honeychurch estate."

"But that's wonderful!" she enthused. "We're going to be neighbors. We're converting the barn in the field behind that old abandoned church."

"It's not abandoned!" Muriel exclaimed. "What a thing to say!"

"Oh, I'm sorry." Jess looked mortified. "It's just that— Aubrey told me that there hasn't been a vicar there for years

and ... well—the churchyard is knee-high in weeds. I mean—
when was the last time there was a service?"

There was an excruciating silence until Muriel finally
spoke. "The last time there was a service was two weeks ago
when I buried my husband, Fred."

Jess paled. "Oh God, I am so sorry—so terribly sorry for
your loss. I didn't know."

"Of course you didn't," I said. "How could you have known?
It's an easy mistake."

Jess shot me a look of gratitude and mouthed, *Thank you.*

Muriel's expression was stony, but then she seemed to re-
lent. "We don't take kindly to outsiders," she said. "We're
Honeychurch folk here, not Carew."

Jess frowned. "I don't understand."

Quickly I explained the centuries-old rivalry between the
Royalist Honeychurches and Roundhead Carews and about
the upcoming re-enactment. "So you could say you're in enemy
territory," I joked. "Don't you agree, Muriel?"

"That's right."

Jess seemed amused. "We outsiders had better stick together, Kat. How many years does it take to become a local?"

"At least forty," said Muriel. And she wasn't joking. "That
reminds me, I have another letter for you. You may as well take
it now since you're here."

Muriel disappeared into the sorting room, leaving the pair
of us alone.

"God, I really put my foot in it, didn't I?" said Jess.

I laughed. "Don't worry. I do it all the time."

"But honestly, that church—I mean, have you been inside?
It's practically derelict."

Muriel emerged from the sorting room. "I hope you feel better before you go to Roscoff."

Jess frowned. "I'm sorry?"

Muriel tapped the return address on the envelope. "Brittany Ferries."

Jess seemed startled. "Oh. Yes. Me too. But it's just a brochure. I think it's junk mail, actually."

"I'll throw it away then, shall I?" I spotted a glint of malice in Muriel's eye.

Jess snatched the envelope. "No need. Thank you. Goodness. I really must be going. Thank you for the Lemsip—but I'll try port and brandy, first."

"I must go, too," I said.

"I hope your mother finds her package," Muriel called after us.

I found Jess waiting for me outside in the sunshine.

"Look, I want to tell you something important." She linked my arm in hers and, before I could protest, drew me away, across the lane and into the churchyard. "I overheard your conversation."

I felt my face grow hot. "I'm sorry—"

"It doesn't matter," she said dismissively. "I'm used to it. I know people are critical of our age difference, but I don't care. Look at Michael Douglas and Catherine Zeta-Jones. You can't help who you fall in love with, can you? And I do love Aubrey. I really do."

This was too much personal information for someone I had known for less than five minutes.

"Jess . . . really, it's—"

"I don't want his money. I have money of my own," she went on in earnest. "Have you been to Carew Court?"

"No," I said.

"It's a very grand house, but it's like a morgue. I hate it. Believe me, I was so happy that Aubrey agreed to move out and convert the barn. It's a bit of an inheritance tax dodge really, because Piers—have you met him—?"

"Not yet—"

"Piers told us that as long as we live somewhere on the estate he avoids the crippling inheritance tax."

"You don't mind giving up the big house?"

"Good God, no!" said Jess emphatically. "I can't wait to move out of that place. Sorry, I've been rabbiting on. Tell me about you?"

"There's nothing to tell really."

"I read somewhere that you'd started your own antique business."

"Well—"

"Sorry. I don't mean to pry," Jess raced on. "It's just that I'm starved of female company. I need a good friend and we're the same age—"

"Are we?"

"Yes; you've just had a big birthday and so have I."

At this, my warning radar went off. It was one of the things I loathed about being in the public eye—everyone knew or thought they knew me personally.

"Forty is a big one, isn't it?" Jess grinned. "It makes you take a look at your life. Get your priorities straight."

"I suppose so." In fact, turning forty had been a real shock for me. Never in my wildest imaginings did I expect to still be single and living so far away from London. But I definitely wasn't about to discuss my feelings with a stranger.

"Aubrey was so sweet," Jess went on. "He bought me a brand-new Prius—a total surprise—and took me to NINE. It's got five Michelin stars. Have you eaten there?"

I shook my head. My fortieth had passed very quietly playing Snap with my mother and Alfred and eating cottage pie.

"NINE is in Plymouth and it's almost impossible to get a table, but Aubrey worked his magic." Jess stretched out her arm. "And he bought me this bangle. It's platinum."

Even if Jess wasn't a gold digger, she enjoyed the good things in life. "It's very pretty." And it really was. For a moment I was taken off-guard by a memory. My ex-boyfriend David had been very big on giving me jewelry. True, some of it had been obtained from seized and unclaimed property from numerous heists, but even so. He had exquisite taste.

Jess cocked her head. "Do you really like it?"

"I really do. I love its simplicity."

"Do you have time for a quick cup of tea?" said Jess suddenly.

"I can't today," I said. "Sorry."

On an impulse, Jess gave me a hug. "I might just pop in and buy Aubrey a slice of homemade cake. How odd that there are two tearooms side by side. Which one do you recommend?"

"Whichever one is open," I said tactfully, and left Jess to it.

I returned to my car feeling unsettled. There was no doubt in my mind that Lavinia was wrong about Rupert having an affair with Jess. She seemed completely enamored with her new husband. But more important, I had no news of my mother's manuscript. It was not at the post office and Muriel was adamant that it had been posted.

I set off for home, but as I crawled past Pippa Carmichael's new abode, Honeysuckle Cottage, Harry Honeychurch came out of the front door. He was dressed as his alter ego, the fictional World War One hero Squadron Leader James Bigglesworth in trademark aviator goggles, white scarf and flying helmet.

I stopped and opened the window. "Harry!" I called out. "What are you doing here?"

Harry hurried over. "Max is the Red Baron. We're about to have a dogfight. You have to watch! Here he comes! Look out! Argh. He's got a machine gun!"

Harry darted across the street in front of my car and threw himself over the churchyard wall just as Max Carmichael raced out of the cottage with a BB gun in hot pursuit. He too was dressed as a World War One aviator. A red T-shirt was emblazoned with the name Red Baron.

Pippa spotted me from the front door and waved. The coil of blond hair that she wore on top of her head had fallen down. Despite looking hot and annoyed, she managed to make her bohemian dress stylish.

"This parking situation is infuriating," she said. "I had to drop the boys off and park up the road." She jabbed a finger at Violet's Morris Minor Traveller. "I reckon old Violent had been waiting for me to do the school run so she could grab that space."

"Violent?" I said.

Pippa grinned. "Do you like her nickname? I caught her

kicking my car yesterday. Put a dent in it, actually. She's got quite the temper."

Pippa's callousness surprised me. "I suppose Violet is disappointed that you've opened a tearoom next door."

"I'm offering healthier options." Pippa glanced behind her and laughed. "There she is, nosy cow, staring at me through the window."

"Honestly, Pippa, I'm saying this as a friend," I said. "Be careful. One thing I've learned is that as a newcomer to the village it's important to get along with everyone."

"I don't care what people think about me."

"This isn't London. You can't be anonymous here," I said. "Everyone knows everybody's business and that's just the way it is."

Pippa gave a heavy sigh. "Sorry. You're probably right. I'm just frazzled. I've had a hellish week. How are you?"

"I didn't know you were moving into the village."

"It was all very sudden," said Pippa somewhat defensively. "Don't give me a hard time, Kat."

"I wasn't going to," I said, stung. "I would have helped you move, that's all."

"It's just hard to juggle everything sometimes."

"I know. I understand it can't be easy." And I guessed it couldn't be. As a single mother Pippa struggled to make ends meet, and Max was a handful at the best of times.

As if reading my thoughts, she yelled, "Max! Harry! Get off those graves! Come here right now!" She turned to me. "Boys will be boys."

Harry and Max darted toward us flapping their arms and making pretty convincing aircraft engine noises.

Harry screeched to a halt and lifted his aviator goggles. "We're getting ready to go on surveillance, Stanford."

"I thought you two fought on opposite sides?" I teased. "Isn't the Red Baron German?"

"I'm only the Red Baron when I am wearing this T-shirt," said Max gravely. "But when I take it off, I'm—"

"Flying Officer Carmichael!" Harry shrieked.

"Go inside and play quietly until it's time for Harry to go home," said Pippa.

"Did you charge my camera, Mum?" Max demanded.

"Yes. I did." Pippa rolled her eyes. "Max is convinced the churchyard is haunted. He wants to take photographs."

"It probably *is* haunted," I said.

"The Hall is haunted," Harry put in. "We've got tons of ghosts there."

"Well, I don't believe in all that ghost rubbish," said Pippa.

"Why don't I take Harry home?" I offered. "I'm going back there now."

"Thanks, but I have to go there anyway."

"Oh?" I was surprised.

"I'm overseeing the catering for the Hog Roast for next weekend's re-enactment. What do they call it . . . a *Skirmish*?"

This was a big surprise. "Oh. But I thought—never mind."

"Kat. Seriously?" Pippa gave an exasperated sigh. "I can't tell you everything that is going on in my life."

Again, I was surprised by Pippa's attitude. "Well, I really must be going," I said, and waved a good-bye.

As I drove home I thought the word "skirmish" summed up what was going on in the village perfectly. The English Civil War had been over for hundreds of years and had been fought for much loftier causes, but right here, in the twenty-first century, I found myself inexplicably embroiled in village trivia and didn't like it one bit.

So far, it had been such a strange day. The discovery of the skeleton, Lavinia accusing Rupert of having an affair with her stepmother—who seemed very nice—Mr. Brown's peculiar reaction about the Jumeau doll and now Pippa Carmichael had moved into the village and was already making waves.

Sometimes I looked back on my life in London and thought everything seemed so much simpler then.

But meanwhile, I had the grim task of telling my mother that *Ravished* was indeed missing.

Chapter Ten

"What am I going to do?" Mum wailed for the umpteenth time.

"Are you positive that you put in the right address?" I said. "Some of these bigger buildings require a suite or floor number."

"I thought you said that the manuscript never left Little Dipperton?"

It was true. I had said that. "But at least Muriel remembered the package," I said. "She asked if you were planning on being the next Krystalle Storm."

"Oh God, that's all I need. Muriel is such a gossip. Why on earth would she think that?"

"Because you are Krystalle Storm."

"Frankly, Muriel is the least of my problems."

I knew that the loss of the manuscript could be disastrous. Even if Mum remembered what the story was about it would take her months to re-type it.

"It's nearly three-thirty," I said.

Mum groaned. "The costumes."

"Did you finish them?"

"Almost."

We headed to my car with the clothes in individual garment bags. I laid them flat on the backseat. Ten minutes later
we had arrived at the Hall.

I always found the front of the house very imposing. The
architecture was described as Classic Revival with its Palla-
dian front and central porte-cochere and Tuscan columns. Four
banks of tall chimneys topped with decorative octagonal pots
confirmed the earlier Tudor core. Additional wings stretched
in different directions, although most of the house and attics
had all been sealed off decades ago.

Thanks to the recent discovery of the Honeychurch mint
and the subsequent sale of several rare silver coins, a large por-
tion of the roof had been repaired. Scaffolding that had stood
"since the millennium"—according to the dowager countess—
had finally been taken down.

Yet, despite the turning circle and graveled forecourt having been cleared of weeds and the fallen cornices and broken
roof tiles moved out of sight, Honeychurch still carried a neglected and abandoned air. True, the stone water fountain with
its rearing horses in the center of the turning circle now worked,
but many of the twelve-pane casement windows on the ground
and first floors remained shuttered and the house was in desperate need of a good coat of paint.

Cropper greeted us at the main entrance. He always stank
of mothballs. I had never seen him wear anything other than
his formal butler attire of starched collar, gray-striped trousers
and tails. Even when he was working in the garden he just
donned a flat cap and threw on a long, heavy waxed coat over
his uniform.

I noticed that Cropper didn't offer to help carry the costumes. Instead, he ushered us into the inner front porch, smiling at me but pointedly ignoring my mother.

I lowered my voice. "Do we have costumes for the Croppers?"

"Over my dead body," she answered.

Mum's petty feud with Cropper's wife over a love affair that had happened half a century ago had been raging for months—yet another *skirmish,* I thought, and a childish one at that.

Cropper motioned for us to follow him into the magnificent two-story galleried reception area where a huge crystal chandelier hung suspended between two domed-glass atriums.

He looked directly at me. "Does Mrs. Stanford have his lordship's coat?"

"Mum?" I asked. "Do you have his lordship's coat?"

"Tell Cropper that yes, I do have his lordship's coat." My mother handed the relevant garment bag to me. I gave it to Cropper.

"I will deliver this to his lordship in the drawing room," said Cropper with a sniff. "Please remain here."

Cropper drifted across the black-and-white marble floor in the direction of the drawing room bearing the garment bag aloft as if he were carrying the head of John the Baptist on a silver platter.

"Hmm," said Mum. "It looks like they're getting ready for a siege."

She pointed to a long oak refectory table where an assortment of antique weapons was displayed. There were polearms and halberds, muskets, vicious stiletto knives, rapiers and basket-hilted two-edged mortuary swords.

"Wasn't all that stuff hanging in the Great Hall?" Mum mused.

I remembered seeing the collection a few months ago in the sealed-off Tudor wing and nodded.

"I wouldn't want to be stabbed by any of those," my mother went on. "Give me a swift bullet to the head anytime."

"I'll remember that for the future," I said drily. "But in the meantime, if you want to learn to use one of these, there's a muster at Carew Court on Saturday morning. I can just see you wielding a rapier."

"If I'm wielding a rapier at anyone, it will be Muriel."

I gave my mother a comforting hug. "I'm sure there is a perfectly reasonable explanation—oh, look," I said, anxious to distract her. "I think they've moved the family portraits around as well."

"Except for the dowager countess." Mum pointed to an ornate portrait of Lady Edith Honeychurch wearing a strapless sapphire-blue evening gown and an exquisite seed pearl necklace. The small gold nameplate stated it was painted on her twenty-first birthday. "She was so beautiful."

"They've moved the William Dobson from the King's Parlor, too." It was nice to see it hanging here rather than hidden away.

The painting portrayed Prince Rupert of the Rhine, Prince Maurice of the Palatinate and Lord James Honeychurch— three Royalists—drinking a flagon of wine. They were seated at a gateleg table and had their glasses raised in a toast presumably to their ill-fated king, Charles I. In the foreground stood Boy, Prince Rupert's white standard poodle.

Two portraits flanked the Dobson painting, neither of

which I had seen before. One was of Lady Frances Honeychurch, who, with her dark-blue eyes and pale skin, bore an uncanny likeness to Edith as a young woman.

"Look, Kat!" Mum exclaimed. "Lady Frances is even wearing the same necklace. That's incredible!" She suddenly shivered. "I just felt as if someone walked right over my grave. Did you feel that?"

"Nope."

"The Roundheads murdered Lady Frances," she declared.

"So Harry is fond of telling me." In fact, each time Rupert's son told the story of how poor Lady Frances was drowned in the pond in the sunken garden he added more and more lurid details. The latest version involved a man-eating octopus.

"What do you know about him?" I pointed to Lord James Honeychurch. He looked dashing, as all Royalists seemed to do in their portraits, with a particularly flamboyant hat and feather, but there was something cold about his eyes that I did not like and I said so.

"And his lips are too thin," Mum agreed.

"I'm surprised you can see them under that mustache."

"I can just tell." She thought for a moment. "This is embarrassing. I really don't remember a James. Perhaps he was a cousin?"

"He must have been fairly important to be painted drinking wine with the two princes."

Mum frowned. "I can't understand why I haven't heard of him before."

I spied the butler emerging from the library. "Maybe Cropper might know?"

"Be my guest," said Mum stubbornly. "*You* ask him."

So I did.

"That's Bootstrap Jim," said Cropper with a sniff.

Mum rolled her eyes. "There's no need to be facetious."

"He sounds like a pirate," I said.

"Lord James was a cousin," Cropper said. "And the correct term is 'a soldier of fortune.'"

Mum perked up. "You mean he really *was* a pirate?"

"According to my grandfather, who was also the butler here, Bootstrap Jim was the black sheep of the family."

"Was . . . Bootstrap Jim born here at Honeychurch?" I asked.

"If he was, his birth and death would be recorded in the Parish registers in St. Mary's church," said Cropper. "But from what's been passed down from generation to generation, he wasn't very popular."

"Did he die in the English Civil War?" Mum mused.

Cropper feigned surprise. "Are you talking to *me*, Iris?"

"Of course I am talking to you, *Seth*," Mum said. "You know I'm researching the family tree for his lordship—"

"I think the less said about Bootstrap Jim the better," said Cropper.

"Surely that's for his lordship to decide?" said Mum.

Cropper turned pink. "Very well. If it's his lordship who is asking." He thought for a moment. "All I can tell you is that if Lord James had been killed in the war it's most likely that he will be found in the Honeychurch mausoleum—"

"Cropper!" The drawing room door opened and Rupert poked his head out and beckoned for us all to join him inside. So we did.

My mother fell into raptures; even I was dazzled.

"Oh, milord! You look *very* dashing!" said Mum. "D'Artagnan!"

Rupert did *indeed* look very dashing in his dark-green doublet with large loose sleeves that were slashed in front and had a collar covered in a falling band of rich lace. He wore long breeches fringed at the bottom that perfectly met the tops of his wide leather knee-high boots that were adorned with more lace ruffles. A red sash and a sword, together with a plumed large-brimmed hat beneath which a cascade of dark ringlets fell to his shoulders, completed the outfit. He'd even managed to curl his mustache.

"Nice job, Mum," I whispered.

Rupert swept his hat off in an elaborate bow.

Mum giggled and curtsied in response. "You look just like a musketeer, milord!"

He grinned broadly. "What an excellent job you've done with my lace cuffs, Iris."

"I replaced them with some Belgian stuff I found," said Mum. "I'm glad you like them. Where would you like me to put the other costumes?"

Rupert's eyes widened. "How many do you have?"

"Lady Lavinia's, Harry's and—although I wasn't asked to make something for the dowager countess, I did so anyway. I found a lovely brushed velvet in midnight blue."

"And Cropper and Mrs. Cropper?" Rupert asked. "What delights did you conjure up for them?"

"We're perfectly happy with the *old* costumes we've been borrowing from the Little Dipperton Players, your lordship," said Cropper in a tone that clearly meant they were not. "And besides, Mrs. Stanford is far too busy."

"I *am* busy," said Mum. "Very busy. But I do need Lady Lavinia to try hers on."

Rupert admired his cuffs for the umpteenth time. "Cropper? Is Muriel here yet?"

"Not yet, milord."

Mum stiffened. "I haven't finished Muriel's costume yet."

"Never mind. But you do need to be paid for the fabric, this wonderful lace and your time," said Rupert. "Fred was the treasurer for the Skirmish, but now he's no longer with us, Muriel insisted on taking over."

"Oh. Good," said Mum. "I'd love to see Muriel."

"You're not going to do anything rash, are you?" I whispered. "Please, Mum."

"It depends."

"Cropper, can you go and find my wife?" Rupert said. "She was supposed to be here."

"Mrs. Cropper is with her now," Cropper replied somewhat cagily.

"Mrs. *Cropper*? Whatever for?"

"I believe she is not feeling quite herself. Shall I—?"

"Yes. Go and get her," said Rupert curtly. Cropper did as he was told and left.

We fell into an uncomfortable silence. I took in the drawing room, always struck by how beautiful it was with its elaborate cornices and decorative strapwork. Shabby silk wallpaper shared the walls with tapestry hangings. Damask curtains fell graciously from the four casement windows that overlooked the park where three enormous marquees now stood.

The furniture reflected the Hall's various incarnations from seventeenth-century oak court cupboards to an ugly

twentieth-century drinks cabinet. There was the usual plethora of side tables, lamps and gilt-framed mirrors as well as an
overwhelming number of miniatures that took up almost the
entire wall to the right of the fireplace. A copper Gibraltar gong
stood in the corner next to a very fine eighteenth-century
French tulipwood and parquetry display cabinet that contained
Edith's coveted snuffbox collection and some early glassware.

Lavinia entered from a side room wearing nothing but a
flimsy silk robe and holding a packet of frozen peas to her
black eye. She made a beeline for one of the two Chester-
field sofas and threw herself onto it with a leg flung over the
arm, allowing anyone who cared to look a view of one pale
skinny leg.

"Lav!" Rupert exclaimed in horror. "For heaven's sake!
Cover yourself up! We have guests."

Lavinia ignored him and waved the bag of frozen peas the-
atrically. "Hello, guests!" she cried. "Golly, Rupey. You look so
yummy in that get-up. Where's my cozzie, Iris?"

"Kat has it, your ladyship." Mum shot me a worried look
and mouthed the word, *Vicodin?*

"I can't wait to see it." Lavinia giggled. "I hope I look as
yummy as Rupey."

"I'm glad you are feeling brighter," said Mum.

"Oh yes. Very much so," she said. "Can't feel a thing. *Ab-
so-lute-ly* no pain. Must get some more of those pills."

"Pills? What is she talking about?" Rupert demanded.

"Nothing," said Mum quickly. "Let's go and try on your
costume. Kat—give it here."

I removed the garment bag to reveal the gown of dark-
burgundy silk with full sleeves and a lace collar. Mum had

embroidered the bodice with fake pearls. Beneath the skirt peeped masses of petticoats.

It was stunning.

Lavinia squealed with delight. "Oh! It's delicious!" She scrambled to her feet as Rupert continued to watch her with growing alarm.

Lavinia touched the gown and promptly burst into tears. "I've never worn anything so beautiful."

"Lav! For God's sakes! Get a grip!" hissed Rupert.

"I told her to only take half," Mum whispered. "She's obviously having some sort of reaction."

Cropper opened the drawing room door and announced, "The Earl of Denby, Lord Aubrey Carew—"

"Oh look, Daddy. Isn't this divine?" Lavinia spun around, clutching the gown to her chest.

"Aubrey," said Rupert. "Allow me to introduce Iris and Katherine Stanford."

As Mum and I turned to meet Lavinia's father, my jaw dropped. I couldn't believe it. Lavinia's father was none other than Mr. Brown.

Chapter Eleven

Mr. Brown turned ashen. For what seemed like eons we just stared at each other.

"Aubrey is our local magistrate, a renowned expert on antique weapons and armory...and leader of the *enemy*," Rupert went on with relish. "Iris is our excellent seamstress and you've probably come across Katherine? She was the TV host for *Fakes & Treasures*."

I suppressed the urge to demand an explanation. Judging by a variety of expressions Aubrey gave me from across the room, I was certain that would come later. But for now, I offered my hand and smiled. "Very nice to meet you."

Aubrey gave a nod of greeting. "Mrs. Stanford. Ms. Stanford... a pleasure."

"If you'd like me to run you up an outfit, you'd better let me know quickly," said Mum. "I've not made a single costume for the Roundheads and I'd quite like to tackle a bit of leather."

Aubrey looked startled. "Oh. Thank you. But that won't be necessary."

"We've asked Aubrey to take a look at the dagger that was

found in the grave this morning," Rupert went on. "Unfortunately, Detective Inspector Cropper isn't here yet."

"Just show me where it is," said Aubrey, who, now he'd recovered from the shock of seeing me and realized I wasn't going to spill the beans, spoke with the unnerving authority of a man used to be obeyed.

"I'm afraid Shawn—Detective Inspector Cropper—took the dagger with him."

"He took the dagger *with* him?" Aubrey exclaimed. "That is highly irregular. It is vital that I see the weapon in situ."

"I'm afraid our policeman considers the grave a crime scene and until we know—"

"I bet pompous Shawn has it in a Ziploc bag," Lavinia said dreamily. "He'll have a plastic shopping bag and in the plastic shopping bag will be the Ziploc bag. I *bet* you a thousand pounds!"

"Be quiet," Rupert hissed again.

Aubrey checked his watch. "How long do you think this Detective Inspector is going to be? I have much to prepare for Saturday's muster."

"Aubrey is our Master of Arms for the Skirmish," Rupert explained. "He'll be organizing the muster on Saturday morning along with Piers— Where is Piers? I thought he was coming with you?"

"You know my son," said Aubrey. "He'll be here in his own time."

Rupert looked annoyed.

"But I do know he has seventeen volunteers willing to play dead," Aubrey said with a chuckle.

"I hope he hasn't offered anyone money this year," said Rupert.

"I believe payment in Scrumpy was mentioned," said Aubrey. "He feels that if someone has to lie in a field full of cow manure on a hot day they should get something for it other than insect bites."

"Well, he should have checked with me first," growled Rupert. "Free Scrumpy was not in the budget."

"He doesn't like you, Rupey," Lavinia said wistfully, still clutching her gown. "I wish you loved each other. I love you, but I love Piers because he's my brother. I can't choose." Lavinia started to sniffle. "Don't ask me to choose. I really can't."

Aubrey rounded on Rupert. "What have you done to her *this* time?"

"I have no idea what she's sniveling about!" Rupert exclaimed.

"Let's go and try on your costume, your ladyship," said Mum cheerfully. "Come along now. Where should we change, milord?"

"Take her to the downstairs loo, Iris," Rupert said, but Lavinia dug in her toes.

"Did you know that we can't use cannon anymore?" she suddenly announced.

Mum looked puzzled. "Cannon, your ladyship?"

"Isn't that right, Daddy? *No* cannon! And *ab-so-lute-ly* no live ammunition! Health and Safety spoil everyone's fun."

"That's quite right, dear," said Aubrey, shooting daggers at Rupert.

"Shatters the windows. Glass *everywhere*." Lavinia nodded

sagely. She paused for a moment. "When you shoot a gun now you have to shout ... *BANG!*"

She yelled so loudly that Cropper fell into the Gibraltar gong with a deafening clatter.

Lavinia screamed. Mum and I collided. Shawn burst into the drawing room in a swirl of cape and feathers making all of us jump. I half-expected him to draw his sword.

"I heard a crash and then a scream." His eyes darted left and right. "What's going on?"

"God have mercy." Mum sniggered, and began to shake with suppressed mirth. I daren't look at her especially when I saw that Shawn was holding his trademark plastic shopping bag.

"Shawn's got the bag!" Lavinia shrieked. "Uh-oh. Someone's in trouble!"

Aubrey fixed Rupert with a glare. "I hope Lavinia's not taking any drugs."

"Drugs?" said Shawn. "What's all this about drugs!"

"Lavinia got kicked by a horse," said Rupert wearily as he helped Cropper out of the Gibraltar gong.

Mum advanced to the sofa where Lavinia had retreated, still clasping her gown. "Come along, milady. Let's try it on and make sure it fits."

Lavinia brightened. "Oh yes. It must fit. I want to look better than Jess."

Aubrey looked pained. Shawn was confused; and Rupert, embarrassed. I felt I was in the midst of a farce.

Mum got hold of Lavinia and we steered her out of the drawing room.

"Ms. Stanford—Kat?" Aubrey hurried after us. "Can we talk privately?"

"You go ahead," I said to my mother.

Aubrey motioned for me to follow him to the far end of the hall and ducked behind a large potted palm.

"I'm sure this will start rumors," I said lightly.

"I feel I must explain," he said. "You must understand that I have a very good reason for not being completely honest with you."

"Antique dolls are quite a change from antique weapons," I teased.

"As I mentioned, the doll belonged to my late wife," he said. "I was curious as to the value, but when I realized it was *indeed* valuable I decided against selling it. Sentimental reasons."

I often came across sellers who wanted to remain anonymous and told him so. "But why the secrecy with me?"

"No secrecy at all," Aubrey blustered. "I didn't want to upset Jess. First wives and all that."

From the Jess I had met earlier in the post office, I found that hard to believe. She hadn't seemed the jealous type.

"Did she mention anything about the message I left on your answer machine?"

Aubrey visibly paled. "You left a *message?*"

"After lunch. When I found the doll in your car."

"But . . . I didn't give you my telephone number!"

"It was on my mobile phone," I said. "My mobile phone logs incoming calls."

"Oh dear," he said anxiously. "Did you mention the doll in your message?"

"No. I just asked you to call me. Nothing more."

This was becoming stranger by the minute.

"Good. Good. Thank you." He gave a brief smile. "First wives and all that."

"So you said. Well, you can pick up the doll anytime. Just call first."

"I wish I had boobs," came an anguished cry from the downstairs loo. "Why did God make me so flat chested?"

"Sometimes I wonder if Lavinia was left by the fairies," Aubrey said with a sigh.

I decided I liked him after all. "I recognized your car in the hedge," I said. "I drove around looking for you. I thought you might have been lying in a ditch somewhere."

"I cut across the fields to Carew Court," said Aubrey. "Those old Volvos are built like tanks. Piers dragged her out with a tractor this afternoon. Apart from some scratches and a broken headlamp, she's perfectly drivable."

"I'm glad you weren't hurt and the Jumeau is still in one piece. What happened?"

"I was run off the road by a madwoman in a Morris Minor Traveller. She didn't even stop to see if I was alright."

Since Violet Green was the only person in the area who owned a Morris Minor Traveller I told Aubrey it was most likely her.

Aubrey frowned. "Violet Green? *Violet Green.* Now why do I know that name?"

"Do you want to see this dagger or not?" Rupert called out from the oak refectory table where Shawn, wearing purple disposable gloves, was holding it.

"Let's go and torment my son-in-law." And with a mischievous wink Aubrey gallantly took my arm, and we went to join them.

Shawn offered Aubrey a pair of disposable gloves. "I must insist on these, sir."

"Do you have a different color?" said Aubrey. "Unlike Prince, I was never fond of purple."

"I'm afraid not," said Shawn. "Please use these. We're trying not to contaminate the item—"

"But since you are holding it, the item has already been contaminated," Aubrey pointed out as he pulled on a pair. "As has the grave, so I'm told. Have you contacted the authorities?"

"Dr. Crane," said Rupert. "Plymouth University of Anthropology. He'll be here on Monday."

"Crane is a good man although a bit unconventional." Aubrey nodded to Shawn. "The dagger please."

Rupert nodded and Shawn obliged.

Aubrey studied the blade in earnest as we all watched the great man.

Finally, Aubrey spoke. "This is an excellent example of a seventeenth-century parrying dagger."

"Of course it's a parrying dagger," said Rupert. "We've already established that."

"It would have been used in combination with a rapier," Aubrey went on. "Historically, the dagger was wielded in the off hand of a swordsman, hence the name main gauche—French for 'left hand.'"

"We know that, Aubrey," said Rupert.

"This dagger was both a primary defense and a secondary weapon—a little brother to the rapier." Aubrey ran his thumb lightly up the blade. "A double-edge blade of Toledo steel." He turned to Shawn. "Toledo in Spain produced the highest-quality steel. It was known as the sword-making and steelmaking center dating back to AD 500. Roman legions were known to carry weapons from Toledo. These are quillons."

"Quillons?" Shawn's voice came from behind my shoulder. I could smell bananas. According to Shawn, his mother-in-law did their laundry and it was the boys' fabric conditioner's scent of choice.

"These two transverse members form the cross guard," said Aubrey. "They're designed to slow an opponent's blade, to block the blows and also protect the hand. The main gauche is also used defensively to create a space so that a swordsman can strike—*OUT*!" With lightning speed Aubrey suddenly lunged at Rupert, who leapt out of the knife's path, "Like so!"

"Good God, Aubrey!" he exclaimed. "You almost had me."

"Steady on, sir," said Shawn, who had leapt back a good three feet himself.

"This is an exceptionally fine example with excellent craftsmanship," said Aubrey. "It would have been highly prized by its owner. These daggers were custom-made—"

"Rather like the wands at Hogwarts," Shawn chimed in. "Sorry. The boys have finally discovered Harry Potter."

"The only thing missing is the sheath," Aubrey went on.

"Surely the leather would have rotted by now—unless," Rupert said. "I think we may have a sheath in the Museum Room. Where's Mother? She'll know."

"I took Edith to the railway station," I reminded him.

"A soldier was married to his sword and dagger," Aubrey went on. "He would never have left his weapons behind—unless he died, too."

"There was only one body in the grave," said Shawn. "A female."

"There were female soldiers, Aubrey," said Rupert.

"Yes…there were, but…" Aubrey looked to Shawn. "Did you find other weapons in the grave? Wouldn't she have carried a sword?"

"She did not have a sword, sir," said Shawn.

"You're the detective, Officer," said Aubrey. "What do you think?"

"We've already assumed she was murdered," said Shawn.

"And it would appear that she wasn't murdered by just anyone, Rupert," said Aubrey grimly. "She was murdered by one of *your* ancestors."

Chapter Twelve

"But that's silly," I said. "How do we know which side she was on?"

"Thank you, Katherine," said Rupert. "Maybe she was a Carew spy and deserved her fate?"

"Ladies, gentlemen," said Shawn quickly. "This is a cold case and it's likely it will remain so—"

"I don't know," said Aubrey slowly. "If it was possible to track down Richard the Third's descendant in Canada—why don't we take your DNA, Rupert?"

"Why don't we take yours?" said Rupert. "But frankly, what does it matter now?"

"I must admit I'm curious as to who she was," I said. "And my mother will be, too."

"Mrs. Muriel Jarvis and Ms. Violet Green," boomed Cropper, putting an end to further speculation. Apart from her shocking-pink Crocs, Muriel was still dressed in black. Violet wore a pale-blue linen suit. Given the current state of their friendship, I was surprised to see them arrive together and hoped that Muriel had kept her promise to talk to Rupert about her financial predicament.

"Violet Green!" Aubrey spun around. "We meet again. I hope your car came off better than mine."

My heart sank. It had been me who had mentioned Violet's name to Aubrey.

"Do you or do you not drive a green Morris Minor Traveller?" Aubrey demanded.

Violet's eyes widened. She turned white.

"Not only did you hit my car with your appalling driving; you left the scene of an accident."

Shawn stepped forward. "Would you like to press charges, milord?"

"Oh, please, please," whimpered Violet. "It's my glasses. They're cracked. I couldn't see properly. I . . . I . . ."

"You should press charges," Muriel declared. "I took my life in my hands this afternoon. She's a maniac on the road."

"And that's the thanks I get for giving you a lift," fumed Violet. "I should have let you walk."

"I wish you had!"

Clearly, Muriel's love affair with her bicycle had been short-lived.

Aubrey regarded the two women with displeasure. "And a good afternoon to you, Mrs. Jarvis. I hope you two ladies followed the orders of the court and made up your differences."

"Unfortunately not, sir." Muriel's expression was pure spite. "Violet still hasn't paid for Fred's hard work. I'm certain it was the stress that did him in." She pointed to Violet. "It's her fault that my poor Fred had a heart attack."

Violet's eyes blazed. "I don't have that kind of money. I've only got my pension and what scraps I make from my tearoom."

Shawn patted his doublet, obviously searching for his policeman's notebook and pencil.

"No need, Shawn." Aubrey waved him away. "Let me handle this."

"She keeps coming up with excuses," Muriel went on. "And me with my money problems."

"Oh yes, *those* problems," said Violet childishly. "The next thing you'll tell us is that all the money for the Skirmish has been stolen. Just like your car."

Muriel gave a cry of distress and, reaching blindly behind, sank—as luck would have it—onto a Dutch marquetry chair.

"Mew?" Violet rushed forward, concern etched on her face. "Are you—?"

"Muriel?" Rupert cut her off. "Cropper, bring Muriel a glass of water."

"I'll get it," I said, but Cropper had glided off with surprising speed.

"I'm alright, really; well, actually, no. I'm not alright at all." Muriel put her face in her hands.

"Is it your heart?" said Violet anxiously. "Tummy? Rheumatism? Phlebitis?"

"Don't you think we should call a doctor?" I suggested.

Muriel finally looked up. "Oh … milord, I don't know how to tell you this. I'm so upset."

"You can tell me, Muriel. We're family."

"Violet is right." She swallowed hard. "All the money for the Skirmish *has* been stolen."

Violet's jaw dropped in astonishment.

"I just ... I just—" She opened the clasp of her handbag and pulled out a clean lace handkerchief. "I only just realized half an hour ago."

"*All* of it?" Rupert exclaimed.

"Why didn't you tell me?" Violet cried.

"Why would I?" Muriel shot back.

"Because ... because ... we're friends."

"Are we?"

Their feud was clearly back on.

"*All* of it," Rupert said again.

Shawn finally produced his notebook. "When was the last time that you saw the money?"

"Just before Fred passed." Muriel began to sniffle into her handkerchief. "He kept it in a biscuit tin."

"A *biscuit tin?*" Rupert cried. "Not under lock and key?"

"Keeping cash in a tin is asking for trouble," said Shawn.

"That's what I told Fred," Muriel agreed. "But he wouldn't listen. He's been the treasurer since 1982 and has never had any problems before."

"Why didn't he put the money in the post office safe?" Shawn asked, which was exactly what I had been thinking myself.

"He didn't like to mix post office business with his treasury responsibilities."

"And you're certain he didn't put the tin somewhere else?" said Shawn. "Perhaps Fred moved it before he died?"

Muriel shook her head. "It was always in the bottom drawer in the kitchen along with the saucepans. I've looked high and low."

"I think it best if you come down to the station and we'll

file a proper report. Perhaps you might like to check for anything else that might be missing—jewelry, perhaps? Unfortunately, since you don't know when the money was stolen, there is no point dusting for fingerprints in the post office or in your kitchen. It's too late for that now."

Muriel nodded. She looked miserable. I glanced over at Violet, who was watching her former best friend with an expression I just couldn't fathom.

"And you mentioned your car was stolen as well?" Shawn said. "Why didn't you report that?"

"I didn't want to trouble you."

"How much money was stolen, Muriel?" Rupert demanded.

After some hesitation, Muriel cleared her throat. "Eleven thousand, five hundred and forty-eight pounds."

"WHAT!" Rupert tore off his hat—and wig—and raked his fingers through his short hair. "But that's an astronomical sum. Surely, not all raised by local jumble sales and church fetes? I had no idea!"

"The Totnes Rotary Club put money in, I believe, milord," said Shawn. "And the Hare & Hounds fronted some hoping to get the funds back from the ticket sales to the Hog Roast."

"This is very serious!" Rupert exclaimed. "The balance of the marquee equipment must be paid for today; and the pig, tomorrow."

"I'm sure we can find a solution to this," said Aubrey. "You know I'm always happy to bail you out. Again."

I caught the implied dig and winced.

"No thank you, Aubrey," said Rupert stiffly. "This is a Honeychurch matter." He turned to Shawn. "Perhaps you can send in a few officers to give Muriel's premises a thorough search immediately."

"I was thinking the same thing only we're a bit short-staffed," said Shawn. "Roxy is on holiday in Majorca." He frowned. "But given there were no signs of a break-in, I can't help thinking someone knew where to find the cash. What do you think, Ms. Green?"

Violet's eyes widened. "Are you accusing me?"

"Not at all," said Shawn. "But we know you're observant. Perhaps you saw something—or someone—suspicious."

"Well . . . I did notice a strange man in the churchyard this afternoon. I expect he's staying at the Hare & Hounds. And of course, we have newcomers at Honeysuckle Cottage."

"Oh?" Shawn turned to Rupert. "Isn't that a tied cottage?"

"Pippa Carmichael and her son, Max," Violet went on. "He's quite a handful."

"Yes," Muriel said suddenly. "Violet's right. I caught him stealing some sweeties yesterday right under my nose. And to be honest, milord, and forgive me for saying this, I don't think Max Carmichael is a good influence over Master Harry—"

"And someone stole my Crown Derby teapot," Violet added. "It's always been on the windowsill in my tearoom and now it's vanished."

"Hardly something a boy would take surely, Ms. Green," said Shawn, pencil poised.

"Maybe not *Max*, but I wouldn't be surprised if it was his *mother*. She wants to put me out of business, you know."

"Your mother is a genius," Lavinia cried as she threw open the door to the downstairs loo and drifted into the reception area in her dark-burgundy gown. She looked quite lovely despite her battered face and the fact that the bodice bore enough pins to sink a battleship.

Mum joined me. "Just a few tweaks needed to the bust."

Lavinia circled Rupert and swished her skirts.

"Not now, Lav," said Rupert crossly.

Lavinia stroked Rupert's arm and then went on to circle her father.

"Oh!" she exclaimed. "What's Muriel doing here? Good. I want a word with her—"

"Pippa Carmichael and Lady Jessica Carew," boomed Cropper. "And Mrs. Cropper."

The trio filed in. I saw Violet stiffen and glare at Pippa. She mumbled something that sounded distinctly like "trollop."

"Good heavens," said Mum. "Quite a party."

I was struck by Pippa's tidy appearance. She had redone her blond hair in a neat French plait and even wore a smidgen of lip gloss. A pale-yellow shift dress showed off her curvaceous figure and tanned legs. She'd swapped her Edwardian button boots for red ballet flats.

Mrs. Cropper was wearing her usual pink-and-white-striped pinafore over a white linen short-sleeved dress. A mobcap completed the resemblance to Mrs. Patmore from *Downton Abbey*.

Jess seemed even smaller than usual sandwiched between Pippa Carmichael and the cook. She greeted everyone with a smile—giving me a friendly wave— before slipping alongside Aubrey and planting a kiss on his cheek. "I hoped I'd find you here, darling."

Aubrey's cheeks turned pink, and judging by the way his eyes softened, it was obvious to everyone that he was enamored with his new wife and—supposedly—she with him.

Aubrey took Jess's hand and squeezed it—a gesture not lost on Lavinia.

"Oh for heaven's sake, Daddy!" she exclaimed. "Do you have to maul each other in public?"

Jess laughed. "I'm sorry, Lavinia, but I think we do." She kissed Aubrey again.

"I think we'll go, Rupert," said Aubrey. "Leave you to this mess—and Ms. Green, I will be in touch, so don't go leaving the country."

Violet looked as if she'd just been given a death sentence.

The lovebirds left.

Lavinia turned her attention to Pippa. "Where is Harry?"

"Out exploring," said Pippa. "You know what kids are like."

Lavinia seemed put out. "I'm sorry? What did you say?"

"They're out somewhere."

"Out somewhere ... *who?*" Lavinia said.

Pippa looked puzzled. "Who?"

Cropper stepped up to Pippa and whispered in her ear. "You're kidding?" He whispered into her ear again.

With a heavy sigh, Pippa said, "Master Harry and Max are out exploring, your *ladyship*." She shot me a look of derision.

"I'm afraid you've all had a wasted journey," said Rupert curtly. "The meeting has to be postponed."

"Cropper filled me in on the theft, milord," Mrs. Cropper said.

"Theft?" Jess and Pippa chorused.

"I'm afraid the money for payment of the marquees and the pig has been stolen," said Rupert.

"That's frightful!" Lavinia exclaimed. "I knew we had a thief in our midst. My riding crop is missing."

"And my Crown Derby teapot," Violet said again.

"I'd like to take some details if I may," said Shawn.

"With due respect, milord," Mrs. Cropper went on. "I don't think we even need to have a meeting. Violet and I have done the Hog Roast for decades. We know what we're doing."

"I'm afraid there is a change this year," said Rupert, looking more than a little sheepish.

"A change?" said Mrs. Cropper.

"Pippa is overseeing the Hog Roast this year," Rupert said. "She has some healthy options on the menu."

"But no one wants healthy options at the Hog Roast," Mrs. Cropper declared. "We've never had healthy options."

"Exactly, so that's why it's time for a change," said Rupert. "Pippa has generously offered her services for no fee."

"But *we've* never been paid a fee, milord," Mrs. Cropper said stubbornly.

"None of us have, milord," said Violet. "Ever."

I saw a nervous tic begin to beat above Rupert's right eye.

"We don't need any help," Mrs. Cooper went on. "Especially from an outsider, do we, Violet?"

"No. Definitely not from *her*."

"Let's go, Mum," I whispered. "All this bickering is making me tired."

"You can. I'm not. I'm thoroughly entertained."

"We need to cater to vegetarians," Pippa said. "My quiches—especially the mushroom and artichoke—are hugely popular. Surely the goal is to make a profit? Not have everyone dropping dead of a heart attack."

There was a ghastly silence. Violet actually patted Muriel's hand in sympathy and Muriel let her.

"Oops," Mum whispered. "She certainly knows how to put her foot in it."

Pippa seemed oblivious.

"So let me get this straight," said Mrs. Cropper, rallying the troops. "You're buying the ingredients for your fancy quiches from the generosity of your heart?"

Pippa turned to Rupert. "Can you just tell them I'm in charge?"

There was a gasp of disbelief from Mrs. Cropper and Violet.

"Excuse me," chimed in Lavinia. "You're being frightfully rude, Mrs. . . . whoever you are."

"Pippa. My name is Pippa. I'm Max's mother. Harry's friend."

Rupert took Lavinia's arm. "Come on, darling; you're not feeling yourself. Let's get you upstairs for a proper nap. I'll make you a cup of your favorite tea."

"Oh, Rupey, you've never made me a cup of my favorite tea." Lavinia gave a heavy sigh. "I do love you. You know I love you, don't you?"

"Yes. Yes. But enough of all this nonsense."

"Can Iris and Kat take me upstairs for my nap?"

"Of course, milady." Mum paused at the door. "Oh—Muriel, why don't you let me take you home afterwards? I've got a burning desire to understand how the British postal system works."

"No thank you," said Muriel. "I am perfectly content to wait here for Violet."

"You've changed your tune," Violet replied. "I thought you couldn't stand my driving."

"I'll take you home, Mrs. Jarvis," said Shawn wearily. "I'd like you to show me where Mr. Jarvis kept the biscuit tin."

"But wait—" Muriel came up to me and slipped a pale-lavender envelope into my hand. "Thank you, again."

Ten minutes later, Mum and I had helped Lavinia out of her pinned-up gown and were tucking her up in her own bed in her own room. She began to snore immediately.

"I can't believe they don't share a bedroom," Mum said. "Oh wait, I remember now. Doesn't his lordship suffer from—?"

"Something like that," I said hastily. I wasn't in the right frame of mind to visualize Lord Rupert Honeychurch's nightly bathroom habits.

Mum took in Lavinia's bedroom. "What a mess! It looks as if a tornado has been through here."

Lavinia's bedroom was chaotic. There was a saddle on the back of an armchair, *Horse & Hound* magazines stacked on the floor along with piles of unfolded clothes. A beautiful walnut dressing table held a set of monogramed silver brushes, old-fashioned glass perfume bottles and used tissues.

Two framed photographs sat on Lavinia's night table. One showed a much younger Rupert dressed in polo-playing attire; and the other, of Harry kitted out in his Biggles regalia looking adorable.

"Don't they have a housekeeper anymore?" said Mum in a low voice.

"Someone from the village comes up once or twice a week," I said. "They tried an agency, but it seems that no one stays for very long. Apparently Edith is very demanding."

"Ah-ha! A fan!" *Forbidden,* Mum's latest book in her Star-Crossed Lovers series, lay open, spine up on the floor. She grabbed it. "Lavinia's dog-eared the pages," she whispered. "Let's see what parts fascinate her ladyship."

"Mum!" I hissed.

"Ah yes." Mum nodded. "I thought so. Look." She jabbed a finger at a paragraph. "That love scene in the stumpery took me a long time to write—oh God."

"What's the matter now?"

"I should have forced Muriel to talk to me," she said. "She would rather drive home with Violet than talk to me. That's guilt. What if my manuscript never shows up?"

"It will," I said firmly. "Did you call the publisher?"

"Yes." Mum nodded. "They are going to have another look in their mailroom. What if whoever stole the club funds found my manuscript and stole that, too?"

"Now you're being silly."

Ten minutes later we pulled into the Carriage House court-yard and found an old blue Mercedes parked on the forecourt. It was in dire need of a wash. Someone had traced the words "Please Clean Me" on the rear window.

Mum frowned. "It looks like we have visitors."

"Perhaps it's the ME or Dr. Crane the anthropologist?" I suggested, although I doubted it.

"Or we're being robbed."

"You're so dramatic."

Back in the kitchen, we heard peals of laughter.

"It's coming from Cromwell Meadows." Mum opened the rear door to the field and pointed to a white canopy and screen that now stood over the grave. "Over there."

"Mum...I think that could be Harry and Max. They shouldn't be there. I'll go and see."

As I drew closer, I also heard a male voice.

I stopped and peeped around the side of the tent. A man in jeans and a short-sleeved white shirt was hunkered down in the grave. I couldn't see what he was doing because Harry and Max were blocking my view.

"Hello," I said.

Startled, the man sprang upright, Swiss Army penknife in hand. He slipped something into his pocket.

"It's Kat!" Harry cried. "Come and see a real skeleton! It's wicked, isn't it, Max? A real skeleton!"

Max grinned in agreement. Both boys were in their flying outfits, but I noticed that Harry's white scarf was missing.

"I'm Kat Stanford," I said. "You must be Dr. Crane."

Chapter Thirteen

The man was in his early forties and handsome in a rak-ish kind of way with shoulder-length dirty-blond hair. He gave me a mischievous smile.

"I *could* be Dr. Crane, I suppose." The man winked at the boys, who started to giggle.

"Detective Inspector Cropper should still be at the Hall. If you go now you just might catch him."

Max continued to snigger. Harry was practically in convulsions.

Something felt off to me. Dr. Crane wasn't wearing any foot coverings, disposable gloves—or even the white coveralls that I would have expected him to wear. There was no telltale bag of tools, either. Although my knowledge of forensic anthropology was limited, I did know that the area was supposed to be tagged and labeled in a specific way.

"Harry, perhaps you could run to the Hall and tell your father that Dr. Crane is here?"

"Perhaps you should." Dr. Crane grinned again.

"Yeah," said Max. "Go on, Harry."

Harry and Max exploded with laughter.

"Okay, boys, enough," said Dr. Crane. "The joke is over."

"What's going on?" I said. "What's so funny?"

"It's not Dr. Crane!" Harry squealed. "It's Uncle *Piers*!"

"Oh. Hello." I didn't know what else to say. I felt a bit of an idiot.

"Biggles has told me everything about you, Flying Officer Stanford."

Piers deftly stepped up and out of the hole. He offered me his hand to shake. I took it, stealing a glance into the grave behind him. It was just as I feared. Piers's footprints were everywhere.

He followed my gaze and shrugged. "I suppose I'll be court-martialed for contaminating a site of historical importance," he said, not sounding remotely concerned.

"We thought we might find some more treasure," Harry enthused. It hadn't been that long ago when Rupert, Eric and I had finally uncovered the missing Honeychurch silver in the old privy next to Jane's Cottage.

"And did you find any treasure?" I was quite sure that Piers had put something into his pocket.

"Unfortunately, not," said Piers. "But of course if you don't believe me, I'm always up for a quick frisk."

A *frisk*? I didn't know how to respond to that, at all. Despite my discomfort, there was something endearing about his boyish charm and wicked sense of humor. What had Edith called Lavinia's brother? A twit?

"But we *did* find something, Uncle Piers!" Harry exclaimed. "The helmet, silly! Look, Kat. You see the soldier? He's still wearing it."

Piers caught my eye. A look passed between us and I knew he knew that the helmet was a scold's bridle and, like me, thought it better if Harry did not know its true purpose.

"But don't you think he should have a sword?" Harry went on. "All soldiers have swords."

"Your father found a small dagger," I said.

"A dagger?" said Piers sharply. "Where?"

"In the grave. Aubrey has taken it, I believe."

"Were there any markings on it? A crest?" Piers's entire attitude had changed. There was no playfulness now. He was deadly serious. "It's important."

"I'm sure Aubrey and Rupert know more than I do," I said carefully. "You should talk to them."

"Here's Father now!" Harry clapped his hands with delight. "Oh look! He's a musketeer!"

We all turned to find Rupert striding toward us looking slightly ridiculous in his seventeenth-century dress. His face was like thunder.

"What the hell is going on here?" he demanded.

"Rupert," said Piers smoothly. "Good afternoon."

"You're trespassing."

Harry looked anxiously to his father and then to his uncle, whom it was obvious he adored.

"Father! Uncle Piers has shown us the dead soldier," said Harry desperately. "Kat says you found a dagger?"

"The lovely Katherine here mentioned you discovered a dagger, Rupert," said Piers smoothly. "I'd like a look at that."

Rupert gave me a filthy look. "I think we should move away from here, don't you? We don't want to interfere with Dr. Crane's excavation on Monday."

"Uh-oh. Looks like I'm in trouble," I heard Piers whisper to the boys. They giggled again.

Rupert shepherded us away from the white tent. "There is a reason why this area has been cordoned off."

"Why does the tape say *Crime Scene*?" Harry asked. "Shouldn't it say *Battle Scene*?"

"The tape doesn't mean anything," I said quickly. "Shawn had it handy in his pocket. He just wanted to keep people out until Dr. Crane came."

"And he was right. We should," said Rupert. "Kat, will you take Harry and Max and walk on ahead? I need to talk to Piers."

"No need for that, Rupert," said Piers. "We're all walking in the same direction."

Harry skipped alongside his uncle and took his hand. Max took the other.

"The appeal for dead bodies has been pretty successful," said Piers.

"Perhaps it's the Scrumpy," Rupert said. "Which I did not agree to, incidentally."

"I'm providing the Scrumpy," said Piers. "So yes, perhaps it is. I seem to have tapped into the eternal life of the zombie and it's attracted a lot of the younger members."

"How does this zombie-soldier thing work?" I said. "In practice."

"We hold a lottery in advance. Every man knows how he is going to die ahead of time and how long he has to wait until he can rise again," said Piers.

"My mum lets me watch *The Walking Dead*," said Max.

"*The Walking* what?" Rupert demanded.

"It's a zombie show on TV," said Max. "It's awesome, isn't it, Harry?"

Harry didn't answer.

"I can't say I've ever seen it," said Rupert. "What's it about?"

"Zombies!" the boys cried.

"That show is far too old for you," said Piers. Personally I didn't think the boys were old enough to watch such a violent show, either.

Max thrust out his jaw. "My mum says I can watch it. I watch loads of horror stuff." He shrugged. "It doesn't scare me."

Piers ruffled Harry's hair affectionately. "And I know it wouldn't scare Biggles, but it certainly scares me!"

Harry looked up at his uncle, clearly relieved.

"And who is your mum, Max?" Piers asked.

"Her name is Pippa," said Max. "We've just moved into the village."

"Ah. So you're Pippa Carmichael's son. *And* you've moved into the village." Piers fixed Rupert with a look filled with contempt. "Fancy that."

"Run along to the car, boys," said Rupert suddenly. "I need to talk to Uncle Piers."

The boys dashed off. I felt as if I should have gone with them so walked on ahead. Even so, I couldn't help overhear snatches of their conversation.

"And before you give me a hard time," I heard Piers say, "Harry and Max were already at the grave when I arrived."

"How did you hear about it?"

"Everyone's talking about it," said Piers. "You can't protect Harry forever, and besides, kids don't regard death the same way as we do."

"Regardless, I'd rather Harry continued to believe it's a soldier in a helmet."

"If you say so," said Piers.

We walked around the side of the Carriage House and into the courtyard where Rupert's Range Rover was parked next to Piers's Mercedes. Harry and Max were jumping on and off the stone mounting block. Mum stood watching them from the carriageway entrance not looking particularly thrilled. She shared my father's old-fashioned view that children should be "seen and not heard." When Max accidentally kicked over a terra-cotta pot of geraniums and it smashed on the cobblestones, she clapped her hands, yelling, "That's enough now, children. Time to go home. Chop, chop, chop."

Rupert piled the children into his Range Rover and drove away.

"Is that your mother?" Piers asked.

"Yes."

He took his arm into mine. "Then please, will you introduce us?"

Mum's eyes widened as we approached. Her curiosity was now replaced by a silly smile, the one I'd seen her adopt when she was once introduced to Bradley Walsh—quizmaster of *The Chase* and someone she has a huge crush on.

Piers reached out a hand for my mother to shake whilst firmly keeping hold of mine. "Piers Carew. A pleasure."

"So you're Lady Lavinia's brother!" Mum was agog. "But you look nothing like her. Did you have a different mother?"

"Mum!" I exclaimed.

"I was joking. I can see the resemblance with Lord Aubrey—he has that same twinkle. I'm Iris. Pleased to meet you."

"You certainly don't look old enough to have a daughter," said Piers. "You both could be mistaken for sisters!"

"Oh God." I groaned.

"Corny but true!" Piers grinned, but Mum fell for that tired old line and turned pink with pleasure.

"Would you like to come inside and have a cup of tea—or something stronger?" she said. "It's never too early for a gin and tonic."

"On any other day, I would happily accept," said Piers. "But unfortunately not today. I am anxious to see that dagger."

"We're certain it bore the Honeychurch crest," said Mum.

"The crest," said Piers slowly. "You're sure of it?"

"Positive. Why? Have you an inkling as to who she might be?" said Mum. "Only, I'm fascinated by the Honeychurch history. You could say that I am the family historian."

Piers brightened. "I'm the Carew family historian," he said. "I'm doing research for a book I'm writing."

"What a good idea. I think the Honeychurches should write one, too," said Mum. "I'd invite you inside to see my family trees if I wasn't finishing up Lady Lavinia's costume for the Skirmish."

"Perhaps I could come tomorrow?"

"Lovely," said Mum, beaming with pleasure.

A match made in heaven, I thought.

"Good-bye." I attempted to withdraw my hand, but Piers wouldn't let go.

"Not so fast. I want to ask you something."

I could practically hear the cogs in my mother's brain working overtime. "I think I left something on the stove top, but that doesn't mean you have to leave, Mr. Carew. Piers. Sir Piers? Do you have a title?"

"Piers will do."

"Alright, Piers-will-do, take all the time you need to chat. Chat here. Do." Mum gave a gay wave and retreated into the depths of the carriageway.

"Your mother is very funny," said Piers.

"Hilarious," I said. "But let's wait for one minute." I motioned for him to keep quiet until I was sure that my mother had really left. "Okay. I think we're safe."

Piers stared intensely into my eyes. "Dinner. Tomorrow night. I won't take no for an answer. I will come to your door at seven."

"Oh." I was so startled that for a moment I didn't know what to say. "I'm not—"

"Cancel your plans!" he said wildly.

"I'm—"

"Then just a drink." He gave another mischievous smile. "Just an hour. What's an hour out of your life? I might even tell you who I think is in that grave—or should I invite your mother instead? Do you think she'd come?"

I laughed. "I'm sure she'd be thrilled to have a drink with you."

"In that case I will take you both out," he said gallantly.

"But seriously," I said. "*Do* you know who it could be?"

"Let's just say that I have an inkling," said Piers. "It's a very sad story—"

"Who is it? I must know!" Mum suddenly materialized. Of course she had been eavesdropping.

"Ah, Iris," said Piers. "I'm trying to persuade your lovely daughter to have dinner with me tomorrow night, but she refuses."

"Nonsense!" Mum exclaimed. "Kat would love to, wouldn't you?"

I was about to protest again when I thought, Why not? "On one condition," I said. "Admit that you took something out of the grave this afternoon."

For a moment, Piers seemed startled. "Me? What an accusation!"

"I saw you," I teased. "You put something in your pocket."

"And if I admit I did," said Piers, "you'll agree to dinner?"

"Oh for heaven's sake, Katherine!" Mum said crossly. "Yes. Yes. I'll make sure she'll go."

"In that case, yes I did," said Piers. "So ... seven o'clock tomorrow?"

"She'll be ready!" Mum cried.

We waved him out of the courtyard.

"Goodness. What a handsome man. What a charmer! I can't believe he is Lady Lavinia's brother."

"And he definitely loathes Rupert," I said.

Mum thought for a moment. "Hasn't he just inherited Carew Court? Now, they're very wealthy. Not like the Honeychurches, who are land rich but cash poor."

"You sound like Mrs. Bennet from *Pride and Prejudice*."

"Well, since you and Shawn never got off the ground, you must keep your options open."

"Mum," I said. "Piers is completely insane; you do know, that, don't you?"

"I hardly think charm can be considered an insanity. It's all that inbreeding within the upper classes that makes them seem insane." She thought for a moment. "What did you mean when you said you saw him take something from the grave?"

I filled my mother in on what had transpired under the white tent, adding, "The whole family is nuts," and went on to tell her about Aubrey pretending to be Mr. Brown. "Of course he claims the doll belonged to his first wife."

My mother didn't seem so enthusiastic now. "Well...at least meet Piers for a drink," said Mum. "Just do it for me. I want to know about this sad story."

I stayed for supper and afterwards helped her finish up the costumes. It was quite late by the time I got home to Jane's Cottage.

Perched on a hill that looked over the Honeychurch Hall estate on one side and distant Dartmoor on the other, the little house had been built in the 1800s on the foundations of the former hunting lodge. Warren Lodge—as it was once known—had been razed to the ground when Cromwell's army came through in pursuit of the Royalists.

The new building was a pretty house constructed of red-brick under a pyramidal slate roof. Two bay windows flanked a Venetian entrance with ionic pilasters that were covered in pink and white climbing roses.

As with the gatehouses, the dowager countess had given me Jane's Cottage for a very low rent. I'd done a few repairs, installed a wood burner stove, decorated and fixed the leaking roof and guttering. I'd had window boxes and planters put around the front that were now filled with flowering geraniums. I liked it, but it still felt temporary and not really like home.

Much to my mother's disappointment, I had kept my place in London. I suppose I still wanted a bolt-hole in case everything went pear-shaped. Mum insisted that I wouldn't really begin to settle into my new life until I had given that up. Maybe she was right.

Having my flat also meant that money was a little tight for me. I didn't want to rent it out, either. I'd left hosting *Fakes & Treasures* with a substantial amount of savings, but those were beginning to dwindle much more quickly than I expected, especially as I was building up my stock for Kat's Collectibles.

I still couldn't get used to the sense of complete isolation at Jane's Cottage. On foot, the Honeychurch tenant cottages where the Croppers and Eric Pugsley lived were half a mile away or a brisk ten-minute walk. Mum's Carriage House was ten minutes farther on from there, with the gatehouses another ten—and that was taking the shortcut through the woods.

At first, I'd been excited about being surrounded by nature and being lulled to sleep by the odd owl—even being awoken by the terrifying shriek of a fox's mating call. But there was something spooky about the place that I couldn't put my finger on. I missed my garden flat by Putney Bridge tube station and the sound of the underground rumbling by, the planes en route to Heathrow and the foreign students in the language school around the corner having late-night parties.

A full moon illuminated my front door. As I let myself in, I was immediately struck by an extraordinary fragrance. It was like something I had never smelled before—a hint of the ocean yet sweet like honey with an underlying musky scent that made my senses tingle. I inhaled deeply, wondering what on earth it could be.

But, without warning, the room turned icy cold.

Gooseflesh crawled up my spine.

The hairs on my arms began to prickle.

I had an intense urge to run, and yet I could not move.

This had happened to me before.

A few months ago, I'd had the distinct impression that Rupert was following me up the stairs to the galleried landing at Honeychurch Hall. In fact, I was getting worried about just how close he was when I felt his breath on my neck. I had turned to confront him. But there had been no one there.

Later, I was told it was probably Harry's great-uncle Rupert, who had been a fighter pilot, and that the Hall was practically overrun with ghosts. Naturally I put that down to Harry's overactive imagination.

Alfred called them uninvited guests but I still wasn't convinced that the spirit world existed. I'd believe it when I saw it with my own eyes.

How I felt then was how I felt now. Scared. Yet Dad always said that it's the living who should be feared, not the dead.

"Come on, Kat!" I said in a cheerful voice. "Let's have a cup of tea."

I marched around the house, singing a silly nursery rhyme for courage, turned on all the lights, switched on the television and then on into the kitchen, where I made a cup of tea.

By the time I returned to the sitting room, the smell had vanished. Whoever it was obviously didn't like my singing, but I still felt unsettled.

I kicked off my shoes and sank onto the sofa. I tried to watch the *News at Ten*, but I couldn't concentrate. What a weird day it had been, and now this.

I couldn't help noticing my fortieth-birthday cards that were ranged along the top of my bookcase. I should take them down.

They were from people from my new life—apart from David, who had the nerve to write inside: *I hope you find happiness. Don't hate me.* I didn't hate him; I just felt incredibly sad. My mother had said that sometimes a relationship is only truly over when you have been hurt enough. When David had renewed his wedding vows with his estranged wife and my nemesis, tabloid journalist Trudy Wynne, he had done just that.

Finally I decided to go to bed, but I found it difficult to sleep. I kept thinking of the woman in the grave and my uninvited guest. Were they linked? Was that her perfume or was I really imagining everything? What could she possibly want with me? I had no connection with her or the past, and yet, seeing the barbaric scold's bridle encasing her skull and knowing that a dagger was found in her breast, I thought perhaps she had a story to tell.

I resolved to swallow my pride and talk to Alfred in the morning.

Chapter Fourteen

I spent a rough night.

My dreams were nightmares where I struggled to breathe. My head felt as if it were being crushed in an iron vise. Earth filled my eyes, my nostrils and my mouth. Shooting pains pierced through my skull, and my chest felt as if it were on fire.

I was drowning in the darkness and utterly paralyzed. I truly believed I was going to die.

And then a shrill, persistent ringing broke through, ringing and ringing before shutting off abruptly.

It was my mobile phone.

Thank God. It had just been a horrible, horrible dream.

I dragged on a silk robe and padded downstairs, heading for the kettle.

My mobile rang again.

"Katherine?" came a male voice. "Aubrey here."

"Ah," I said, suddenly jolted back to reality. "You want to come and collect the doll?"

"I'm already at the gatehouse and I don't have a lot of time."

He sounded impatient. "I left you two messages. One was over an hour ago. Hardly good business practice."

Stung, I glanced at the clock and was shocked to see it was almost ten.

"Just give me fifteen minutes and I'll be right there."

Cursing, I threw on some clothes—a pair of black jeans that were already too tight and a black V-neck long-sleeved T-shirt. I dragged a comb through my curly hair that seemed to have expanded to three times its usual size for no reason at all.

To reach the gatehouses by car was a pain—I had to take the service road, exit the tradesmen's entrance and circle back to the main gates. But if I walked it would take me twice as long.

I drove.

Aubrey's damaged Volvo was parked in front of the gate-house. The colorful banner that Eric had struggled to put up yesterday morning now lay in a heap in the middle of the drive.

"Help me with this," barked Aubrey as I got out of my Golf. We moved the banner against the stone wall moments before a large truck with *Tasty Trotters* emblazoned on the side swung into the entrance, nearly mowing us down.

There was a lot of work involved in setting up this annual event. I wondered if it was worth it.

"I'll phone Eric to come and put the banner back," I said. "Can I offer you a cup of coffee?"

"No. Busy day," Aubrey said curtly. I would imagine that he could be quite intimidating in court.

I led the way inside. "I apologize for the chaos," I said. "I'm still getting organized. I'll fetch the doll."

I kept the high-value items locked in a large safe that I'd installed in a small box room beyond the galley kitchen. I hadn't yet got the gatehouses alarmed and made a mental note to do so this coming week. With hundreds of strangers descending on the estate coupled with the random thefts that had been going on in the village, I didn't want to take any chances.

As I returned with the Black & Decker box I heard Aubrey gasp. "Jess! What are you doing here?"

"I saw your car outside, darling." She looked elegant in white jeans, a white shirt with the collar up and the pale-blue leather jacket. She was carrying a tiny gift bag.

"I've got to see Rupert," said Aubrey. He took the box from me. "I'm returning this . . . I'm returning his power drill."

"I just passed him in Little Dipperton." Jess looked at the Black & Decker box and then at me. "Don't ask him to hang a picture, Kat. He's hopeless at D-I-Y."

I really didn't know what to say so just smiled.

"What are you doing here anyway?" said Jess. "Should I be jealous?"

Aubrey seemed to pull himself together. "Kat has a lobster-tailed pot helmet that she very kindly offered to loan our farm manager."

"Oh. *That.*" Jess gave a dismissive wave. "I feel like I'm the only person in the world who is not going to the ball."

"I'm sure my mother would make you a costume," I heard myself say, then wished I hadn't.

Jess pulled a face. "Not my thing."

"Must be getting on," said Aubrey, and began to sidle to the door. "Oh, are the workmen at the barn this weekend?"

"No," said Jess. "There seems to be some delay with the materials—don't forget your fish helmet thing."

"I need to clean it up a little first," I said, and again wondered why I would lie for someone I barely knew. Maybe my mother's penchant for storytelling was in my genes, after all.

"Wait!" Jess darted to Aubrey's side and kissed his cheek. "I made you a curried chicken sandwich by the way. You know how caught up you get and forget to eat. Love you."

Aubrey turned scarlet and mumbled something incomprehensible before making his escape.

"Isn't he adorable?" said Jess. "I love it when he blushes."

"Very," I said, and wracked my brains for something to say. "How is the barn conversion coming along?"

"Excruciatingly slowly, especially when they don't turn up for work. But we'll be in by late October, I hope," said Jess. "There is no way I'm spending a winter at Carew Court. It's freezing cold inside even now and we're in the middle of a heat wave. There are no showers. Just old claw bathtubs, and when the heating is turned on the pipes rattle so hard that I fear the radiators will fall off the walls. The entire place smells of mold and mothballs. The house is on a hill and gets the north wind whistling down through the valley. I've seen the carpet on the landing literally levitate because the windows don't fit."

Despite myself, I laughed.

"It's like the upper classes were born with a gene that protects them from draughty hallways." Jess grinned. "I've told Aubrey I want under-floor heating and a state-of-the-art kitchen."

"It sounds lovely," I said.

"Sorry! I am going on as usual. I almost forgot why I came this morning." She passed me the bag. "Happy birthday!"

"Oh—thank you. But really, there is no need."

"Of course there is. Turning forty is huge. I hope you like it."

The little bag was stuffed full of tissue paper and sparkles.

I brought out a clump and unwrapped it to reveal an identical bracelet to the one Jess had been wearing the day before.

"Jess! I can't accept this!"

"You admired mine and I thought . . . why not. We're going to be firm friends, after all."

My heart sank. I'd been through this kind of thing many a time before. Fans would send inappropriate gifts in the hope that I would become their friends. But back then I didn't have to worry about hurting any feelings. My publicist would send the giver a warm and appreciative thank you letter and then promptly donate the gift to a hospital or a women's shelter. But here I was faced with a truly awkward situation.

"I'm sorry, I just . . ."

"You hate it," she said.

"No, not at all." And I didn't. I liked it a lot.

"It's just a little something. A trinket," said Jess. "I bought it from a jeweler in Dartmouth. I always like to support local artists, don't you?"

"Well, in that case, thank you," I said.

"Try it on. The catch can be a little tricky," said Jess. "I hope it fits. I had to guess your size. The idea is to collect charms. But I prefer a more simple look."

"Can I get the key?" came a familiar voice. Eric strolled through the front door.

And then the most extraordinary thing happened.

All the color drained out of Jess's face.

Eric turned beet red. "*Maureen?* What on earth are you doing here?"

Chapter Fifteen

Jess made a swift recovery and flashed Eric one of her dazzling smiles. "Maureen? Who is Maureen?" She laughed. "Sorry, but you must have mistaken me for someone else."

Eric's color deepened. "But you look—"

"I've got a common face," she joked. "I always look like someone somebody knows—or they call me Tinker Bell because of my pixie cut." She turned to me. "Not like you, Kat. I wish I had your hair."

Jess held my gaze just a little bit too long. I knew that look; my mother had perfected it over the years and it usually meant she was lying.

I'd never seen Eric so flustered. I wasn't blind, nor was I stupid. They obviously knew each other.

"Well!" said Jess. "I really must go. I've got to stop by the barn. Happy belated birthday, again." And so she left.

Eric still stood there, beanie in hand. Neither of us spoke until we heard Jess's car drive away.

"Are you alright, Eric?"

"So . . ." He hesitated. "Is she a customer?"

"That's Mrs. Carew—or should I say Lady Carew."

Eric's jaw dropped. "Carew's *wife*? I never heard that Piers got married?"

"Not Piers," I said. "The earl. Jess is Lavinia's stepmother."

"She married the old man? But ... he's—" Eric seemed upset. "When did this happen?"

I shrugged. "I think they've only been married a few weeks."

"*Weeks?*" Eric's frown deepened and so did his pallor. "I don't believe it," he muttered. "The ... I don't bloody believe it."

Now I was really intrigued. "Why did you call her Maureen?"

Eric's head snapped up. "She's not the Maureen I remember. I must have been mistaken after all." He cast about the room, scowling. "Where's the ladder?"

"In the other gatehouse." I opened the desk drawer and handed him a key. "I locked it in there. Here, help yourself."

Mum suddenly burst through the door. Eric sprang aside.

"Good heavens," I said. "It's like Piccadilly Circus in here this morning! You are my fourth visitor, Mum."

Eric nodded a greeting. "I'll get the ladder," he said, and vanished.

"You look annoyed," I said mildly.

"Annoyed? Whatever gave you that idea?" Mum stood arms akimbo, eyes blazing. "You will never believe this, but Muriel must have had my manuscript all the time!"

"They found it?" I said. "That's good news."

"Is it?" Mum shouted. "*Is it?*"

"Yes. It is."

"There are *five* pages missing!" she shrieked. "And a lot of pages are covered in strawberry jam!"

"Oh."

"And it wasn't my jam," said Mum. "I am very careful with my manuscript. And besides, you checked the pages, didn't you?"

"Twice." I agreed. "So what do you think happened?"

In between bursts of indignation and the most colorful language I had ever heard my mother utter aloud, she told me that Goldfinch Publishing had indeed called to tell her they had found the missing manuscript.

"It was stamped *Next Day delivery!*" Mum raged on. "I knew she went through the post. Didn't I tell you? I knew it!"

"Yes, you did."

"You do realize what this means, don't you?"

"Muriel sent it yesterday after I paid her a visit," I said calmly.

"But don't you see?" Mum's nostrils were actually flaring. "Muriel must know that I am Krystalle Storm. She *knows* and if she knows everyone in the village will know. And if they know . . . it won't take long for HM Revenue & Customs to know. And if they know they'll find out I haven't paid taxes for years and have been stashing my loot in the Channel Islands, and when they find that out—oh! It's all too much." She collapsed into the Knole sofa.

"Oh, dear," was all I said. I wasn't that hard-hearted to say, "I told you so."

"What should I do? Give her hush money?" said Mum.

"What for?"

"No." Mum shook her head vigorously. "That won't do. Won't do at all. It'll open me up to blackmail." She frowned, then brightened. "I know. I'll get Alfred to threaten her. Tell her to keep quiet or else . . . or else . . . or else—"

"Or else what?"

"She'll end up meeting her husband in heaven sooner than she thinks."

"Whilst you languish in prison not just for tax evasion but for murder, too?" I said. "Perhaps you should invite Muriel into your confidence? Tell her she's the only one who knows the truth—"

"Are you mad?" Mum exclaimed.

"Well, I think you're missing a much more important issue."

Mum looked blank.

"The pages?" I said.

"Oh God, yes," said Mum.

"So you might have to come clean so you can ask her where they are. They have to be in the post office or her cottage." Which was probably where she had had the manuscript all the time.

"There's a small sitting room and kitchen behind the post office and two bedrooms upstairs," said Mum. "And that Clara St. James called me unprofessional. She said how *disappointed* she was to receive a manuscript in such poor condition from one of her top authors."

"But at least she acknowledges that you are one of her *top* authors."

"Not for much longer if I don't find those pages." All the wind seemed to have gone out of my mother's sails. She seemed defeated. "They want the missing pages first thing Monday morning."

"Oh dear," I said again. "I don't suppose your editor told you exactly what pages *were* missing?"

"Of course not," said Mum.

"Then we have no choice," I said. "Today is Friday. We will go to the post office and confront Muriel right now."

"My life is over."

"Don't be dramatic."

"She wants a four-page summary of the next book. Also by Monday."

"Then you'd better get busy," I said. "Let me handle Muriel, okay?"

"I'm coming with you. I'm too upset." Mum spotted Jess's gift bag. "A birthday present? Who from? Shawn?"

"No. Jess Carew."

Mum's eyes widened. "Why?"

"Exactly. Why indeed."

"Let me see." Mum grabbed the bag before I could protest. "There's a birthday card in here. You didn't open it."

"You can if you like."

Mum showed me the card. "You seemed to have made an impression. *I'm excited we'll soon be neighbors. Looking forward to getting to know you better. Love, Jess.* At least I think that's what it says. Her writing is atrocious. Is that a heart over the letter *i*?"

"Oh dear," I said, yet again.

Mum unwrapped the bangle. "This was expensive."

"I know!"

"Is she trying to buy your friendship?" Mum regarded the bangle. "This will never fit you. Your wrists are too thick. You've got big bones."

"Thanks, Mum. You really know how to make a girl feel attractive."

"And she's so dainty. Like a little elf, but all the same,

it's very nice of her. You always found it difficult to make friends."

"Actually, I'm a private person and I am very particular about who I want to let into my life, thanks." I was beginning to get irritated. "I'm going to talk to Muriel."

Mum glowered. I locked the gatehouse and we headed for my car.

"I suppose you can always change it for a much bigger size."

"There!" I exclaimed. "You're doing it again!"

"Unless you don't plan on wearing it," said Mum. "I would."

"Actually, I like it. So yes, I do. I don't have much jewelry anymore."

"I told you not to get rid of all that stuff that David bought you."

It was true. I had. I had put everything he had ever given me into an estate auction and then donated the proceeds to the RSPCA.

"I knew you'd regret it," said Mum. "What on earth made you do that?"

"Every piece I owned reminded me of him," I said simply. "Can we change the subject?"

"You're so snippy today."

I bit back the obvious retort. I had been in quite a good mood until my mother had mentioned the size of my bones.

We drove on in silence for what remained of the short trip to Little Dipperton.

As we turned into the village a panda car and the familiar sight of Dick-the-forensic—I never knew his last name—were parked outside the post office, making it very difficult to squeeze by. I could see the large figure of DC Clive Banks moving a few bystanders away from the front door.

"That's just my luck," Mum declared.

"What do you mean?"

"If Muriel's dead then I'll never get my pages back."

"Mother! Why would you say such a thing?" At that moment, Pippa emerged from the post office with Muriel on her arm.

"Luckily for you, Muriel seems very much alive," I said. "Stop the car. I'll find out what's going on."

I opened my window as the pair drew alongside us. Muriel looked as white as a sheet.

"Whatever's happened?" I said.

"Muriel has been robbed again," Pippa declared.

"Robbed! *Again?*" Mum exclaimed. "What rotten luck."

"Well, not exactly again," said Muriel. "I just realized that other things had been stolen, after all."

"Poor you," I said. "I am sorry."

Muriel nodded. "All the jewelry that Fred bought me."

"Are you insured?" I said.

"I don't know," said Muriel. "But if I am, how long do you have to wait until you get compensation?"

"Why don't you let me help you," I said. "Obviously the pieces are of great sentimental value. If you give me detailed descriptions of what was taken, I might be able to help you find them again."

"Oh. Really. I don't want to put you out."

"In fact, there is a website called *It's Been NICKED*—"

"I don't have the Internet—"

"All I'm saying is that we should explore unclaimed property websites first."

"It must have been stolen at the same time as the money for the Skirmish," Muriel went on. "I bet it was the same people. But I was so upset when Fred died, I couldn't face looking for anything that reminded me of him."

"Really?" Mum said with ill-disguised disbelief.

Muriel shot my mother a mutinous look. "It was only when Detective Inspector Cropper asked me if anything else had gone missing that I thought to check my jewelry."

"And where did you keep that?" said Mum. "In a shoe box at the bottom of your wardrobe?"

Muriel looked astonished. "Yes. Yes I did." Her eyes narrowed. "How did you know that?"

"It's one of the first places burglars look, Muriel," said Mum. "And the other place is in a tea caddy or a biscuit tin that's on a shelf in the kitchen."

"The biscuit tin was *not* on a shelf in the kitchen. It was in the saucepan drawer." Muriel broke down. "I don't think I can go on. First Fred. Then the money and now this." She shook her head. "And I'm quite certain his lordship might evict me as well."

"Don't be silly," Pippa said in a soothing voice. "Why would he do that?"

"He's let me live rent-free ever since Fred died," she said. "But now . . . with all this kerfuffle—"

"There does seem to have been a lot of shoplifting going on," Mum declared. "Are you sure that nothing else was taken?"

"Like what?"

"Letters? Papers? You are a post office, after all."

"Not that I am aware of," said Muriel. "Did you read in the papers about that man who escaped from prison?"

Mum and I exchanged blank looks and then I remembered. "The one who masterminded some elaborate car theft ring?"

"That's the one," said Muriel. "I think it was him who stole my car."

Mum pulled a face. "The canary-yellow Kia? Hardly an easy car to sell on the black market."

"It was a special edition," said Muriel. "Fred chose the color."

Pippa rolled her eyes. "I doubt it, dear," she said. "What would he be doing down here and why would he be targeting your post office if he's a car thief?"

"Speaking about the post office," said Mum. "I really need to talk to you. It's important."

"I don't want to talk to anyone anymore," Muriel wailed. "My bunions hurt. I have a headache. I don't feel very well."

"Let's go and make you a nice cup of chamomile tea," said Pippa.

"Don't you have PG tips?" Muriel whined.

Paarp! Paarp! Paarp! Three insistent blares of the horn made us all jump.

"Oh dear," said Pippa. "It's Violet." She gave a mischievous grin. "Looks like she'll have to park behind the churchyard."

I closed my window and we drove on.

"For someone who has just moved into the village," said Mum, "that Pippa Carmichael seems to have got her feet under the table pretty quickly."

"I think when you actually live right in the middle of the village it's hard to avoid it. Plus she's opened that rival tearoom.

I'm disappointed in her, Mum. She's nothing like I thought she was at all."

"No one ever is," said Mum gloomily. "I happened to like Muriel until she stabbed me in the back."

"Maybe just for once you can enlist Shawn's help," I said. "After all, he knows who you are. I'm sure he'd understand."

"Alright," said Mum. "Let's park and go and find out."

We followed the lane around the churchyard and into an oblong-shaped area of hardened mud with a sign that optimistically said: CAR PARK. There was just enough space for half a dozen cars, and this morning that's exactly how many cars were there.

"How infuriating," my mother said.

But just fifty yards farther on was the entrance to Jess's barn. A flurry of signs covered the five-bar gate. There was a notice from the Devon County Council stating that there was planning permission to build a house; another sign said: NO PARKING AND THAT MEANS YOU in large red letters and a third was in pale green and beige that read: DELUGE CONSTRUCTION. And next to *that* was a brand-new American-styled mailbox—just as Muriel had said.

"How odd," Mum said. "Fancy having a mailbox and no house."

The thought had crossed my mind, too.

"Let's park there," said Mum.

"You mean next to the NO PARKING AND THAT MEANS YOU sign?"

"Your new best friend won't mind." Mum gave a snort of derision. "DeLuge Construction? That doesn't exactly inspire confidence, does it? Who names their company *deluge*?"

We left the MINI as close to the hedge as possible, but just as we got out Jess roared around the corner and had to hit the brakes. She opened the window. "Sorry! I'll never get used to these narrow lanes."

"Do you mind if we park here for a minute or two?"

"Please do. I saw the police cars in the village," said Jess. "What's going on? Has there been another burglary?"

"Apparently, Muriel remembered she had a load of jewelry," said Mum with a sneer. "So now the police are taking a proper look and trying to see if anything else has been stolen."

"Aubrey told me about the missing funds for the re-enactment," said Jess. "Awful. Do they have any idea who it might be? It sounds like it could be someone who knew where to find the money. Poor Muriel. First her husband dies and now this."

"And that hideous car of hers was stolen, apparently," said Mum. "Who would want to drive a canary-yellow Kia?"

"A canary-yellow Kia?" Jess frowned. "Stolen? When?"

"Last Friday. In broad daylight—didn't you say, Kat?" Mum went on. "Right outside Tesco."

"But I saw it!" Jess exclaimed. "I was in Dartmouth last Friday and I saw a canary-yellow Kia being towed away from Tesco."

"You should tell Shawn," I said.

"Good idea. Do you have his phone number?"

"It's on my iPhone. I'll give it to you." I took out my mobile and scrolled through the numbers as Jess rummaged in her handbag.

"Ready?"

"Yes—" She produced a cheap pay-as-you-go phone—"Wait, sorry"—and quickly put it back and pulled out an iPhone instead. "I'll program it into my mobile right now."

"If you knew Muriel like I know Muriel," said Mum darkly, "you'd be singing a different tune."

"Mum," I protested. "That's not fair."

"I know you make excuses for her, Kat," Mum went on. "But I'm afraid I've seen Muriel's true colors."

"Why? What has she done?" said Jess.

Mum pointed to Jess's brand-new American mailbox. "You'd better be careful."

Jess looked to me, but I just shrugged.

"Muriel Jarvis goes through everybody's post," Mum declared.

"But...but that's illegal!!" Jess exclaimed. "I don't believe you!"

"We don't know for sure, Mother," I said, adding hastily, "we don't have proof."

"Oh yes we do," Mum cried.

"But that's terrible!" Jess said again.

"I always knew she was a busybody," Mum went on. "*Always* knew it. How else can she know all the gossip in the village?"

"It's not just Muriel who gossips," I said. "You do, too. You're doing it now."

"I do no such thing!"

"Well...she won't find anything interesting out about me," Jess said lightly.

"I'm just warning you, that's all."

"So what are you doing now?" Jess demanded.

"Going to talk to the police officer about some missing letters," Mum lied. "That's what." She pointed to the American mailbox again. "And if you're expecting something and it hasn't arrived, I suggest you come with us, too."

Jess looked at her watch. "Gosh, is that the time? I had no idea. I must get back in time to make Aubrey's lunch."

And with that, she closed her window and drove away.

It was then that I remembered she'd already made Aubrey's lunch. He was going to have a curried chicken sandwich.

I thought back to earlier that morning when Eric had stepped into the gatehouse. He had definitely known her before. I was sure of it. He had called her Maureen.

"There's something not quite right about that woman," Mum mused.

I was inclined to agree.

Chapter Sixteen

We entered the churchyard and immediately Mum plunged down a narrow path between two lines of moss-covered headstones.

"Where are you going?" I exclaimed.

"Have you seen how old some of these headstones are?" Mum yelled over her shoulder. "It's like everyone from below stairs is buried over here." She foraged around for a good five minutes before working her way back.

"They're all there," she said. "Stark, Cropper, Pugsley, Banks and Jones. I saw the same names in those photographs in the downstairs loo at the Hall. I was looking at them whilst her ladyship was changing into her gown. They date back to the 1880s, you know."

"You mean the loyalty portraits." I'd been as fascinated as my mother at the formal tableaus of the Honeychurch family and their staff—all in uniform—through the decades.

"Didn't you mention something about Parish registers?" said Mum.

"Edith did. She told me that if they were still in the church they would be in the Parish chest in the vestry."

"Let's do that after we've spoken to Shawn," said Mum. "Just imagine seeing the name of everyone who was born, married and died over the last five centuries or so."

"It makes our life seem rather insignificant, doesn't it?"

"Speak for yourself," said Mum.

As we rounded the stone buttress of the Norman church, Mum saw Fred's wheelbarrow blocking the path.

"So that's where Fred Jarvis dropped dead," said Mum.

"I heard Muriel say that she couldn't face moving the wheelbarrow."

Mum scanned the area. "And that's where he's been buried—oh, Kat. That's what your father used to say to me. 'You'll miss me when I'm gone.' And I do. I really do."

I gave my mother a hug. "I know. I do, too. But come on, let's find Shawn and get this over and done with."

As we left the churchyard, Shawn emerged from the post office with DC Banks. Shawn was holding a white scarf. He tucked it inside his trench coat.

"Morning, Officer," said Mum. "Can I have a quick word with you?" She glanced over at DC Banks and added, "In private."

DC Banks nodded. "I'll wait in the car." His heavy beard seemed even heavier than usual today. I felt like all he needed was to clamp a cutlass between his teeth and put on an eye patch.

"Are you going to confess?" said Shawn.

Mum's eyes widened. "Confess to what?"

"It was a joke." Shawn looked at me and actually winked.

It was so unlike him to have a sense of humor I was momentarily taken off-guard.

"Oh. Very funny," said Mum.

"Let's go back inside," Shawn suggested.

I followed them into the post office. This was something I was determined to witness.

"And what can I do for you, Iris?" said Shawn.

"I left something of mine in here yesterday," said Mum. I gave her an encouraging nod. "About five pages—just a list of furniture."

I gave a heavy sigh.

"I'm trying to get a new quote for house insurance." She smiled broadly. "It was accidentally attached to my shopping list. I came in here and got chatting as one does, and it was only this morning that I realized I must have left it somewhere here. Do you mind if I take a look around?"

"I'm afraid that won't be possible."

"Please can you make an exception?" said Mum. "Some of the items on the list were very valuable. Do you remember that gold necklace, Kat?"

I didn't answer. I was too annoyed.

"It sounds like whoever took that money and also Muriel's jewelry is a professional," Mum went on. "And what with her car being stolen."

"Ah! The stolen car." Shawn brought out his pad and presumably made a note of it.

"Have you searched Muriel's flat yet? Upstairs, perhaps?"

Shawn looked surprised. "Did *you* go upstairs?"

"Oh. Yes." Mum nodded. "Yes I did. I popped up there for a quick cup of tea. Didn't I, Kat? Remember?"

"I have no idea," I said wearily.

"The kitchen is downstairs," said Shawn. "The bedrooms are upstairs."

"Oh yes, that's right. I was getting confused for a moment." Mum flashed one of her too-bright smiles.

"Have you asked Muriel if she found this very important *list*?"

"Not yet. She's seemed too distressed, which is why I thought I would take a quick look myself."

"She's still with Pippa Carmichael," said Shawn. "Why don't you go next door and ask her."

"I don't want to bother her," Mum said. "But I'm quite sure she won't mind."

"I'm afraid the answer is still no, Iris." Shawn turned to me. "Can we speak alone for a moment? Outside?"

Mum looked worried. "What about?"

"Nothing that concerns you," said Shawn lightly.

"Okay." I suddenly felt self-conscious about my appearance.

"I'll stay here," said Mum.

"I don't think so." We trooped after Shawn, who motioned for DC Banks to stay with my mother.

"I don't need a guard, you know," she grumbled. "I'm not six."

Shawn gently took my arm. "Let's just pop down there." He led me into the narrow passage between Muriel's post office and Violet's cottage. We had to step over mounds of dead roses. The wall looked awful with its broken trellis and cracked, graying brickwork.

Shawn stopped halfway down the passageway. It was dingy, dank and smelled of moss.

To my surprise, my heart began to pound. I couldn't remember ever being in such an enclosed space with Shawn. He
was making me nervous. "Is everything okay?"

Shawn withdrew the white scarf.

I remembered Harry hadn't been wearing it yesterday.
"That's Harry's, isn't it?" I said. "Where did you find it?"

"Behind the post office counter. He must have dropped it."

The implication was clear. "I don't believe it of Harry."

"I tend to agree with you, but I'd like you to talk to him
just the same."

"Why me?" I exclaimed. "He does have parents, you know."

"You're good with Harry," said Shawn.

"Alright, but I am quite sure he wouldn't have taken money
or jewelry. Muriel just mentioned sweets."

"I know she did," said Shawn.

"And if anything, I would think Max Carmichael is the one
who is leading Harry astray."

And Harry could be so easily led. I knew how much it
meant to him to be part of the gang at his new school. I also
thought of how he looked up to his uncle Piers, who was definitely not a good example if his blatant disregard for the burial
site in Cromwell Meadows was anything to go by.

"Violet Green claims that she sees the boys loitering in the
churchyard at all hours of the night—"

"That does surprise me!" I exclaimed. "Harry hates the dark."

"Maybe he's grown out of it," said Shawn mildly. "I'm on
Harry's side, Kat. Talk to Pippa Carmichael as well. She's your
friend, isn't she? Just find out where they were on Thursday
night."

"Of course I'll speak to him. But I don't think it's right that I speak to Pippa about her son. That's your domain."

Shawn paused for a moment before taking a deep breath. "But there's something else." He cleared his throat. "I wanted to tell you why I haven't been in touch these past few weeks."

"Oh." I felt my face grow hot. "Honestly. You don't need to explain anything. Really."

"No! I must tell you. I want to."

A flash of movement caught my eye. I looked over Shawn's shoulder and saw Violet duck back behind the net curtain in her cottage. Startled, I jumped, making Shawn leap back and hit the wall.

"Yes, we are being watched," I said.

"All I wanted to say was that I am working on a special case at the moment with New Scotland Yard."

"That sounds intriguing," I said. "I suppose that's all you're going to tell me, too."

"I'm afraid so," he said. "I just didn't want you to think that I was ignoring you—"

I felt oddly pleased.

"And when I haven't been working," Shawn went on, "I've got the boys—"

"Of course," I said. "I understand."

"But I really want to see you again, Kat." He regarded me with such intensity that my stomach turned over. "Would you be able to have a drink with me this evening?" He must have seen something in my expression, because he gave a rueful smile. "Okay, okay. I know I've canceled before, but—"

"Why don't you call me later on this afternoon," I said.

"I will. I'm ninety-nine percent positive tonight will work. My mother-in-law has the twins every Friday."

There was a sudden explosion of frenzied barking coming from the churchyard opposite. I recognized that distinctive bark anywhere.

"What's Mr. Chips doing here?"

"Shawn! Shawn! Where are you?" came a shout. DC Banks peered around the corner. "What are you doing down there?"

"We're having a meeting," mumbled Shawn. "What seems to be the problem?"

"That little Jack Russell has made a discovery, sir. He's in the churchyard. Come and see."

At the mouth of the passageway I could see my mother waving from the other side of the churchyard wall. She was with Alfred. "It's here! Right here!"

We joined them at Fred Jarvis's graveside, where, to all of our astonishment, stood Mr. Chips with a very muddy nose. Alfred reached down and fondled the little dog's ears.

Peeping out from the earth was the top of an old biscuit tin.

Chapter Seventeen

"Yes." Muriel nodded. Her face was ashen. "That's Fred's tin. That's the tin that had all the money in it. Why would someone do such a terrible thing?"

"It is a particularly unkind way to dispose of the evidence," said Shawn.

DC Banks scratched his head. "I still don't understand why they just didn't take the tin, sir."

I couldn't have agreed more.

Alfred said nothing. He was watching Muriel very carefully.

"But why not leave the tin in the kitchen?" Mum went on. "Why go to all the trouble of burying the biscuit tin, at all?"

"I think I know why," Muriel said slowly. She gestured to Violet's cottage. "*She* wanted to get paid, so she took my money."

"*Your* money?" Mum said.

Muriel reddened. "That's not what I meant."

"I thought Violet owed you the money for Fred's gardening services," I pointed out. "Not the other way around."

"I meant . . . I meant . . . Violet took it so she could pay me and not get into trouble with the magistrate." Muriel nodded. "Yes. That's what I meant."

"What about the kids playing in the churchyard?" Mum put in. "Max can be quite a naughty boy."

"Let's not go hurling accusations quite yet." Shawn pulled on his disposable gloves. "Thanks, little fella," he said to Mr. Chips, and scratched his chin. "We'll take it from here. Let's go back inside, shall we? Perhaps a cup of tea is in order?"

"It's on the house." Suddenly Pippa was standing at the graveside, too. No one had seen her coming. "I've just made a delicious carrot cake, and for the record, Max would never do anything like that, Iris. He's a good boy. It's Harry you need to watch out for. Muriel told me she found his scarf in the post office."

"Let's go and have tea and carrot cake, Mrs. Jarvis," Shawn said. I sensed he was getting irritated. "Right now!"

Mum stepped in front of the postmistress. "I really need to talk to you."

Muriel waved her away. "I can't. I'm just too upset."

"Iris, can't you tell she's upset?" Pippa threw her arm around Muriel's shoulder and the merry group headed over to Pippa's tearoom, leaving me, Mum and Alfred standing by Fred's grave. We all looked at one another in bewilderment.

"Interesting new friendship," said Mum.

"An interesting discovery, if you ask me," Alfred mused.

"I wouldn't be surprised if that Max had something to do with it," said Mum. "Why else would Pippa be so friendly with Muriel? She probably knows her boy has been stealing and hopes Muriel won't press charges."

It was possible but not likely, and I said so—although I was puzzled by their unusual friendship myself.

Mum turned to her stepbrother. "As an expert on this sort of thing, what do you think?"

"Not Harry. I'm sure about him." Alfred shook his head firmly. "I've got my theories, but I'd never accuse someone without proof."

"Oh, come on, Alfred. I'm your sister," Mum said. "Who do you think it is?"

Alfred scowled. "You're wasting your time. My lips are sealed."

I had a suspect, too, but I wasn't going to say anything without proof, either. Muriel was desperate for money, because she had asked me for a loan and written a touching thank-you letter, too. The cash had been there in the kitchen—nearly twelve thousand pounds. Perhaps the temptation had been too much. I was in a dilemma. Should I mention it to Shawn?

"And anyway, why were you in the churchyard with the dog?" Mum demanded.

"Lady Lavinia asked me to fetch her *Horse & Hound* magazine," he said. "Mr. Chips saw a squirrel and raced into the churchyard. When I found him, he was digging up that biscuit tin."

"Well . . . I think we should let the police do their job," I said. "And you do yours, Mum." I pointed to St. Mary's. "Didn't you want to see if the Parish registers were inside?"

"You're right. I do."

Alfred whistled for Mr. Chips and they headed back to Mum's MINI.

"Why can't Alfred get his own car?" I said. "Why does he always have to borrow yours?"

"I'm sure he has his reasons," Mum said. "Why don't you ask him?"

"Does he have a driver's license?"

Mum fixed me with a look that I was beginning to know all too well. It was none of my business.

I turned my attention to the beauty of the twelfth-century Norman church. It had stood here for nearly one thousand years, something that I couldn't get my head around. What amazing things these stones had witnessed. I felt an overwhelming sense of humility and marveled at how insignificant our lives were in the great scheme of things. Ever since I had moved to Devon, I'd become just as fascinated by the history of the place as my mother had. Kings and queens had been on the throne, wars had been fought, plagues had swept the countryside and yet this little church had withstood everything that time had thrown in its path and still stood proud. I found it oddly comforting knowing that no matter how good—or how bad—life could be, "this too shall pass." And on we go.

We headed to the main entrance.

Neither of us had been inside the church before.

"It's not locked," said Mum as she grasped the heavy iron handle and opened the oak door. Despite the bright sunny morning, it was dark and gloomy inside.

As we entered I was assaulted by the pungent smell of what I could have sworn was cooked bacon mixed with the scent of ancient prayer books, damp and mildew.

Mum sniffed, then whispered, "Do you smell . . . bacon?"

"Yes," I whispered back. "Why are we whispering?"

Mum shrugged and said loudly, "Come on, let's see if we can find the Parish chest."

"What an amazing place!" I exclaimed. "It's like a little time capsule."

According to the pamphlet we picked up inside, the medieval bell tower and the south two-story porch with its pretty molded battlement had been added late in the fifteenth century. The bell tower still held the three medieval bells in their original cage. There was also an underground crypt.

St. Mary's church was small, with just a long north and south aisle separating late medieval box benches of unvarnished oak. Some still had their original latch doors.

"Gosh! Those are the original pews!" I exclaimed.

"They don't look very comfortable." Mum shivered. "And it's very cold in here."

"Apparently there is no electricity or heating." There were dozens of partially burned-down beeswax candles in candelabras dotted throughout the church.

Mum pointed to the organ where, just behind it, a fire extinguisher stood next to a portable propane heater. "I see they're taking no chances over there."

"At least the organist was warm."

In front of the curtain that screened the entrance to the bell tower was a Norman font beneath a Jacobean cover. On the wall were the remains of a mural painting depicting the coat of arms of Queen Elizabeth I with an illegible Gothic script below.

I gazed up at the fifteenth-century wagon roof with its four-petal flower carvings and the Grenville coat of arms, marveling at the extraordinary workmanship. A procession of brass and marble plaques ran along the walls between the windows, commemorating the Honeychurch clan way back to the 1500s. The ancestral names were now familiar to me—I saw them almost every day on the family tree that my mother had in her office.

"Oh look!" Mum exclaimed. "There's that pirate, Bootstrap Jim. So he did die in Little Dipperton, but not until 1667."

"The war officially ended in 1651."

"It's rather like visiting old friends—oh, oh dear." She wiped away a tear.

"What's the matter?"

"Your father," she said. "I should never have had him cremated. He would have been much happier here. He could have had a plaque and we could have left flowers for him just like Muriel does for her Fred."

"It's a bit late for that now, Mum," I said. "I'm sure he's very happy floating along the River Dart."

"But—I don't have anywhere to *go*," she went on. "I don't feel him around me anymore and I'm sure it's because he's probably floated all the way to South America by now."

I gave Mum a hug. "Why don't we get a memorial plaque or something? Perhaps Edith will allow you to have that put in the churchyard?"

"I'll think about it," she said. "But I'm not sure he would have approved of my new life."

"Mother," I said, exasperated. "It's also a bit late for all that, too. I think Dad would have been very proud of what you have accomplished. I really do."

"I sometimes feel you missed out on so much because we eloped," said Mum. "In fact, I don't even know where half of my family are buried. Does that mean they'll get forgotten over time?"

"I can assure you that you won't get forgotten," I said, jollying her out of what I could tell was turning into one of her maudlin moods. "You'll be immortalized by all your books."

"It's not the same," Mum said. "We never put down roots. Or had a place to call home."

"That's not true," I said. "We all lived in Tooting for decades and now this is your home."

"It's not the same," she said again. "Six hundred years of Honeychurches and all their tenant families worshiped here—were born here, loved, married, died . . . right *here*." Mum turned to me in earnest. "Who was the woman in the grave, Kat? I know you want to know as much as I do."

"Of course I do," I said as I stood in front of the plaque commemorating Lady Frances Honeychurch. "Mum! Did you know that Lady Frances had a sister?"

"What do you mean?"

"Read that plaque. It says beloved sister of *Eleanor.*"

"*Eleanor.* I don't know anything about an Eleanor Honeychurch." Mum's excitement was plain. She whipped out her Post-it notes that she always seemed to carry on her even when it appeared she had no pockets. "There's no portrait of an Eleanor Honeychurch hanging at the Hall, either."

"Well—that doesn't really mean much. It could be in one of the abandoned wings," I said. "That's why we need to find those Parish registers. Eleanor's birth would have been recorded there—"

"And her death," Mum pointed out.

"To the vestry!"

We walked up the aisle. Mum paused at the rood screen beneath the chancel arch. Behind the Elizabethan pulpit a moth-eaten velvet curtain covered a low archway. The smell of bacon seemed more pungent here.

My mother pulled it aside. "Not through here. Just a narrow flight of stairs."

"That would lead to the rood loft," I said. "The vestry will be off the chancel. Don't you know these things?"

"I have never been a churchgoer, but that doesn't mean to say I don't believe in Him."

She gestured to a stone pillar where a hymn board with sliders bore three hymn numbers. Mum shivered. "I suppose those were the hymns sung at Fred Jarvis's funeral."

I pointed to a pair of eighteenth-century torchieres that were topped with vases of wildflowers and gladioli. "But I'm quite sure those were not his flowers. It was two weeks ago. Someone is still doing the church flowers. How strange."

"Maybe it's the same person who likes bacon sandwiches."

We passed through to the altar that sat beneath a beautiful stained-glass window. Traditional scenes from the Bible were mixed with knights riding white chargers bearing fluttering pennants with the Honeychurch motto *ad perseverate est ad triumphum.*

The door to the vestry stood open. It was a sparsely furnished room. There was just an oak table, a high-back chair, an ambry set in the wall and the Parish chest. The chest was made of oak and had thick iron bands, a lock plate and an iron hasp from which dangled a shiny new padlock. It was enormous—big enough for me to climb into and lie down flat.

"The key must be somewhere," said Mum.

"The padlock looks new."

"I thought you said that her ladyship hadn't been here for years."

"Edith hasn't, but someone obviously has."

"The flower lady who likes bacon sandwiches?"

We scanned the room. Scattered around were various odds and ends—a chipped headstone, a stack of moth-eaten Bibles and, bizarrely, four croquet mallets.

Behind the door stood a plastic bucket containing a mop, bleach cleaning fluid, disposable gloves and several old rags.

I opened the ambry. At one time it would have housed altar artifacts, but today it held a half-empty box of beeswax candles and a box of matches.

Mum searched all three of the black cassocks and grubby white surplices that hung from a row of pegs for vestments. "No. Nothing here, either."

"Maybe whoever does the flowers and cleans the church has it." I ran my hands over the Parish chest. "This oak tree was probably felled in the late fifteenth century. Isn't that amazing?"

"Let's hope that since this chest is locked, the Parish registers are still inside. Let's go and find out who cleans the church."

As we left St. Mary's, we bumped right into Shawn. "Good, I was hoping that I hadn't missed you."

"Do you know who arranges the flowers and cleans the church?" Mum demanded.

"Violet Green," said Shawn. "She's been doing it for decades. Why?"

"Even though there aren't any regular services?"

"I have no idea. Why don't you ask her?" Shawn looked at

Mum and then again at me. "A quick word with Kat, if you don't mind?"

"I'll meet you back at the car, Mum."

For once, my mother did as she was told.

Shawn looked sheepish. "It's about tonight," he said. "I'm afraid something came up—"

To my surprise I was actually really disappointed. "It's fine, honestly."

Shawn looked wretched. "I really am sorry, Kat."

"Don't give it another thought." Of course I understood his reasons, but I couldn't help thinking that if he really wanted to see me as he claimed, then he would have found a way—even if it had been for just an hour.

"I'm pretty tired anyway," I said, and I was. "I could do with an early night."

When I got to the car, Mum said, "He canceled you again, didn't he?"

I turned on her angrily. "It's none of your business, Mother."

"I'm only trying to help," Mum bleated. "And how many times *has* he canceled? Five? Six?"

"Did you want to ask Violet about the key now?" I snapped.

"I don't need to see Violet," said Mum. "I have a better idea."

"What about Muriel?"

"I don't need to talk to her, either," said Mum. "I have a better idea on that, too."

"Fine. Well, whatever it is, I don't want to know."

"Fine. I won't tell you."

We drove back to the Carriage House in an icy silence until Mum said, "Where's Jazzbo?"

She was right. My Merrythought Jerry mouse was not sitting in his usual place on my dashboard. "I must have left him in my tote bag."

"No wonder we had difficulty parking in the village. What good is a parking mascot if you don't put him in the car?"

I didn't bother to answer.

Alfred and Mr. Chips were waiting in the courtyard. Alfred gave a friendly wave and came over.

Mum got out of my car and slammed the door extra-hard.

I opened the window to say hello.

"Thought I'd stop by for a spot of lunch," said Alfred.

"Well, you won't have the pleasure of Katherine's company," said Mum stoutly. "She's not staying."

"I've got work to do this afternoon," I said equally stoutly. "I do have a business to run, you know."

"And so do we," Mum retorted. "Did you get that tracking device for his lordship's car, Alfred?"

"Iris!" Alfred said sharply. "Loose lips sink ships."

"Oh my God!" I exclaimed. "You're not seriously going to track Rupert's movements, are you?"

"I was just joking," said Mum, but I knew she wasn't. "Alfred prefers the old-fashioned surveillance method, don't you? And perhaps you can put your lock-picking expertise into good use? I need to get into the Parish chest in St. Mary's. Probably better to do it after dark."

"That should be easy." Alfred gave a toothless grin. "I like to keep my hand in. Those skills need practice."

"So will your table tennis if you get arrested again," I said.

"I also need you to take a look for five pages that are somewhere in that wretched Muriel's cottage," Mum went on. "I told you I had a better idea, Kat."

"It sounds like you're going to have a busy night," I said. "I'll leave you both to your scheming."

I drove back to the gatehouse and spent the rest of the afternoon going through my stock. My mother had upset me, but it was also my fault. I shouldn't let her push those buttons and take the bait. Why did she exasperate me so? I was sure I did the same to her, too.

It had been a trying day and I welcomed the distraction of putting my office in order. In fact, I was so absorbed that I lost all track of time until I heard a smart rap on my front door.

It was Piers Carew. He was holding a bunch of gerbera daisies. "Are you ready?"

Chapter Eighteen

"They mean innocence, purity and cheerfulness," said Piers.

I must have looked horrified, because he laughed. "We can have a drink if you're too busy, which"—he peered over my shoulder—"I can see that you are."

"I d-d-idn't think we had a definite p-p-lan," I stammered, and gestured aimlessly to the chaos behind me. "I was—"

"Unpacking?"

"Unpacking and packing," I said. "I've brought my stock down from London—I was going to open a shop in Shoreditch, but my plans changed."

"And I'm glad they did."

I groaned. "Seriously?"

"But I *am* glad!" He laughed. "However ... why are you packing? I hope you're not thinking of leaving when we've only just met."

"Not leaving *yet*," I teased. "But I *am* thinking of renting a space at Dartmouth Antique Emporium."

"Good idea," he said. "You're a bit off the beaten track up here."

His comment echoed Muriel's and justified my decision—all being well. "I'll still use this gatehouse as a showroom and an office, though."

"Good."

We hadn't moved from the front door. I noticed that Piers had Lavinia's blond coloring, but his eyes were hazel with dark-green speckles. He exuded an aura of confidence that Shawn did not have. For a moment I felt a twinge of guilt that was really ridiculous. It wasn't as if Shawn and I had ever been an item.

"Do you want me to put those gerbera daisies in water or should I hold them until they wilt?" he said.

"Yes. I mean, no," I said. "You may as well come in."

"Kitchen?" he said as he breezed on by.

"Left-hand door," I said, and watched him pick his way through boxes of toys, bears, dolls and other random items that I'd taken a fancy to or hoped would sell well.

He returned with the daisies in a water glass. "I couldn't find a vase."

"I don't have one here."

Piers scanned the room. "I hear you specialize in toys."

I remembered Aubrey's comment about his first wife. "Didn't your mother collect antique dolls?"

Piers seemed incredulous. "You obviously never met Primrose Carew. My mother was the proverbial tomboy. Hated the name Primrose and insisted everyone call her Prim, which she was—prim to the extreme. But she was a great shot, stag-hunted, raced at point-to-points...knew how to fix a car... that sort of thing."

"And your father never owned a Jumeau?"

"A what?"

"It's an antique French doll," I said, "very valuable."

"Why do you ask?"

I hesitated. Aubrey had lied to me, but I certainly didn't know Piers well enough to tell him so. "No reason."

"But I prefer bears," he said. "I still have a Steiff bear called Mortimer."

"How very Sebastian Flyte," I teased.

"But Mortimer is far more dashing than Aloysius," said Piers. "And besides, *my* bear kept all the bullies away when we went to boarding school. You must meet him."

There was no denying that Piers was charming. I could feel myself begin to thaw. What kind of man admitted he still owned a childhood bear? So I told him all about my Merrythought Jerry mouse Jazzbo Jenkins.

"Well . . . where is he?" Piers demanded. "Introduce us!"

But when I picked up my tote bag Jazzbo wasn't in there after all. "I must have left him at Jane's Cottage. Another time."

"I like the fact there will be another time," said Piers.

I groaned again. "Please. No more corny lines."

"But I mean it!" He pretended to look hurt, but I wasn't fooled. "Did you want some help with unpacking and packing?"

"No. I think I need a break. Would you like a cup of— actually, I only have tea here."

"I was supposed to be taking you out."

"Oh, but—I didn't think—I'm hardly dressed for going out." In fact, I was still wearing the same clothes I'd thrown on so hastily that morning. I had also scraped my hair back with a bandana because it kept falling over my face. I hadn't even showered, but I had cleaned my teeth.

"This is Devon, not London, and besides, you're so beautiful, no one will notice," said Piers. "And I meant that, too." He moved closer and undid the bandana from my hair and helped my curls cascade onto my shoulders. It was an intimate moment and I felt myself blushing like a sixteen-year-old. "There. Much better." He gently brushed a lock away from my face. "You remind me of a Pre-Raphaelite painting."

I hesitated. What was wrong with me? Piers was an attractive and entertaining man. And—best of all—he was *single*!

"It's just a drink, Kat," he said gently. "I'm not going to ravish you."

I found myself blushing *again*. "Well—"

"Besides, don't you want to know what I found in the grave yesterday?"

I gasped. "You admit it!"

"I admitted it when I asked you out and we struck a bargain."

I relented. "Alright. You win. Just give me a couple of minutes."

I grabbed my tote bag again and retreated to the small bathroom. Fortunately, I always kept lipstick and mascara in a tiny makeup bag. I dabbed both on and hastily dragged a comb through my unruly hair. I also remembered that I kept a pair of heels and a red silk scarf in the gatehouse just in case a client turned up unannounced.

Moments later the Mercedes—which had been "washed in my honor"—was roaring through the narrow country roads so fast that I instantly regretted my decision. I had my eyes closed at every hairpin bend.

"Relax!" said Piers with a laugh. "I know these lanes like the back of my hand."

"You'll get caught for speeding."

Piers pointed to a gadget below the dashboard. "Allow me to introduce the Target Blu Eye. It spots a police car or emergency vehicle up to a thousand yards away."

"Isn't that illegal?"

"Nope!" said Piers. "Although the police did try and ban it."

As we turned onto the main road toward Plymouth, I said, "Where exactly *are* we going?"

"It's a surprise."

Piers handled the Mercedes with such skill that I was embarrassed to admit that I felt a tiny frisson of excitement. I couldn't deny that being driven to a mysterious location with a very attractive and entertaining man was an adventure. I began to get used to his insane driving and the constant warning beeps and flashing lights from the scanner.

Piers put on some music. It was Cuban, sultry and sexy. To my surprise, I began to relax.

Maybe my mother was right. I did need to take a chance.

When my relationship with international art investigator David Wynne ended, so did my social life. With David, it had revolved around mixing with other TV celebrities and his well-connected cronies. As mini-celebrities ourselves, we were always out at the theater or a concert, attending a gallery opening, having a box at Wimbledon, to name just a few in-the-public-eye scenarios—in fact, David and I epitomized the clichéd London scene that graced the pages of society magazines.

But tonight, I felt alive again and it felt good! And yet, as we approached the bright lights of Plymouth I began to feel a twinge of alarm and when we pulled up outside a very fancy restaurant called NINE and two valet parking attendants swarmed around the Mercedes, I began to have serious second thoughts.

"I thought we were just going to a pub for a drink," I protested. "I'm hardly dressed to go here."

And then I remembered where I'd heard of this restaurant before. Jess had celebrated her fortieth birthday here. She'd also said it was virtually impossible to get a reservation, and here we were, just rolling up.

Piers leaned over and grabbed a jacket from the rear seat.

"You came prepared!" I said crossly. "Look at me!"

"They're just strict on men wearing a jacket," he said. "Stop worrying. You look gorgeous."

We left the Mercedes with the valet parking attendants and headed for the restaurant.

"Did you make a reservation?" I demanded.

"Why?"

"I'm told it's impossible to get in without one."

"Just wait and see," said Piers with a wink.

"You're not going to embarrass me and use my name, are you?" I whispered.

"Do you still have that kind of influence?" he teased. "Stop worrying."

"You make me feel worried," I said, and I meant it. I felt off-balance and unsure of myself.

NINE was all smoked glass, slate and marble. A huge fish tank stretched the length of the rear wall, filled with exotic angelfish of every color imaginable.

We approached the hostess station.

I hung back as Piers greeted an impossibly thin hostess dressed in black. Her dark hair was severely pulled back into a tight knot at the nape of her head. She wore crimson lipstick and had accentuated her eyebrows and eyes in kohl pencil. The name pin said "Sabrina."

Self-consciously I readjusted my scarf.

"What was the name again?" I could hear the hostess say, flipping the pages of the reservation book back and forth.

"Roger Matthews," said Piers easily. "That's 'Matthews' with two *t*'s."

My heart sank. Who on earth was Roger Matthews?

Sabrina's frown deepened. "And you called and made a reservation?"

"My personal assistant called three weeks ago. She then called and reconfirmed yesterday. Is there a problem?"

"Piers!" I hissed, but instead of answering, he reached back and pulled me closer.

Sabrina was getting flustered. "Let me check again." She shot me an apologetic smile. "I'm so sorry to keep you waiting."

Piers leaned over the hostess station and lowered his voice. "Now look, Sabrina, I don't want to make a fuss, but I'm here on behalf of the Air France in-flight magazine. I'm writing a restaurant review for the December edition."

I wanted the floor to open and swallow me up. The word "embarrassed" didn't even come close to how I was feeling. It was beyond mortifying. Really, my mother should have taken my place. The two would have been brilliantly suited.

Complaints from behind began to rumble. I turned to see a few disgruntled patrons who clearly did have reservations at NINE.

"Why don't you have a quick word with your manager," said Piers.

"I shall. Please wait here." She stepped away whilst the line behind us grew more vocal. I heard someone say, "Isn't that Kat Stanford?" followed by, "Seems they don't have a reservation, but I suppose she's pushing her way in."

"Piers," I begged. "Please. Let's just go."

I saw his jaw harden, and although his eyes were sparkling, he really was being a complete and utter twit. Edith was right.

"Aren't you hungry?" he said.

But before I could answer, Sabrina returned all smiles. "I apologize, Mr. Matthews," she said. "Please let me personally show you to your table. Come this way. After you, Ms. Stanford."

She had recognized me, too.

Somehow I had a feeling that the evening was going to get extremely awkward.

Chapter Nineteen

Sabrina weaved through the tables and mounted the steps into a private alcove with floor-to-ceiling windows. The view of Plymouth Sound was spectacular. It had to be the best table in the house.

As Sabrina left us to settle in I said, "I can't believe you did that."

"I just like to prove how shallow people can be."

"Shallow?" I exclaimed. "That's hardly fair. She was being polite and you put her in an awful position. If you were writing a review and she questioned your identity, wouldn't that garner an automatic black mark?"

"True," Piers admitted. "But she should have asked for my business card."

"What would you have done if she had?"

Piers reached into his jacket pocket and withdrew a business card. Although it carried the Air France logo, it was made of flimsy paper and was so obviously fake that I laughed.

"You've done this before!"

"Only when I need to impress beautiful women."

I noted the plural. "Oh *please*. Save me from your charms."

"Just kidding," he said. "I had this one made specially for this evening."

"I don't believe you."

"I'm not asking you to," he said. "Ah, here they come."

The maître d', the sommelier and an earnest headwaiter surrounded our table. Napkins were placed on our laps, menus were presented, iced water was poured into cut-crystal glasses and warm bread was offered along with olive oil and balsamic vinegar.

The sommelier handed Piers the wine list with a flourish. As Piers seemed to study it forever, the sommelier began to get nervous.

Finally, Piers gave his nod of approval. "Very extensive. Good."

"Our manager, Mr. Roberts, insists on selecting your wine this evening. With his compliments, naturally," said the sommelier. "That is, if Sir and Madam would allow?"

Piers smiled. "Please thank Mr. Roberts," he said. "I am looking forward to sampling his selections."

The headwaiter stepped forward. "And if Sir and Madam would also allow, the chef would like to create a personal menu for this evening. And again, with his compliments."

"I think we'd like that very much." Piers turned to me, "Wouldn't we, darling?"

I was so dumbfounded all I could do was nod.

The three bowed obsequiously and moved away.

"I can't believe you could do this!" I said again. "With their *compliments*? Does that mean we don't have to pay for dinner?"

"*You* wouldn't have to pay regardless." Piers picked up my hand and kissed it. "Thank you for joining me—"

"What if we're arrested for impersonating this Roger Matthews? Who is Roger Matthews anyway?"

"A chum." Piers grinned. "We play pranks on each other all the time."

I thought for a moment. "Who do you think you are? George Clooney and Brad Pitt?"

"We were playing pranks years before they started. They must have got the idea from us. Roger and I went to Eton together."

For some reason this made me feel better, although logically I couldn't think why.

"So Roger *is* a food critic?" I ventured.

"Good God, no. He's a hedge fund manager in the City."

"And you're doing this because you wanted to prove how shallow they are or because you wanted to impress me?"

"Both."

"You're incorrigible."

The evening passed in a whirlwind. Wave after wave of courses appeared with sorbets in between to clean our palates. As each arrived, so the wineglasses were changed and the sommelier told the story of each wine and why he had carefully paired it to each course.

The food was spectacular and the wine incredible. I was becoming light-headed and felt I was laughing too loudly, but Piers was so entertaining, I couldn't help it. I noticed he hardly drank at all—just sampled each glass and left it relatively untouched.

"So what do you think about Father's new bride?" Piers said suddenly.

"I've only just met her, but she seems nice enough," I said. "Do *you* like her?"

"When Lavinia and I found out that he had eloped with a woman almost thirty years his junior we were horrified." This time he did take more than a sip of wine. "I was so sure she was after his money."

"And is she?"

"I don't know," said Piers. "There was no prenuptial agreement, and the moment the barn is finished they're moving out and leaving Carew Court to me."

"Isn't that good news?"

"Hell, yes!" he exclaimed. "Of course I've been managing the estate for years, but Father will be officially relinquishing the reins and giving me one hundred percent control."

"In that case, this is good news. Your father is happy and so are you."

"I've got great plans for the Court," Piers went on. "All I need is a television company to come along and make a series like *Downton Abbey*. Do you still have connections?"

"Not really, but—"

"It doesn't matter," he said dismissively. "Lady Carnarvon is a friend. She told us that before *Downton Abbey* was filmed at Highclere they were going under. Thanks to the show, tours are booked months in advance. Now the castle's financial future is assured."

"It sounds like a great plan."

"Of course we're listed with the Historic Houses Association, but tours are by appointment only. I want to ramp that up to regular openings. Look into holding weddings, shooting parties, that kind of thing."

"I'm happy to know that you don't plan on selling any of it." I thought for a moment. "How much land do you have?"

"Put it this way, we have more land than Honeychurch and we've never sold off so much as a tree."

"That's amazing."

"The Honeychurches had just as much as we had two hundred years ago but began selling it off to repay gambling debts." Piers sounded more than a little gleeful. "The Carew estate stands exactly as it was the day King Edward the Fourth gave the land to my ancestor. But of course, Rupert likes to blame us for his financial misfortunes."

"You mean his ancestors lost at cards to your ancestors?"

"No. The war."

I laughed. "Which one?"

"When Cromwell became dictator after the English Civil War, massive fines were levied on the Royalists. Naturally, we collected the money in the West Country. Didn't make us very popular with our neighbors who picked the wrong side."

"But that was all so long ago!" I exclaimed. "Can't you bury the hatchet—no pun intended?"

"Edith's alright, but it's Rupert I have a problem with."

I didn't like where this particular conversation was heading, but thankfully the sommelier reappeared. "Would Sir or Madam care for a glass of port? We have a very good Graham's 1966."

"I'd love a glass," I said.

"I'm driving." Piers shook his head, adding, "And if you paid attention, you'd see that I drink a quarter of a glass to every one of yours. I want to keep my wits about me." He reached across and took my hand, gently kissing my fingers. My stomach lurched. Flustered, I snatched my hand away.

"You're incorrigible," I said again. "And a terrible flirt."

"You're different from all the others, Kat," he said quietly, and looked deep into my eyes. I couldn't hold his gaze and struggled to find something else to say.

"I kept my side of the agreement," I said. "You must keep yours. What was it that you found in the grave?"

Piers reached inside his jacket pocket. He took out a gold ring. "I took this."

"But…but…you can't just do that!" I was appalled. "That's stealing. It was found on Honeychurch land."

"I'm well aware of the Treasure Act of 1996," said Piers mildly. "I know that legally it should belong to the landowner, but I don't care. The ring belongs to me—or should I say, the family."

"Oh. And you're sure of that?"

"Here, be my guest." He handed me the ring.

I rummaged in my tote bag for my loupe. "I'd say it is a posy ring—late sixteenth century or perhaps early seventeenth? It's very pretty."

"There is an inscription inside the band." Piers turned on my iPhone flashlight so I could see it more easily.

I tried to read it, but it was hard to decipher.

Piers leaned forward and beckoned me to move closer. I could smell his aftershave—it was subtle, with just a hint of sandalwood. "*Two Hands, One Heart, Not e're in Death Shall Us Part,*" he said.

"It's beautiful," I whispered—and romantic.

"I removed the ring from Eleanor's finger—or rather what was left of it."

"Eleanor Honeychurch," I said excitedly. "Frances's sister. How can you be so sure it is her?"

"You've heard of Eleanor?" Piers seemed incredulous.

I told him that my mother and I had seen Lady Frances's plaque in St. Mary's church that mentioned she had a sister.

I thought for a moment. "A posy ring was given as a love token—"

"Or a wedding band," said Piers. "Eleanor was married in secret to my ancestor Nicholas. A Royalist Honeychurch marrying a Roundhead Carew. Can you imagine the scandal were it ever to come out? The repercussions in a time of war?"

"Yes. Terrible." For a strange moment I had thought I felt a tingle in my hand. I gave him back the ring. "So the dagger with the Honeychurch crest must have belonged to her—oh." With a sickening jolt I remembered that it had been found embedded in Eleanor's rib cage. "You mean—you think she was *murdered* because of this marriage? Murdered by someone in her own family?"

Piers shrugged. "What do you think? All I know is that Nicholas was told Eleanor had run away to France. He never stopped searching for her."

"But how do you know all this?"

"Family papers," said Piers. "Love letters."

"Can you show me these love letters?"

"Of course."

"You're quite the romantic, aren't you?" I teased.

"I was born in the wrong century," he said.

And, looking at him, I had to agree.

"What are you going to tell Rupert?" I said.

"I want to bury Eleanor where she belongs. With us."

"You don't like Rupert very much, do you?" I said. "And it's got nothing to do with the Royalists and the Roundheads."

"Damn right I don't like him," said Piers. "Pippa Carmichael is your friend, isn't she?"

The change of subject threw me completely. "Yes. Why are you asking?"

"I want you to tell her to stay away from my brother-in-law."

"You think there is something going on between them?" I was shocked. "I can't imagine Pippa doing that," I said. "Her own husband cheated on her, so the fact that she would do that to another woman is hard for me to accept."

"You don't know Rupert."

I didn't really know Pippa that well, either. True, we had exchanged conversations about Harry and Max and we'd even gone out for a glass of wine once or twice. But when I had asked Pippa about her love life, she'd been evasive and, to be honest, if she was sleeping with Rupert she'd hardly tell me.

"Lavinia is my sister," said Piers. "I'm sick of Rupert cheating right in front of her face. It's humiliating. His affairs have been going on for too many years, but she won't leave him. And he'll never leave her because it's *our* money that keeps Honeychurch Hall afloat."

Lavinia's comment about Piers cutting her off hit me afresh.

"Surely that was Lavinia's choice," I said quietly. "She knew what Rupert was like before she married him."

"It's my duty to protect her," said Piers somewhat pompously.

"This is really nothing to do with me, Piers," I said firmly.

"It's making me feel very uncomfortable. Can we change the subject?"

Fortunately, the maître d' and a tall man in glasses approached our table and stopped all further conversation.

"Allow me to introduce our manager, Mr. Roberts," said the maître d'.

Piers smiled and made some joke that I didn't hear. I was still unsettled by the turn of our conversation. It had cast a pall over the evening.

"I hope that everything was to your satisfaction, Mr. Matthews?" said Mr. Roberts.

"Delicious," said Piers. "You can count on a five-star review."

"Ms. Stanford?"

"Yes. It was very good. Thank you."

"We're delighted to have you here at our restaurant, Ms. Stanford," Mr. Roberts went on. "My wife was so disappointed when you retired from *Fakes & Treasures*. The new host isn't nearly so charming—or beautiful."

"Thank you. I really enjoyed doing the show." And frankly, at this moment, I would do anything to turn back the clock.

"Kat's started her own business," Piers said. "I think she should have a grand opening party here at your restaurant."

"What an excellent idea," beamed Mr. Roberts. "We could have an auction or invite guests to bring their fakes … and treasures!" He laughed, but I could only just force a smile. Of course I appreciated Piers trying to drum up business, but had he forgotten that as far as Mr. Roberts was concerned, Piers was a food critic for the Air France magazine?

"Do you have a business card?" Mr. Roberts asked as he produced his own.

I took one from my purse and we exchanged.

"Would you mind very much having a photograph taken?" Mr. Roberts waved Sabrina over. "We have a very active Facebook page and I know our fans would love to know that you dined at our establishment."

A feeling of dread settled into the pit of my stomach.

"And of course it's an honor to have you review our restaurant, Mr. Matthews." Mr. Roberts gestured for Piers to be included.

For once Piers faltered a little and didn't seem so confident now. My good mood had evaporated and I was no longer amused at his immature bet with his childhood *chum*. He suddenly retrieved his iPhone and glanced at the caller I.D. "Sadly, I have to take this, so you will have to go ahead without me."

I suspected there was no phone call. He just needed an excuse to leave.

Piers jumped up and headed in the direction of the toilets, leaving me fuming.

Moments later the diners in the restaurant were not only watching me having my photograph taken with the manager but also snapping many of their own.

The moment the fuss had died down, Piers reappeared. "Time for us to go."

"Would you be able to stay for a tour of the kitchens?" said Mr. Roberts.

"Another time," said Piers, flashing a hasty smile. "You've been more than gracious."

"Can we validate your parking?" said Mr. Roberts. "Do you have coats?"

Just as we got to the hostess station, my heart practically stopped. I couldn't believe it.

There, emerging from the cloak cupboard, was Detective Inspector Shawn Cropper.

Chapter Twenty

For a moment I felt as if I'd been caught in a lie, but it was Shawn who had claimed to be working—or was he?

Shawn was dressed in a pair of neat trousers and sports jacket—no trench coat for him tonight—and when a very pretty strawberry blonde in her mid-thirties emerged from the cloak cupboard brandishing a cloakroom ticket it was obvious he was on a date.

And then he saw me.

He looked horrified. "Kat? What on earth—?"

"Damn it," I heard Piers hiss in my ear. "What's Cropper doing here?" Piers took my elbow. "We've got to go."

Shawn looked from Piers and then to me with confusion that turned into first disbelief and then disapproval, but before he could say a word Sabrina slipped between us. She gave Piers his validated parking ticket. "Your car is already waiting outside, Mr. Matthews. Mr. Roberts didn't get your business card. Do you have one handy?"

"Another time," Piers shouted, and propelled me out of the restaurant to the waiting Mercedes.

Piers walked so quickly I had to break into a jog to keep up, and yet even though I could sense he was agitated, he remembered his manners and opened my passenger door. He also took a moment to tip the valet parking attendant—quite generously, judging by the man's happy smile.

We sped away in silence.

Slowly the full implication of what had just happened began to sink in.

After a good ten minutes, he finally spoke. "I'm sorry, Kat," he said. "I'm afraid my joke backfired."

"You're telling me it backfired," I said angrily. "You do know that Shawn will tell the manager who you really are."

"Yes."

"And it's me who is going to look the idiot." I was really upset. "They took my photograph for their wretched Facebook page. It will look like I scrounged a free meal."

Piers gave a snort of laughter.

"It's not funny!" I exclaimed.

"Well . . . it is a little bit."

"No. Not even a little bit!"

Piers stole me a sideways glance, but when he realized I wasn't joking he seemed contrite. "Let me make it up to you."

"No. Just take me home, please."

"Of course. Right away." He floored the engine and the car surged forward. I lost count of the number of times the police scanner beeped, but he didn't seem to care.

Finally, we turned off the A38 into the myriad of country lanes that led to Little Dipperton.

"Look, I really *am* sorry," said Piers again. "It was a stupid idea."

"Yes, it was stupid."

"Have dinner with me again and this time I swear I will book the table in my own name."

"No."

"I'll make it worth your while."

"Yes, I'm sure you would," I said drily. "But the answer is still no."

As the village of Little Dipperton loomed, Piers slowed down a little—but not much. As we passed the entrance to Jess's barn conversion, Piers narrowly missed hitting a man who was standing in the middle of the road. Just *standing* there! He actually had to vault over the low stone wall by the churchyard to get out of our way.

"Careful!" I shrieked. "You nearly hit him!"

"Bloody tourist," Piers mumbled under his breath, but he did reduce his speed for just a moment. We crawled past St. Mary's at a snail's pace. I could have sworn I saw a light flickering in the chancel, but I couldn't be sure.

It was when we descended the steep hill to Bridge Cottage that Piers was forced to hit the brakes. Suddenly a black Range Rover swerved out of a concealed track and cut us off. It raced up the other side heading for Honeychurch Hall.

We both knew who was at the wheel.

"What's Rupert doing out so late?" I said, and wished I hadn't.

"Why don't we ask him?" Piers slammed his foot on the accelerator and we tore after him.

"Piers," I begged. "Please. Let him go."

But Piers ignored me. I was beginning to wonder if he was mentally unstable.

Piers rode the Range Rover's bumper and flashed his lights, but Rupert accelerated all the more. I kept my eyes closed and hung on to my seat. I didn't care if Piers knew these lanes like the back of his hand ... I was terrified.

"Piers!" I screamed. "If you don't slow down I'm throwing myself out." I unbuckled my seat belt.

We came to a screeching halt.

"God. I'm so sorry," he said. "I don't know what came over me. I just— Kat, forgive me."

"Take me home!" I shouted. *"Now!"*

Without another word, we set off again. Piers turned into the tradesmen's entrance and we bumped our way along the service road, trying to avoid the numerous potholes.

All too late I remembered that I had left my Golf outside the gatehouse, but there was no question of me asking to be taken back there now. I'd have to collect the car in the morning.

Moments later we had arrived at Jane's Cottage.

Piers cut the engine.

"I won't come in," he said sheepishly.

"Probably a good idea."

Piers got out of the Mercedes and came around to open my door. He walked me to the entrance and waited for me to find my latchkey.

I turned to say good night.

Piers leaned in and for a moment I thought he was going to kiss me, but instead, he whispered in my ear, "I could easily fall in love with you, but don't fall in love with me, Katherine Stanford."

"Don't flatter yourself," I said coldly. "I can assure you that there is no danger of that."

Suddenly he cupped my chin and then he *did* kiss me. He kissed me so fiercely that my head spun. I felt a rush of electricity that was so unexpected that I had to reach out to steady myself against the pillar.

Piers broke away as abruptly as he had begun. And, without another word, he turned on his heel and strode back to his car, leaving me with a racing heart and feeling more than a little confused. I stared after the receding taillights as the Mercedes sped away.

But all thoughts of Piers vanished the minute I stepped inside my door.

Someone was here, but this uninvited guest was human.

I grabbed the fire poker and stood still. Listening.

And then I heard a strange ping. It seemed to be coming from the kitchen.

Gingerly, I crept forward and slowly peered into the tiny room.

The blue light from my electric kettle glowed in the darkness.

There was a creak overhead.

I walked to the bottom of the spiral staircase.

"Mother!" I shouted. "I know you're up there."

"Are you alone?" came the reply.

"Yes. I am."

"Piers didn't come in?" Mum descended the staircase.

"How did you know I went out with Piers?" I said. "Are you *spying* on me?"

"What? Oh—yes. No. Alfred saw you."

"Even for you that is pretty low—Mum?" Her face was deathly pale. She seemed upset. "Are you feeling alright? Whatever's the matter?"

She swallowed hard. "Something awful has happened to Muriel. I think she's dead."

Chapter Twenty-one

"**What do you mean, you** *think* **she's dead?**" I said. "Did you call for an ambulance?"

"Now calm down," said Mum. "It's not all bad."

"Calm down?" I exclaimed. "And what do you mean, it's not *all* bad! You just said Muriel was dead."

"Alfred said she looked it."

"Did he feel for a pulse?"

"I'll let Alfred tell you what happened— Alfred!" Mum shouted. "You can come out now!"

Alfred emerged from the downstairs cloak cupboard.

"You did call for an ambulance, didn't you?" I said.

Mum and Alfred exchanged looks. "Of course he did," she said, but I wasn't sure whether to believe her or not. "We need to talk to you. I put the kettle on, but I think—no, we *all* need a brandy."

"Sit down. I'll get it." I retreated to the kitchen and took out my emergency bottle of brandy that seemed to be used so regularly these days that the term no longer qualified.

"Just bring out mugs," Mum called from the living room. "We don't need your fancy glass."

"Just like we don't need your fancy coronation china to drink our tea." I brought out my fancy glass—three Pall Mall brandy balloons with the Lady Hamilton pattern—set the tray on the table and sank into the armchair. Even though I was shattered from my own disastrous evening, I was filled with such anxiety I hardly knew what to think.

"I know you didn't walk here," I said. "So where is your car?"

"We parked in the undergrowth," she said. "I didn't want to cramp your style if . . . well, you know . . . if Piers—"

"How can you even be thinking about my social life after dropping such a bombshell."

"I wasn't," said Mum. "You were. You asked me if I had walked up here."

"I have this weird sense of déjà vu," I said. "The three of us drinking brandy in the middle of the night following a catastrophe masterminded by you. And you're certain that Muriel is alive?"

"He didn't hang around, if that's what you're asking," said Mum. "We had nothing to do with it this time, did we, Alfred?"

There was a long silence. In fact, Alfred didn't say a word. I realized he was dressed entirely in black and was clutching his balaclava. I guessed what must have happened.

"Alfred broke into the post office. Muriel caught him and fainted from shock," I said.

"Nothing like that," said Mum. "But at least I now have proof that Muriel read my manuscript."

"I thought we had already established that."

"He found the missing pages." My mother took a big swig of brandy and grimaced. "I still prefer gin."

"Where were these pages?" I asked.

"In her kitchen. Under an armchair."

"So Alfred not only broke into the post office, he also broke into her flat?"

"The door wasn't *locked*, Katherine," Mum said, "So technically, no. He just let himself in. Actually, Alfred saved her life."

"I'm confused. You just told me Alfred thought she was dead."

"You won't believe this," said Mum. "But Muriel was trying to do herself in."

"What are you talking about?"

"Muriel tried to kill herself. She was going to put her head in the gas oven."

"What!" I was truly horrified. It wasn't what I expected to hear at all. "Oh. But that's terrible."

"And she left a suicide note on the kitchen table, didn't she, Alfred—?"

"Not exactly." Alfred scratched his head. "It was the start of a suicide note. It just said, *Dear Friends. I'm sorry, but I can't*... and that was it."

"Can't what?" I said.

Alfred shrugged. "I suppose the fumes just got to her before she had a chance to finish it."

"Alfred couldn't risk being seen," said Mum. "That's why he had to leave in a hurry."

I thought for a moment. "But how can she have written a suicide note with her head in the gas oven?"

"Her head wasn't *in* the gas oven," said Alfred. "She was lying on the floor on her back *next* to the gas oven."

I was more confused than ever. "But the oven—?"

"Door was open."

"Didn't you smell any gas?"

"Nope," said Alfred. "But the kitchen window was open as well."

"Wait a minute...the kitchen window was *open?*"

"Why are you repeating everything Alfred says?" Mum demanded.

"Just the top bit was open," Alfred continued. "On a latch."

"Wait a minute, wait a minute. Let me think." I tried to steady my racing thoughts. Something didn't feel right to me. I thought back to one of my English literature classes when we discussed the suicide of Sylvia Plath. "Doesn't the room have to be sealed up?"

"And the door to the hall was wide open," Alfred went on. "Come to think of it, there was quite a breeze. And she was only wearing one shoe."

"One shoe," I said.

"Shocking pink, it was," said Alfred.

"Maybe it was a cry for help?" Mum suggested.

"Poor Muriel," I said. "We must call the hospital in the morning."

"Whatever happens," said Mum, "I thank God for the suicide note—"

"Which was unfinished," I pointed out.

"Doesn't matter. Alfred is off the hook."

"Was he ever *on* the hook?"

"And he didn't take anything else, did you, Alfred?"

"Of course I didn't," said Alfred. "I left all her electronics and whatnot. You've never seen so many new appliances. A bloody enormous TV for starters."

We fell quiet. Mum reached for the brandy bottle and topped us all up.

"Why the gas oven?" I said suddenly. "Why not take pills?"

"Oh everyone used to do it in the old days," said Mum dismissively. "It's quite painless."

"So if you're not worried, why did you come up here in the middle of the night to tell me all about it?" I demanded.

Mum looked to Alfred, but he kept quiet. He seemed distracted, lost in his thoughts.

"Just in case . . . just in case Alfred needs an alibi . . . we thought we might say we spent the evening with you."

"Well, unfortunately, that won't work," I said. "Because I saw Shawn tonight in Plymouth and he saw me with Piers. Sorry. This time you're on your own."

Mum brightened. "Was he jealous?"

As I bundled the pair of them outside, Alfred stopped. "You go and get in the car, Iris. I'll be with you in a tick."

"Don't tell her anything," said Mum.

"I know you don't believe in the spirit world, Kat—"

"I didn't say I didn't believe in the spirit world, Alfred," I said. "I'll believe it when I see it with my own eyes."

Alfred nodded. "I have a message for you," he said. "You must take care. Someone is not who they seem."

"I think that goes for everyone I know," I said drily.

"*Shush!*" Alfred cocked his head and listened, then nodded.

"Now you're going to tell me you can hear voices."

He looked puzzled. "She says you can't help who you fall in love with."

My heart lurched. "That makes no sense to me," I said. "But I'll bear it in mind. Good night, Alfred."

But of course Alfred's message did make sense, but it seemed too far-fetched to be real. Alfred's channeling was infamous, but weren't all psychics just extra-sensitive and able to pick up on people's emotions? Call me a cynic, but that's what I believed to be true. Mum and Alfred knew I'd gone out with Piers, who was completely unsuitable. There was no danger of me falling in love with him at all. But what about the tragic love story between Eleanor Honeychurch and Piers's ancestor Nicholas Carew?

Unexpectedly, a rash of goose bumps raced up my spine just as my birthday cards toppled onto the floor, one by one. There had been no wind—not even a draft—and the front door was closed.

She came to me a few hours later. A sudden crash sent my bedroom window flying open. Startled, I sat up in bed, shivering with cold despite the mildness of the night. Once again I was overwhelmed by the distinctive scent of sweet honey mixed with the salt of the ocean.

This time I called out her name, "Eleanor. Is that you? Oh for God's sake, Kat, don't be ridiculous."

I felt foolish, but I was scared.

I switched on the lamp, got out of bed and closed the

window. The smell vanished. I daren't go back to sleep for fear of having the same horrific dreams returning from the night before. Grabbing my pillow and the duvet, I went downstairs and spent the rest of the night on the sofa with all the lights on, falling into a deep sleep just as the dawn chorus began.

Chapter Twenty-two

"The police are coming," Mum's voice shrieked on the other end of the line.

Once again I'd spent a miserable night, only this time I was stiff from sleeping on the sofa. My neck was killing me.

"I told you you're on your own on this one."

"It'll be Shawn. He likes you. You like him."

And that was all the reason for me to stay away. He was the last person I wanted to see after my humiliation of the night before.

"Please," Mum said. "I promise I won't ask you to do anything like this ever again."

"This makes me all the more suspicious, but alright. Put the kettle on and I'll be there in twenty minutes."

"Can't you get here sooner? Why twenty minutes?"

Of course I'd left my car at the gatehouse "It's too complicated to explain," I said. "Did you find out if Muriel is okay?"

But Mum had already hung up the phone.

I was about to pull on a pair of jeans when I remembered that Saturday mornings I usually rode out with Harry. I put on jodhpurs instead. They were quite a struggle to get into. I had to lie flat on the floor to get the zipper all the way up to the top. I really needed to go on a diet. Fortunately, the polo shirt was long, so I wore that tucked out rather than in. On an impulse, I put on mascara and a dab of lipstick, then brushed my hair. I slipped my slumber net into my pocket. Shawn and I might well be finished before we began, but I didn't want him to think I was a complete slattern.

As I strode into the kitchen Mum gave me a knowing look. "Makeup for Shawn?"

"Pearls for Shawn?" She was wearing a smart Marks & Spencer dress that looked as if she were about to open the village fete. "Where's Alfred?" I demanded.

"I told him to stay away." Mum looked worried. "Why would the police want to talk to me?"

"Well, we'll soon find out why, won't we? I'm going to have some toast."

"One piece, Katherine," she said. "Judging by the state of your jodhpurs, I don't think they could accommodate two."

I busied myself in the kitchen and made some tea and toast—two pieces—whilst my mother paced about the room.

"And make a cup of tea for Shawn," said Mum. "Give him the Duke of Edinburgh mug—the nice one. We need to soften him up."

"Soften who up?" came the familiar voice of Detective Inspector Shawn Cropper.

Mum and I both gave a guilty start.

Shawn looked terrible. Dark rings sat beneath his eyes. He seemed exhausted. As he was wearing his trench coat over his uniform trousers, shirt and tie, this was clearly an official visit, and this official visit was marked by his trademark plastic shopping bag that always seemed to contain incriminating evidence.

He barely gave me a nod of acknowledgment. My stomach was in knots. It was most unlike me. It wasn't as if anything had happened between Piers and myself apart from that electrifying kiss, but—judging by Shawn's haggard appearance—it was obvious that something *had* happened between Shawn and his pretty young strawberry blonde.

"You left the door open, Iris," said Shawn. "And you want to be careful. With the upcoming Skirmish there are a lot of strangers in the vicinity. Kat, I hope you have an alarm installed at the gatehouses."

"They're installing them next week," I said.

"Working on a Saturday, Officer?" Mum beamed. "And all alone? Coffee? Tea? Me? That was a joke." Mum laughed and showed too many teeth. "Alfred's not here."

"Why do you think I need to talk to Alfred?" said Shawn.

"D-d-don't you?" Mum stammered. "I mean. I thought you might want to . . . talk to everyone who knows Muriel."

"What about Muriel?"

Mum's jaw dropped. "Well . . . I heard . . . I heard she had tried to commit suicide."

"Suicide?" said Shawn sharply.

"What with losing her Fred," Mum went on. "And the money for the re-enactment. I heard she was worried she was going to be evicted by his lordship."

"Who told you that she had tried to commit suicide?" Shawn demanded.

Mum looked to me for help. I just shrugged.

"Violet Green," Mum said wildly.

"Violet *Green?*" said Shawn.

"From the tearoom." Mum nodded furiously. "That's right. As you know, she lives next door to Muriel. I suppose she found her."

"Mum, the ambulance—"

"*Ambulance,* you say?" Shawn whipped out his notepad and pencil.

"Ignore Katherine; she doesn't know what she is talking about."

"You were right, though," said Shawn. "It was Violet Green who found Muriel."

"Good." Mum nodded.

Shawn gave her a look I couldn't fathom. "There was another break-in last night."

"Really? Wh-h-atever f-f-or?" Mum gave a hollow laugh. "What was taken this time?"

"Nothing was taken from the post office or the general store."

"How odd," Mum said.

"That's what I thought until I found this."

Shawn brandished his plastic shopping bag.

"Here we go," Mum muttered under her breath.

Shawn donned disposable gloves and withdrew one of his much beloved Ziploc bags that contained a folded piece of paper covered in type. He smoothed it out on the kitchen table. "Does this look familiar, Iris?"

Even I could see the traces of jam smudged in the margin.

Mum looked to me in a panic.

Shawn pointed to the top of the paper where the name

Storm/Ravished was typed in boldface. "I believe this belongs to you."

"Why?" Mum whispered.

"Seriously, Iris?" Shawn rolled his eyes. "You want to play the ignorance card *again*? Just tell me the truth. Do you recognize this extract from your novel?"

"What page number is it?"

"Page fifty-nine."

"Is that the scene where the squire takes the vicar's daughter into the stables—?"

"Yes." Shawn's cheeks flushed a little, but he steadily met her gaze. "Judging by the contents of that one page, I would like to congratulate you on the title. It's a good choice."

"Thank you," said Mum. "It was a toss between *Conquered* and *Ravished*, but I thought that *Ravished* had more pizzazz."

"Oh, Iris, what am I going to do with you," Shawn said with a weary sigh. "You know very well that I am aware of who you really are. I am also aware of your desire for utmost secrecy, and that is why I have come here alone. You can't carry on like this."

"I couldn't agree more!" I exclaimed.

Mum looked miserable. "I don't know who knows about me and who doesn't anymore. I get so confused."

"I can't vouch for the officers at other Devon & Cornwall Constabulary stations, but I can assure you that our satellite office has kept quiet. And I'm confident that those at the Hall are far too terrified of the dowager countess to let the cat out of the bag. But the truth now—did Muriel Jarvis find out?"

Mum opened her mouth and shut it again.

Shawn frowned. "This page was found in Muriel's sitting

room under the sofa. I put it to you that *you* went back there to look for it. This is obviously a page from your manuscript and—given the typos and Wite-Out—I suggest it has not yet been published and is therefore of the utmost value to you."

Again, Mum stayed silent. She had absolutely no defense whatsoever.

"Mum," I said finally. "Please ... can't you be honest for once?"

My mother took a deep breath. "Oh alright. It's true. *Ravished* is my latest novel and you are quite right, it has not been published—you're such a clever detective."

"And?" Shawn prompted.

"I have a horrible new editor who doesn't like me very much. When she told me that the manuscript arrived with pages—a page actually—missing, I was very upset."

Shawn picked up the sheet of paper and inspected it closely. "This was written on an old typewriter."

"Yes. I always use my late husband's Olivetti," said Mum.

"Don't you use a computer?"

"No."

"So this page here—" Shawn flapped it at my mother. "Is the original? It's not a carbon copy? Presumably there is a copy of the entire manuscript somewhere?"

"No, there isn't," I chimed in.

"Now don't you nag me, too," said Mum. "When I got a phone call telling me that the book never arrived, of course Katherine here—tell him, Kat—"

"I tracked the package," I said. "It never left Little Dipperton post office. I asked Muriel. She swore she'd sent it. The next day the package arrived minus the pages."

"Pages?" said Shawn sharply.

"Page!" Mum put in. "Page, Katherine. *Page!*"

Ignoring my mother's eyebrow gymnastics that were clearly telling me to keep quiet about Alfred's nighttime mission, I told Shawn what I could.

"So if this sheet of paper is missing in the manuscript, it would be a great loss to the story."

"But it's not missing," said Mum brightly. "You found it!"

"Look, Iris, we know that Muriel had a habit of opening everybody's post."

"You *knew?*" Mum and I chorused.

"Everyone in the village knew that, but no one could ever prove it. No checks were ever reported stolen and the post might well be slow, but it always reached its destination in the end."

"That's disgusting!" Mum fumed. "I hope you're going to press charges!"

"You have a lot to lose, Mrs. Stanford." Shawn's voice hardened. Whenever Shawn dropped the friendly "Iris" and substituted "Mrs. Stanford," he meant business. "Did she ever attempt to blackmail you?"

Mum's jaw dropped. *"Blackmail!"* I could practically hear the cogs in my mother's brain turning.

"Where were you last night?" Shawn demanded.

"Alfred and I were home playing Snap," said Mum.

Shawn's eyes narrowed. "Alfred Bushman was with *you?*"

"Yes."

"Now that is interesting," said Shawn. "Because according to Lady Lavinia, Alfred spent the evening with *her* caring for a sick horse."

"That's right," said Mum quickly. "And then he came over for a quick game of Snap, didn't he, Katherine?"

"I don't think your daughter will be able to help you, Mrs. Stanford," Shawn said coldly. "She was otherwise engaged all night."

"It wasn't all night," I protested. "It was just dinner."

"Dinner with a certain *Roger Matthews*. Food critic of the Air France in-flight magazine?" Shawn's voice was dripping with sarcasm.

My heart sank. Shawn had confirmed my worst fears. He knew everything.

Mum rounded on me. "Who is Roger Matthews?"

"I'll explain later," I said wearily.

"Did you go to the post office last night, Mrs. Stanford?" Shawn asked.

"No. Cross my heart and hope to die."

"I'm sorry, but what is really going on here?" I exclaimed. "I thought you said that Muriel was going to be okay."

"I said nothing of the sort," Shawn exclaimed. "I just said she didn't commit suicide. Muriel Jarvis was murdered."

Chapter Twenty-three

"Murdered!" I exclaimed.

Mum gave a small cry. "No!" She pulled out a kitchen chair and sat down heavily. "I don't believe it."

"I'm having another cup of tea—Mum? I'm making one for you, too." I could see Shawn watching my mother like a hawk. "Shawn? Another cup?"

"Alright. Thank you." He sat at the table, too. I made more tea and brought out what was left of the packet of McVitie's chocolate digestive biscuits. Shawn dived in, adding apologetically, "I didn't get much to eat last night."

I was tempted to ask him why not, but my mother cleared her throat and said, "What happened to Muriel?"

"We're waiting for the results from the autopsy," said Shawn.

"Won't that take weeks?" I asked.

"I have a friend who can get things done quickly," he said, reaching for his third chocolate digestive. "She's doing me a favor."

I thought back to the pretty strawberry blonde from the

night before and was astonished to realize that I actually felt jealous.

"Well," said Mum, rallying around. "I've already given you my alibi. Thank you for bringing back that page. I had no idea that it was missing. What are you doing?"

Shawn put the page back in the plastic carrier bag. "We'd like to hang on to it for a little bit longer, if you don't mind."

"I *do* mind," said Mum. "Please. I've never asked you for anything, but having that page is very important to my career."

"I'll tell you what, I will photocopy it and you can send that off to your publisher. That's all I'm prepared to do."

"Thank you," Mum gushed. "I can't thank you enough."

"You can thank me by telling me the truth."

"I have."

"Not even about your red MINI—"

Mum blinked.

"That is your car, isn't it?"

"Yes."

"And you're not going to insult me by telling me that someone stole your car?"

"Muriel's car was stolen," said Mum.

"Muriel's car was repossessed," said Shawn. "We learned that this morning."

"So not stolen at all," I said.

"It seems she was in some financial straits."

"Actually, Muriel asked if she could borrow some money," I put in.

"You never told me that!" Mum exclaimed. "I hope you said no. Remember what your father said, *'neither a borrower nor lender be'*?"

"I gave her three hundred pounds," I said.

"Very kind of you, Kat," said Shawn.

"Are you suggesting that she staged her own robbery?" Mum said. "Do you think *she* buried that old tin in her husband's grave?"

"It's something we are considering," said Shawn. "It looks like Fred Jarvis was heavily in debt."

"You think he spent the money for the re-enactment?" I said.

"We're exploring all lines of enquiry," said Shawn in that annoyingly pompous way he had.

"Poor Muriel," I said, and I really meant it. "And you think she was trying to hide it?"

"But let's get back to you, Mrs. Stanford," said Shawn. "Your MINI was seen in the car park at the Hare & Hounds pub last night, but I have already spoken to Stan and Doreen Mutters and no one saw you there."

"Oh."

"But you *were* seen in the churchyard," said Shawn.

"The *churchyard?*" Mum's astonishment was genuine. "Why would I go to the churchyard? Who told you that?"

"Violet Green's cottage overlooks the churchyard," said Shawn. "She saw two people moving around."

Mum was incredulous. "Well, that was definitely neither me nor Alfred."

"Unfortunately, it's your word against Ms. Green's."

"She's as blind as a bat!" Mum exclaimed. "And what time did she say she saw something?"

"I'm not at liberty to say."

"I did see some lights inside the church," I said suddenly.

"That would have been around midnight, wouldn't you say, Mum? You and Alfred would have been at Jane's by then."

"Jane's?" said Shawn. "Why would they be waiting for you at Jane's Cottage?"

"I know this sounds hard to believe, but Snap—you do know the card game I assume?" said Mum—"it's addictive. Kat just had to play a quick game before bedtime."

Shawn gave a heavy sigh. "I know you are hiding something, Iris. Luckily for you, this is Little Dipperton; otherwise I would have you in the back of my car and you'd be down at the police station in Dartmouth, where they would not be treating you so leniently."

"But I haven't done—"

"There is also the problem of the re-enactment," Shawn went on. "Unfortunately, his lordship is adamant that the festivities go on next weekend. We'll be keeping this under wraps for the time being."

"You mean no one knows that Muriel is dead?" I said.

"We're suggesting that she died of natural causes until after the Skirmish is over." Shawn regarded my mother with open disdain. "You might want to think about getting a solicitor, Mrs. Stanford. In fact, perhaps you should keep a solicitor permanently on call given your track record for getting into trouble."

"I'm innocent!" Mum exclaimed.

Shawn got to his feet. "Thank you for the tea. I'm off to have a word with Alfred now. Oh, I almost forgot." He reached into his trench coat pocket. "I brought you today's newspapers. They were outside your front door. I'll see myself out."

The moment Shawn was out of earshot, Mum said, "I wonder if there are any more pages still at Muriel's? The assistant told me there were only five missing, but she was obviously wrong. And that Violet Green is such a troublemaker. Why would she say she saw me in the churchyard?"

I stared in dismay at the front page of *Star Stalkers*, the trashiest newspaper in the country, and one I was all too familiar with.

"Katherine?" said Mum. "Are you listening?"

"I thought you canceled this newspaper!"

"I didn't think I needed to," said Mum. "You gave all that glamor up when you moved down here. Why?"

I pointed to the headline.

"Oh dear," she said.

Splashed over the front page was:

SCROUNGING A FREE MEAL?
EX–TV HOST OF *FAKES & TREASURES* CAUGHT
IN PRANK WITH NEW BOYFRIEND!
5-STAR MICHELIN RESTAURANT FOOLED!

There was a photo of me standing with Mr. Roberts smiling for the camera along with "Roger Matthews" and a quote: *"I've personally admired Kat Stanford for many years, so of course I accepted her friend's credentials on trust."*

I was stunned.

Mum snatched the paper up. "Piers called himself Roger Matthews?" She skimmed the article. "A seven-course meal estimated to cost two hundred pounds a head—good heavens! No wonder those jodhpurs are tight!"

"It wasn't my idea."

"Blah blah blah... tour of the kitchen?"

"That bit is untrue," I protested. "We didn't go—"

"Blah blah blah... half a dozen bottles of wine for... wait a minute... reviewer... Air *France*?" She began to laugh. "I didn't think you had it in you!"

"It's not funny!"

"Ooh... what a change from stuffy old David Wynne and pompous Shawn," Mum said gleefully. "And see here... Piers is described as an international playboy. Listen to this—"

"No thank you."

"Viscount Carew, son of the Earl of Denby, is well known for his pranks among the European jet set."

"Great."

"But how nice to see you on the front page again, darling," Mum said. "Although why you wore that old T-shirt? You've got plenty of other nice outfits. You don't want to let yourself go, especially if Piers is used to going out with models."

"I'm not going out with Piers ever again," I said. "He told me we were going for a quick drink. I did it for you in fact."

"You'd better tell me the whole story," said Mum. So I did.

Before long we were both laughing. "Serves them right if they are too caught up in their own self-importance not to check the facts!" Mum tossed *Star Stalkers* aside and picked up the weekly local paper that came out every Saturday. "I wonder what the *Dipperton Deal* has to say. Let's see."

"It won't be in there yet, Mother."

As expected, there was no mention of Muriel's murder given that it had happened after the newspaper had gone to print. A national tabloid could easily have done so, but the *Dipperton Deal* didn't have that kind of modern technology.

The front page was devoted to the upcoming Skirmish, with a warning to keep all valuables safe given a spate of thefts in the area. There was a paragraph on the discovery of a skeleton in Cromwell Meadows with the promise that the illustrious Dr. Crane from Plymouth University would be sharing his findings in next week's edition. In fact, the *Dipperton Deal* promised a one-page "splash."

I turned to page 2. "What about this?" I said. "You could have blamed your MINI being parked in the Hare & Hounds car park on him." I showed Mum a photograph of a clean-cut, good-looking man in his early forties wearing a suit and tie. He grinned mischievously at the camera. "*Danny Coverdale,*" I read aloud, "*leader of an international car theft ring, is still at large following his escape from Ford Open Prison in West Sussex.*"

"At large?" Mum mused. "Do they still use that old-fashioned term?"

"Apparently so," I said. "Did you know that according to this report there are over ninety prisoners who have escaped from Ford Open Prison over the last few years and many are still on the run!" I had a thought. "Where was Alfred staying at Her Majesty's pleasure?"

"This last time?" said Mum. "Wormwood Scrubs. Why?" Her eyes widened. "Alfred is not an escaped prisoner! And besides, he would never have hurt Muriel."

"Well, someone did," I said. "And it sounds like there were quite a few people who she upset along the way."

"Maybe it was a loan shark?" Mum suggested. "If Muriel's Fred had been in debt, maybe they came to collect their money? They obviously took back that awful canary-yellow Kia."

"*Maybe* that's what they were doing when Alfred turned

up," I suggested. "*Maybe* he interrupted them in Muriel's kitchen?"

Mum pulled a face. "That's a bit of a stretch. But I suppose it would explain why they didn't finish staging the job and why the suicide note hadn't been finished."

I shook my head. "But that doesn't make sense. If it were a loan shark, wouldn't they have taken whatever they could in repayment? Alfred said they left the TV and the new appliances. And what about the post office safe?"

"If Muriel didn't die from gas fumes because the oven was never turned on, how *did* she die?" Mum mused.

"We won't know that until—"

"The autopsy, true. This is all so depressing. Tell me something cheerful. Did Piers take something from the grave after all?"

"Yes," I said, and went on to tell her all about Eleanor and Nicholas being in love and supposedly marrying in secret.

"How romantic!" cried Mum. "And to accuse a Honeychurch of murdering his own kin—how exciting!"

"Hopefully there might be some information in the Parish registers," I said. "They'd have to have their marriage recorded whether it was secret or not. We should ask Violet for the key to the padlock."

"But if it is true . . . ," said Mum slowly, "then they ghosted her."

"They what?"

"Ghosted. Apparently that's what young people do these days. Rather than end a relationship, they delete the other person from their life and pretend they no longer exist. Charlize Theron did that to Sean Penn."

"For someone who doesn't have the Internet or social media you seem particularly well informed."

"Stacey—that's my hairdresser at Snipx—tells me everything," said Mum. "It must be awful to be young in this day and age."

"You might have a point about the ghosting," I said. "We wouldn't have even known of Eleanor's existence had I not seen Frances's plaque in St. Mary's."

"Hmmm," said Mum dreamily. She had adopted a look I knew all too well. "Kat!" she exclaimed. "That's it! Nicholas Carew and Eleanor Honeychurch—that's my new Star-Crossed Lovers story. It's so Romeo and Juliet."

"Well, don't thank me; thank Eleanor."

"I must strike while the iron is hot. I think I can redeem myself with my new editor with this idea—do you mind if I go and get cracking on this story?"

"Be my guest," I said. "I'll see you later. I'm off to ride with Harry."

Chapter Twenty-four

"Ah, there you are, Katherine." Lavinia emerged from the tack room. The bruises on her face had now turned an ugly yellow. "Poor Muriel. What rotten luck."

"Yes. Terrible."

"First Fred drops dead, then she's robbed not once, but twice, and then ... well ... you know ... we're not supposed to talk about ... you know ... her ... *misadventure* until we get further instructions."

I suppose "misadventure" was one way of describing poor Muriel's demise. I still felt very upset about it all. She'd only been sitting in my living room two days ago. I wondered if Muriel had already spent the three hundred pounds I'd given her and then thought what a terrible thing to even think about.

"Where's Alfred?" I scanned the stable yard. It looked particularly beautiful in the morning sunshine with wooden barrels filled with red geraniums. I was always struck by the neatness here in comparison to the Hall. Not even a piece of straw was out of place.

"Shawn has taken Alfred off to help with their enquiries," Lavinia said. "But I don't want you to worry."

"I already know what's going on. Shawn came to the Carriage House this morning."

"Ah. Well. He came here first... and then he came back again about thirty minutes ago," said Lavinia. "But as I say. Nothing to worry about." She lowered her voice to a whisper. "Alfred is in the clear."

"In the clear?"

"As you know, he's being doing a bit of... undercover work for me so to speak," Lavinia went on. "I would hate it to get out that he was roaming the countryside last night."

"Of course," I said.

Lavinia cast about. "Harry will be here in a moment. He took Mr. Chips into the kitchen. That dog is such a handful with Edith gone. Thank heavens she'll be back soon. But I did want to have a quick word with you. Shall we go somewhere private?"

"Of course." Why did everyone want to speak to me alone?

We took refuge in the tack room. Lavinia closed the door. She gestured to the old sofa that was oozing stuffing and covered in dog hair. "Do sit down, Katherine."

"I'm fine standing," I said. "Is everything okay? Are you feeling better?" Off Lavinia's blank look I added, "The bruised ribs?"

"Oh golly, yes. That Vico stuff that Iris gave me was *ab-so-lute-ly* super. I felt like I was floating on a cloud. You don't suppose she has any more, do you?"

"Why don't you ask her?"

Lavinia perched on the edge of a huge pine chest that

contained horse blankets. She inspected her grubby finger-
nails and gave a heavy sigh. "This is frightfully difficult."

I decided to sit after all. Her sigh sounded serious. "I'm
listening."

Lavinia fell quiet.

Whilst I waited for her to begin, I took in one of my favorite places. There was something warm and cozy about the tack
room. Whether it was the smell of oiled leather or just the feeling of much-loved horses I wasn't sure. One wall was lined
with saddle racks and bridles, each bearing the name of its
owner on a brass plaque. There were also a dozen racks holding ancient saddles, the owners of which lay buried in the
equine cemetery that overlooked the river Dart.

A pegboard was tacked to another wall, covered in rosettes
along with photographs of Edith, Lavinia and William, Alfred's
predecessor, the three of them pictured driving four-in-hand
when they used to compete in carriage-driving competitions.

"This is frightfully difficult," Lavinia said again. "But I
really *have* to talk to you."

"Well, here I am."

"Pippa is a friend of yours, isn't she?"

My heart sank. Piers must have voiced his suspicions about
Rupert and Pippa after all.

"I know Pippa, but we're not exactly close," I said carefully.

"Whenever I try to talk to her, she avoids me," Lavinia went
on. "It's most extraordinary. The thing is, I'm really worried."

"I'm sure you don't have anything to worry about. Rupert
loves you," I said, and then wondered why I would say such a
thing.

"What's Rupert got to do with it?"

"Nothing," I said quickly.

"It's not just about poor Violet and her tearoom, although I do think it's frightfully thoughtless to set up a rival business next door—I really need you to talk to Pippa."

"You want me to talk to Pippa about Violet?"

"Violet. No. Why would I want you to talk to Pippa about Violet?"

"You just mentioned Violet."

"Did I?"

I was getting exasperated. Edith was right about one thing. Lavinia was as thick as two short planks.

"I think Max is a bad influence on Harry," Lavinia declared.

"Oh, *that*!" I exclaimed, breathing a sigh of relief.

"You agree? You've noticed it, too?"

"Isn't it just high spirits?" I thought back to the pair of them playing in the churchyard on Thursday after school. "It's nice that Harry has a friend."

"Is it?" Lavinia pulled a face. "Harry has begged me to let him stay the night there again and I don't think they are supervised."

"I can't believe they'd get into trouble in the village."

"Have you read the newspapers? Ninety prisoners have escaped from Ford Open Prison."

"Not in one go," I said. "I think that has happened over the past few years and I'm quite certain they wouldn't have all come to Little Dipperton."

"Oh. Yes. Good point. But even so, we'll be expecting a lot of strangers in the village for the Skirmish. The Hare & Hounds is completely sold out for B and B, so I'm told. No...the thing is *apparently* Max is convinced the church is haunted and he wants to capture it on his camera. Every time I broach the subject with Rupert and suggest he talk to Pippa, Rupert leaves the room. I don't think he likes Pippa very much."

I had a pretty good idea why he pretended not to. Sadly, pretending to loathe the woman you're secretly sleeping with was as old as time.

"The thing is—" She sighed again. "I have an awful feeling that Harry and Max stole all that money for the reenactment."

"I don't believe it!" I said. And I absolutely didn't. "Who told you that? Shawn?"

"Not in so many words," said Lavinia. "But... Harry's white scarf was discovered inside the post office. Shawn found it there yesterday morning and gave it to me."

"That's a big accusation," I said.

"And then... the empty biscuit tin that Mr. Chips dug up from Fred Jarvis's grave." She gave a shudder. "What a cruel joke. Harry would never do that unless someone made him."

"Have you asked Harry?"

"Good grief no!" Lavinia exclaimed. "That's a father's domain, but as I said, Rupert refuses to talk about it. Will you ask him? Find out what sort of tricks he and Max get up to? You're so good with Harry. He really likes you." Lavinia gave *another* heavy sigh. "I just don't want him turning out like—"

"Rupert?"

"Good grief no!" Lavinia exclaimed again. "No. I mean like my brother, Piers. As a child he was always getting into mischief, and as a man he hasn't changed."

She regarded me with an expression that I couldn't gauge. "And there is something else."

"Fire away," I said.

Her face turned pink. "I like to think we are friends, Katherine—"

"I like to think we are, too—" Although I couldn't ever imagine confiding anything to Lavinia.

"I know you've met Piers."

"Yes."

"Piers is ... Piers is a little *wild*," she said. "I wouldn't want you to get hurt."

I felt my feathers distinctly ruffle. "There is no danger of that," I said. "Honestly. We just went out for dinner."

"Yes, I know," said Lavinia with yet *another* sigh. "It's just the sort of thing he loves to do and I'm afraid it made you look bad. I saw it on the front page of *Star Stalkers*. He's done that heaps of times—it's some sort of silly bet with his chum Roger Matthews. Piers is always getting into scrapes. It's frightfully lucky that Daddy is a magistrate. He knows all the right people to get Piers off."

"I can assure you that it's unlikely that we will be going out again."

"But that's what they all say." Lavinia was earnest. "My brother is a hopeless romantic. He falls in love all the time."

"I gathered that," I said. "I'm immune to hopeless romantics."

"Did he ask you for a drink and then before you knew what was happening you are miles away and dining at a super restaurant?"

I grudgingly agreed that was true.

"The next thing he'll do is send you flowers."

"He already brought me flowers—"

"Yes—gerbera daisies? The flower of innocence, purity and cheerfulness?"

"I don't believe it," I muttered. "Yes. True."

"Don't worry. You'll get *masses* of flowers next. And *then* he'll surprise you with a weekend trip to Paris."

"You really don't need to worry," I said, and meant it. I was beginning to feel a bit of a fool for being so easily duped. Even so, I found myself on the defensive. "But as I said, it wasn't a date. We were talking about the identity of the woman in Cromwell Meadows. Piers believes she is Eleanor Honeychurch. Apparently she married one of your ancestors, Nicholas Carew?"

"Oh God. You poor thing! Did he bore you to death?" said Lavinia. "Piers has always been obsessed with the family lineage."

"I told you, you have nothing to worry about," I said again.

"Oh goody. I'm so relieved." Lavinia smiled. "You see, the thing is, Piers is sort of betrothed to my best friend, Cassandra Bowden-Forbes. Do you know her?"

"No, I don't." So Piers hadn't been single at all! How infuriating!

"She's a bit like you actually," Lavinia went on. "Does a bit of antiquing."

Antiquing? Lavinia made my profession sound like a hobby. I knew she meant well, but I was surprised to feel disappointed despite my earlier resolve not to see Piers again. If there was the shadow of another woman in any shape or form on the horizon, I was *definitely* not interested. Ever.

Lavinia brightened up. "I'm so glad we understand each

other. I've been frightfully worried about having this conversation. I'm so glad it's all sorted out."

"Me too."

Harry burst into the tack room dressed as Squadron Leader James Bigglesworth *and* wearing his white scarf.

"Ready for today's mission, Stanford?"

I had never been happier to see him.

Chapter Twenty-five

"If you had to die in the English Civil War," said Harry, "what method would you choose?"

"I'd like to think I survived, thank you," I said.

"No, you have to pretend! You have to answer!" Harry exclaimed.

I was used to Harry's delight in describing all manner of deaths in gory details, but today my mind flashed not just to poor Eleanor's appalling end, but to Muriel's, too. "Let me think about it."

I was riding Duchess, the dapple-gray mare, and Harry was on his beloved black pony, Thunder.

We were trotting along Hopton's Crest, a rough track that ran along the top of a ridge and had the most spectacular views. It was one of my favorite places to ride.

On one side nestled the small village of Little Dipperton and the tiny church of St. Mary's. On the other, tucked between trees and centuries-old dry stone walls, spread the Honeychurch Hall estate with the peculiar equine cemetery, ornamental grounds, Victorian grotto and vast walled garden that was lined with near-derelict glasshouses.

During the winter Eric's scrapyard would have been easy to see, but now that summer was around the corner the rows of old cars or, as he called them, end-of-life vehicles were screened by banks of trees. I could just make out Mum's Carriage House and beyond that the white tent that covered Eleanor's remains.

In the distance I could see the Greenway Ferry pleasure boat cruising gently up the River Dart.

"Don't you think they all look like ants," said Harry, pointing to all the activity in the park. There were now four enormous marquees.

"I'm so excited about the Skirmish," he went on. "I'm going to carry the king's colors."

"Congratulations," I said. "That's quite an honor. Who is playing the king?"

"It's a secret." Harry grinned. "But you're changing the subject. Tell me how would you want to die?"

"I'll tell you on one condition," I said.

"A condition?" Harry exclaimed. "Good heavens, Stanford. Are you forgetting who you are talking to?"

"My apologies, sir," I said. "But it's very important. I've had orders from above about last night's surveillance activities in the churchyard."

"Orders from above? Well . . . in that case, I'll tell you, but first—"

"Alright," I said. "What are my options?"

"Let me think," said Harry. "I know! Being pierced by an

eighteen-foot-long pike. It's like an axe with a steel spike at the end, and when the enemy charges and you are in the way you could get skewered and it would go right through your body and there would be blood everywhere and it would take you ages to die."

"No. That sounds gross."

"A cannonball?" said Harry. "The balls are lead and when they are fired from cannon they can smash you to smithereens. Bits of arms and legs everywhere! There's a few cannonballs in the Museum Room."

"Sounds messy."

"What about a musket? Father has two. The barrels are four feet long and you load them from the muzzle with gunpowder and little lead balls," Harry went on cheerfully. "But sometimes the guns didn't fire in the rain, so it was quicker to use them as clubs."

"That sounds painful."

"They're all painful, silly," said Harry. "But if you did get wounded, there wasn't any anas … anas—"

"Anesthetic?"

"Uncle Piers told me the doctors would use bullet extractors and bone saws and skull elevators—"

"*Skull* elevators? That sounds disgusting. What other options do I have?"

"Being mowed down by the cavalry?"

"Trampled on, you mean?"

"Although you could live longer if you had an Albert to pull the enemy from their horses—"

"Albert? Oh. You mean a halberd?"

"That's what I said."

"What about good old-fashioned sword fighting?"

"That's boring." Harry thought for a moment. His goggles glinted in the morning sunshine. "Or I suppose you could allow yourself to get captured by the enemy."

"And why would I do that?"

"In those days you could change sides if you wanted to. Uncle Piers said that people only had to swear an oath not to take up arms again and they could go home for dinner. Jolly lucky, don't you think?"

"Then I would change sides all the time," I declared.

Fortunately, we had reached the end of Hopton's Crest and had to fall into single file. The track narrowed to a steep path that wound down through sloping woodland.

At the bottom, Harry waited for me to ride up alongside him. He looked worried. "If there was another war, whose side would I be on? Father is a Honeychurch and Mummy is a Carew."

"First of all, there won't be another war like that one," I said. "And one day you're going to be the Earl of Grenville, aren't you?"

"Yes."

"In which case that makes you a Honeychurch."

"Oh." He still didn't seem convinced. "But let's not tell Uncle Piers that."

"Okay," I said. "Now it's your turn to tell me about last night's surveillance in the churchyard? Was it successful? Did you see any ghosts?"

Harry nodded eagerly. "It was wicked."

"Wow. So you actually saw a ghost?"

"Mrs. Jarvis from the post office saw it, too," said Harry. "She was scared."

"Muriel Jarvis?" I said sharply. "You saw Muriel last night in the *churchyard*?"

Harry nodded. "She was saying good night to Mr. Jarvis at his grave. Mummy told me that Mr. Jarvis had a heart attack and died when he was doing the weeding. I hope Cropper doesn't die when he does the weeding. He's much older than Mr. Jarvis."

"I hope Cropper doesn't, either," I said. "What did this ghost look like? Are you sure it wasn't a zombie?"

Harry laughed. "Of course it wasn't a *zombie*! It was white."

"And where did you see this white ghost?"

"It came out of the church, so we hid behind the tombstones and then there was a scream, so we ran back to Max's house."

I wasn't sure what to make of this. "What did Max's mother say?"

"She was asleep," said Harry.

"So she didn't know that you crept out of the house in the middle of the night?"

"It was a top-secret mission," Harry protested. "I dropped my scarf, but luckily, I got it back again."

This was even more puzzling. According to Shawn, he'd found Harry's white scarf in the post office.

"And I found this!" Harry pulled out a mobile phone from his pocket. "Finders, Keepers, Losers, Weepers!"

"Let me see that!"

Harry passed it up to me. It was a cheap pay-as-you-go mobile phone. Something similar to the one I'd noticed in Jess's handbag. Perhaps she had dropped it.

"It doesn't work yet," said Harry. "Max says I have to charge the battery."

"Where exactly did you find this?"

"In the churchyard," said Harry. "Max has a phone, so now we can phone each other. Can I have it back please?"

I gave it to Harry. "You'll need a power cord, though."

"We're going tonight to see if we can get photographs of the ghost," Harry went on.

"I thought you already took photographs?"

"We were scared, but tonight we'll be ready and then we can sell them to the newspapers and be millionaires and then I can give the money to Father so he can paint the windows."

"I think you should ask your parents if that's okay, Harry," I said. "They may not like you hanging around the churchyard in the middle of the night."

"You won't tell them, will you?"

"I won't tell them," I said firmly. "But only on the condition that *you* do. And please, tell them about seeing Mrs. Jarvis in the churchyard."

"Why?"

"It's on a need to know basis, but it's important. I'd tell you if I could. I promise."

Harry nodded. "Alright. Yes."

Once again we had to break into single file as the track narrowed into an animal path that wound through the trees. Eventually it opened into a grassy bridleway. We cantered past Harry's tree house, skirting Coffin Mire, and turned down another track that led by Bridge Cottage.

A blue Prius was parked under a bank of overhanging trees, but as we trotted on by I noticed that it was empty.

It was only when we approached the five-bar gate that I spotted Eric sitting in his Land Rover. Next to him was none other than Jess Carew.

Chapter Twenty-six

"Hello," said Harry cheerfully as he peered into the front of the Land Rover. "What are you doing here? I didn't know you were friends."

Eric's face was scarlet and Jess looked like a deer caught in headlights. I too was stuck for words.

"Yes. We're just friends." Jess flashed me an earnest smile. "Nothing more."

I thought back to the gatehouse and how the pair had obviously recognized each other back then. If Jess was having an affair with anyone, it was—hard to believe—Eric.

"Where's Gramps?" Harry demanded.

"He and your uncle Piers are rehearsing today," said Jess.

"But why are *you* talking to Eric?"

"I had a message from your grandfather for him," said Jess smoothly. "He's hoping that Eric will help organize the weapons for next Saturday."

"He can't do that," said Harry, and then clapped his hand over his mouth. "Oops. It's a secret."

"I love secrets," said Jess.

"But why are you here?" Harry said again.

Jess laughed. "Goodness, Biggles, I feel like I am being interrogated!"

Harry didn't laugh. "You are."

"I was driving along Cavalier Lane and saw Eric's Land Rover," Jess went on—not so confident now. "I wasn't going to interrupt his day, but then I changed my mind and parked my car just a little farther up the road and walked back."

"But why are you both *sitting* in Eric's Land Rover?"

"Oh, Harry, does it matter?" Jess snapped, but quickly smiled again. "Well, I must say time is moving on, so I really need to get going."

"And we should go, too," I said to Harry.

We left the guilty pair and headed for home at a brisk trot. Harry didn't mention it and neither did I, but I couldn't stop thinking about them.

The rest of our ride passed uneventfully, but my mind was filled with Eric and Jess. I was disappointed. I liked her and had begun to believe she actually cared for Aubrey. I just hoped she wasn't expecting to draw me into her confidence. I was growing weary of being the keeper of secrets for all and sundry.

I found Mum in the kitchen making sandwiches. "Did you post your pages?"

"Oh yes!" Mum exclaimed. "And guess what? I saw the shop in Dartmouth where Jess must have purchased your bangle. I can tell you that it was not cheap."

"Oh?"

"I popped in and told them you'd received a gift and would they change it for a larger size and they said it wasn't a problem at all."

"I have to go to Dartmouth tomorrow," I said. "I'll go in and see them."

"I'd avoid tomorrow, dear," said Mum. "It's the Dart Music Festival. The place will be a zoo."

"By the way, Lavinia wondered if she could have more Vicodin—"

"Who does she think I am?" Mum grumbled. "Her dealer? Ah—here is Alfred now. Lunch?"

Alfred strolled into the kitchen looking furious.

"Whatever's the matter?" Mum cried.

"That bloody stupid woman—Violet whatever her name is—insists she saw me in the churchyard," Alfred snarled. "And she heard a scream."

"I think she saw Harry and Max," I said, and relayed Harry's conversation with me. "The boys also saw Muriel in the churchyard last night."

"What time was that?" Alfred demanded.

"I didn't ask. Sorry."

"What about Pippa Carmichael?" Mum suggested. "Wouldn't she have been woken up by Muriel's screams—if it was Muriel screaming, of course, and not the ghost?"

"Apparently Pippa was in bed fast asleep."

"So we've just got to deal with Violet and her appalling eyesight," said Mum with a sigh. "What a load of gossips."

"The boys must have crept out very late." I was worried. Little Dipperton may seem safe, but with the re-enactment coming up sightseers had started to trickle in. I thought of the man who had been hitchhiking and who might have been the same man who had been standing in the middle of the lane the night that Piers drove me home in such fury. I made a mental note to mention it to Shawn. I assumed the stranger would be staying at the Hare & Hounds, but it was odd that he'd been lurking around the village so late.

Alfred slammed his hand down hard on the kitchen table. Mum and I jumped. "I didn't go into that churchyard," he fumed. "I tailed Rupert until the A38 but gave up to go back and find your damn manuscript, Iris."

"You left one page behind," Mum snapped.

Alfred glowered. "You told me five pages were missing. I brought five pages back. I wasn't to know there was another page. If I had, I would have looked for that page."

"Did the police ask for your fingerprints?" said Mum. We all knew that if Alfred's fingerprints were put into the system his criminal record spanning over fifty years would be out in the open. Of course I knew that Alfred was on parole, but I never thought to ask him if he reported to a parole office every day or what the terms were for that parole.

"No. They did not," said Alfred. "And that's the last time I do any of your dirty work, Iris."

"You won't do mine, but you'll spy on his lordship for Lady Lavinia?"

Fortunately, a rapping on the front door allowed me to escape. "I'll go," I said, and left the pair of them bickering in the kitchen.

For the second time today, I was caught off-guard. There, standing on the doorstep, was Jess. She looked worried.

"Can I talk to you?"

I hesitated. "Now?"

"Please. I need to tell you the truth," she said earnestly. "It really isn't what you think."

"Okay. Follow me."

The Carriage House formed part of a quadrangle. A range of outbuildings still in varying states of decay formed two sides; and a half-dilapidated barn, the fourth. I opened the door to the disused feed shed and ushered her inside.

"I knew Eric before I met Aubrey," she blurted out. "I love Aubrey. I really do."

I tried to remember when Eric's wife, Vera, had died. It had been shortly after I first moved to Devon. That was nine months ago. As far as we all knew, Eric had never had a girlfriend since then—at least not one we had been aware of.

"I had just got out of an ugly relationship and didn't want anything serious."

"Okay."

"I mean, when you and David Wynne broke up—"

"We're not talking about me," I said. "We're talking about you."

"Yes. Yes. You're right. We are." She took a deep breath. "So I tried online dating."

"Okay."

"I told you, I didn't want anything serious. Eric didn't want anything serious. It was just a fling. I didn't expect to see Eric ever again."

"Didn't you know where Eric lived?"

"I never asked," said Jess. "We used to meet in Taunton. In a hotel."

"But why the secrecy? Why couldn't you be out in the open about it?"

"Eric was married."

"Oh." Of course I'd known that Eric's marriage to Vera had been volatile, but even so.

"My ex-boyfriend was the jealous type and I didn't want to risk him finding out."

"Why are you telling me all this?"

"I wanted you to hear it from me," she said. "Eric was cut up about the fact I ghosted him."

It was the second time I'd heard that term in twenty-four hours. "Poor Eric."

"Why poor Eric?" Jess exclaimed. "*He* was the one who didn't play by the rules. Everyone knows what you sign up for with adult online dating."

"*Adult* online dating!" I exclaimed.

"You know, Ashley Madison? Life is short. Have an affair, or something." Jess blushed. "It's for people who don't want a commitment. It's non-exclusive, no questions asked. Just sex. You know how it is."

In this case, I didn't. I had never been that kind of girl.

"We, I mean me . . . I was moving around a lot at the time for work and it suited me."

"I thought you had a jealous ex-boyfriend?"

"Oh. Yes. And that, too."

"Is that why Eric called you Maureen?"

"He called himself *Christian*!" Jess exclaimed. "He told me he was an entrepreneur and ran a successful car dealership— not a scrapyard!"

Despite myself I had to laugh.

A flicker of a smile crossed Jess's features. "He was actually very skilled in the bedroom."

"Argh! No details please!" I said.

"You can't tell anyone about this."

"Who am I going to tell?"

"Lavinia. Piers."

"That's not my style," I said. "But be careful. This village is a hive of gossip."

"Like the postmistress?"

"Yes."

"Did she really go through people's post?"

"Supposedly."

"Maybe that's why she committed suicide?"

I was surprised. "Is that what you heard?"

"Didn't she? I thought there was a note."

"Who told you?"

"Violet. You mean she didn't?"

"Have you spoken to Shawn yet?" I asked.

Jess shook her head. "Why would he want to talk to me? Carew Court is miles away." She cocked her head. "Shawn's nice. He's single, isn't he?"

"Don't play matchmaker."

"Honestly, you should be open. Look at me! I never thought in a million years that I would end up married to Aubrey!"

"You never told me how you met."

"I was waiting tables for a charity gala and we got talking. He was—is the most fascinating man I've ever met. He makes me feel safe. He's so kind to me, Kat." She looked miserable. "Do you think Eric will cause any trouble? I think I hurt his feelings."

"Even if he said something, why should it matter?" I said. "This was before you met Aubrey anyway."

"Yes. Yes. You're right. It was. It's just—" She bit her lip. "I suppose it's not Aubrey that I'm worried about. It's Piers and Lavinia. Piers loathes me. He thinks I'm a gold digger, but I've already proved that I'm not. I didn't sign a prenup or anything like that." Tears brimmed over and trickled down her face. "I really love Aubrey, you know. I've done things in my past, things I'm ashamed of that I would never want to come out. But I'm changed. Really I am. Doesn't everyone deserve a second chance?"

"Yes," I said. "I believe we all do."

And with that, Jess left the feed shed and went back to her car. I was troubled. I knew she wasn't telling me everything. She was hiding something, but I didn't know what. Didn't Shakespeare say, *"The lady doth protest too much"*? Why bother to convince me of her love for Aubrey? Why the need to prove something to me? We weren't friends, much as she liked to think otherwise.

As Jess's Prius left, so Piers, in his Mercedes, arrived.

I could tell it was going to be another one of those days.

Piers got out of the car clutching two bouquets of roses and holding a leather portfolio under his arm. "What was *she* doing here?"

"Just saying hello," I said.

He scowled. "You should watch her. She's not who she seems and I'm going to prove it."

Piers's words echoed those of Alfred when he supposedly channeled my "uninvited guest." But what could Jess possibly do to me?

"I come bearing gifts and an apology," he said, all smiles once more.

"The flowers are beautiful. But two bouquets is a little extravagant."

"I have to claw my way back into your affection," said Piers. "But in fact, one is for Iris. There is something that you both should see."

Chapter Twenty-seven

"Kat said that you were the self-appointed Honeychurch historian, so I thought you might be interested in these."

"Of course I am!" My mother stared in wonder at the six parchment letters with their broken wax seals that lay on the kitchen table. The script was spidery and very difficult to read, but Piers had copied them into a notebook in surprisingly neat handwriting.

"The Carews keep everything," said Piers with more than a hint of pride. "Nicholas and Eleanor were friends from childhood. But Eleanor had been betrothed at birth to her cousin, James Honeychurch."

"Ah, the pirate," said Mum. "Bootstrap Jim."

"But he was a cousin," I said. "Wasn't it illegal for first cousins to marry?"

"The monarchy were always marrying first cousins and cousins once removed," said Mum. "In fact, the entire line of succession to the British throne stems from a first-cousin marriage between Frederick William the First of Prussia and

Sophia Dorothea of Hanover. There are over five thousand descendants who are currently alive—"

"Including Emma Bunton?" I teased.

Piers looked confused.

"From the Spice Girls," said Mum helpfully. "Emma is one hundred and third in line to the throne."

"Sorry, private joke," I said. "You were saying?"

"The war broke out and Nicholas and Eleanor eloped. He returned to fight but got caught up in the Battle of Naseby. By the time he got back, Eleanor had vanished," said Piers. "No one knew what had really happened to her until now."

I looked up from reading one of the transcriptions. "Listen to this." I read, *"How it doth pain me so but I do this willingly for you my love and would suffer a thousand more barbs just to see your face once more."*

"Do you think that refers to the scold's bridle?" said Mum.

"You can't help who you fall in love with," Piers said.

He had echoed Alfred's words from the night before. I looked at Piers with his tousled hair and boyish face and for a moment—just a moment—wondered if I was being too cynical and that I should give him a chance to redeem himself.

"Why would someone put a scold's bridle on her?" I said with a shudder.

"No one really knows. Punishment? Jealousy? Spying?" he said. "Or just plain spite."

"What about her sister, Lady Frances?" Mum said suddenly. "She must have known what was going on. Wouldn't she have intervened?"

"The role of women was very different in those days," I

pointed out. "There would have been nothing she could do—particularly in wartime."

"Didn't Nicholas try to find her?" Mum asked.

"I've found traces of correspondence that seem to imply he did, but the country was falling apart. It was all people could do to survive."

"But who killed her?" said Mum.

"The dagger in her grave was proof enough for me," said Piers. "As well as confirming the crest on the blade, my father found James Honeychurch's initials engraved in the hilt."

"But that's terrible!" I exclaimed.

"She was betrayed by her own kin," Mum declared. "Just like me—oh, wait.... Betrayed! That's it. *Betrayed*! Excuse me. I must write this down." She turned away and grabbed a block of Post-its and began scribbling away.

Piers caught my eye. I gave a shrug. "Taking notes," I said.

"We must tell his lordship," Mum went on. "Lady Eleanor should be buried in the family mausoleum at St. Mary's church."

"Absolutely not," said Piers forcefully. "She must be buried with her husband in our family chapel. That's where she belongs." He got to his feet, picked up the parchment letters and carefully slid them back inside the plastic protector sleeves.

"What about his lordship?" Mum said.

"You can tell Rupert whatever you like."

"Thank you for showing us these letters," I said. "And for the flowers."

"And the ring is exquisite," Mum chimed in.

I walked Piers out to his car.

"Have I redeemed myself?" he asked.

"A tiny bit. Yes. Although I fear that my reputation is in tatters."

I watched him drive away. There had been no mention of another date and I wasn't sure if I was relieved or disappointed.

"Come on," said Mum, who suddenly materialized at my elbow. "Let's go and get Alfred. We need to go back to St. Mary's."

"Why do we need Alfred?"

"Given the circumstances, I'd like to know the exact date Eleanor died," said Mum. "We've got some lock picking to do."

We climbed into Mum's MINI and headed for Little Dipperton. Twenty minutes later the three of us were walking into St. Mary's church.

Alfred wrinkled his nose. "Can you smell that?"

"Bacon sandwiches," Mum and I chorused.

"That's good, because perhaps Violet is here and we can ask for the key—I can't think who else would be eating bacon sandwiches."

We headed up the aisle and into the vestry and approached the enormous Parish chest.

"That's weird," I said. "It looks as if the chest has been moved. It was flush against the wall when we were here last time, but now it's not." In fact, it stood a good three inches away from the wall.

"It's still padlocked," said Mum. "See what you can do with that, Alfred."

Alfred knelt down and withdrew a lockpick from his pocket.

"Shouldn't someone stand watch?" I said nervously.

"*Shush,*" said Mum. "Look and learn."

Alfred began to noodle away on the padlock.

I looked around the vestry. It was then that I noticed a bottle of bleach cleaning fluid. It was under the chair—a strange place to leave such a thing. I picked the bottle up.

"Keep still!" Mum hissed. "Alfred needs absolute silence; otherwise he can't hear the clicks."

I stopped.

"*Shush!*" Mum said again. "Listen! Someone's coming!"

She was right. I could hear footsteps and they were heading our way.

"Quickly, Alfred! Leave it!"

Alfred jumped to his feet just as Violet walked into the vestry.

She regarded us with suspicion. "I thought I saw you heading for the church. What are you doing in here? Stealing candles?"

"Candles?" Mum exclaimed. "Why would we want to steal candles?"

"Well, someone is." She marched over to the ambry and brought out the box. "I've been counting them. You see? This was a full box last Wednesday."

"And you have no right to accuse poor Alfred here of lurking in the churchyard last night," Mum went on.

"I know what I saw," Violet said stubbornly. "And I saw you with him, too, and that's what I told the police."

"But I was nowhere near the church!" Mum shouted. "You need your eyes tested." She pointed at poor Violet's cracked glasses. "What you saw were two little boys playing ghosts. Isn't that right, Kat?"

"Harry and Max *were* in the churchyard last night," I said to Violet.

"I know. I found Master Harry's scarf," said Violet. "I posted it through Muriel's letterbox. Master Harry is very fond of that scarf."

Well, that explained how the scarf ended up in the post office.

"It was a man and a woman," Violet insisted.

I thought for a moment. "Did you see Muriel in the churchyard as well, Violet?"

"Yes," said Violet. "She always goes to Fred's grave to say good night."

"You see!" Mum exclaimed. "It must have been Muriel that you saw, not me."

"Did you hear anything?" I asked. "A scream perhaps?"

"The boys make a racket," said Violet. "I'm always hearing them. It's wicked. They shouldn't be allowed to climb over the graves in the Lord's garden. It's disrespectful. Poor Muriel."

"You've certainly changed your tune. I thought you couldn't stand Muriel."

"When it comes to outsiders, blood is thicker than water."

"How can that be?" said Mum. "Although it wouldn't surprise me if you were related. Everyone seems to be related to everyone here."

"We're cousins twice removed," said Violet with a sniff.

"What are you doing in here anyway?" Mum demanded.

"I've come to do the flowers," said Violet. "I keep the church clean." She snatched the bleach bottle from my hand but then paused, wrinkling her nostrils. "Can you smell bacon sandwiches?"

"Yes," said Mum. "It's hard not to. For someone who likes to keep this little church clean, your standards are slipping."

"I told Lady Carew not to eat bacon sandwiches in here."

"Jess?" said Mum. "We haven't seen her this morning. Why would she be eating a bacon sandwich in the church?"

"I make them for the workmen at the barn," said Violet. "That Pippa doesn't fry anything. Says it's unhealthy."

"What's going on in here?" Shawn entered the vestry.

"You called the police?" Mum gasped. "Why? Why would you do that?"

"Ms. Green did no such thing," said Shawn. "Thanks to Kat, Harry told his mother, and she urged him to call me about what the boys witnessed in the churchyard last night. I'm afraid this is now off-limits."

"Why?" Mum demanded.

"We're quite certain that Muriel was not killed in her own home—"

"Muriel was murdered!" Violet cried. "But I thought . . . thought . . . no, who would do such a thing?"

"Eyewitness accounts and the expertise of our forensic maestro have proved otherwise," said Shawn.

"You think she was killed in the churchyard?" I said.

"She visited Fred's grave every night," Violet whispered.

Shawn suddenly spotted the bleach that Violet was holding. "Where did you find that?"

"I found it," I said. "It was under the chair."

"Under the *chair*?" Violet said with a frown. "I always put my supplies away in the bucket behind the door. I would never leave it under a chair."

"I'll take that if you don't mind," said Shawn.

"Can't you just tell us what is going on?" I said.

"I'm sorry. No." Shawn paused. "Can you smell bacon sandwiches?"

"I make them for Lady Carew," said Violet again. "She gives them to the workmen at the barn."

Shawn regarded Mum, Alfred and me. I noted that Alfred hadn't uttered a word since the police officer had arrived. "And what are you all doing in here?"

"I was doing some research for his lordship about the Honeychurch family and wanted to look through the Parish registers." Mum pointed to the Parish chest. "But it's locked."

"You wouldn't have had much luck anyway," said Shawn. "All the Parish registers were moved to the county record office twenty years ago."

"We thought Violet would have a key to the padlock."

Violet frowned. "But why would I have a key?"

"You didn't put the padlock on?" said Mum.

"I would never do that," said Violet.

"Perhaps the dowager countess knows," Shawn suggested.

"She's in London. I'm picking her up from the railway station tomorrow," I said.

"Oh, I'm so relieved her ladyship caught the train to London," said Violet. "I've been so worried."

"If only my worries were as small as yours, Violet," said Mum rather unkindly, I thought.

We were a subdued party on the drive back home. The thought that the boys may have heard Muriel's dying screams just made my blood run cold.

"You don't think it's remotely possible that Muriel saw something and died of fright?" said Mum.

"You mean, she teleported her way from the churchyard to her kitchen, tried to write a suicide note and—"

"It was just a theory," said Mum crossly.

"Alfred?" I said. "You're very quiet."

"I'm thinking," he said. "That wheelbarrow had been moved."

"Wheelbarrow? What are you talking about?" said Mum.

"Yesterday, when Mr. Chips dug up the biscuit tin, the wheelbarrow was in the middle of the path. This afternoon, the wheelbarrow was behind one of the headstones."

"You think someone *wheeled* Muriel's body back to her kitchen?" Mum gave a snigger. "You're daft, you are. Are you going to tell the policeman?"

"Never," Alfred snarled. "Matter of principle. I'd never snitch."

"Didn't you say Muriel was only wearing one shoe when you saw her in the kitchen?" I said suddenly.

"That's right."

"And you expect Alfred to tell the police?" Mum scoffed.

"But that's really important," I said. "But no, of course he can't."

Back at Jane's Cottage I felt inexplicably depressed. I couldn't stop thinking about the letters that Piers had shown us. It was all so tragic. And there was poor Muriel. The more I thought about her death the more I was certain she had to have seen something in the churchyard. Perhaps the boys knew more than they realized. Could Alfred have done something after all? It could have been an accident and he'd tried to cover it up by making it look like a suicide—but then why not finish the job? As Alfred liked to say, he *was* a professional.

I climbed into my pajamas even though it was only eight o'clock, poured myself a glass of wine and ate scrambled eggs on toast.

I must have dozed off, because I was jolted awake by the shrill ring of my mobile phone. To my astonishment, Pippa's name flashed up on the caller I.D.

I looked at the clock. It was just past midnight.

"Come quickly," she said. "Something terrible has happened."

My stomach gave a sickening lurch. "Is Harry alright?"

"Yes, yes, of course he is." Pippa gave an anguished sob. "Everything is ruined. I don't know who else I can trust."

"Slow down," I said. "What's happened?"

"I think she's dead."

"Who!" I exclaimed.

"Violet."

I tried to take this in. "What on earth is Violet doing at your house so late?"

"Oh, Kat, I'm not home." She paused to control herself. "A car accident. I don't know why she was out so late. We saw it happen."

I was horrified. "The boys saw it?"

"No, no, of course not. They're not here," said Pippa. "You have to come. Please, Kat."

"Where are you?"

"Bridge Cottage," she whispered.

"*Bridge Cottage!*" I exclaimed. "Whatever for? But . . . but what about Harry and Max?"

"Don't judge me! Not now," Pippa sobbed. "Just come. Quickly!"

Chapter Twenty-eight

Pippa was waiting for me as I pulled up outside the ruins of Bridge Cottage. In the full moon I caught sight of her clothing—a short skirt, a low-cut T-shirt. Not the usual clothing I ever saw her wear.

Violet's Morris Minor had hit a tree at the bottom of the hill just before the bridge where the lane made a sharp curve.

It wasn't the first time something awful had happened in this cursed part of the village.

"Thank you for coming," Pippa said miserably. "Violet's still in the front seat."

"Did you call for an ambulance?"

Pippa nodded. "After I spoke to you. I had to walk up to the top of the hill to get a signal."

"Is she alive?"

"I don't know," Pippa said miserably. "She's slumped over the steering wheel. I didn't want to touch her. She wasn't moving."

I hurried over to the car. Violet had a bloody gash across her forehead, but thankfully she was wearing a seat belt. Fortunately, I was able to open the door. I reached out for her neck. The pulse was there. Faint but, thankfully, still there.

"What on earth was she doing out driving so late?"

"We heard a car coming," said Pippa. "It was coming so fast! She didn't even attempt to brake; she just—" Pippa struggled to control her emotions. "It was horrible. I'll never forget the sound of the crash or her screaming."

I was deeply troubled. Was it Violet who had been creeping about the countryside at all hours of the night?

"You'll have to tell the police," I said.

"No! I can't. I can't do that."

I had a sudden thought. "Where's your car?"

Pippa couldn't meet my eye. "I walked."

"I'm not stupid!" I exclaimed. "Were you meeting someone here? Is that it?"

"I...I can't tell you. Please, *please* don't ask me," she begged.

I was stunned. "So whoever it was just drove off and left *you* to deal with it?"

"It wasn't like that," she whispered. "His car was stolen."

"What do you mean?"

"We were...distracted. He'd parked it a little far away and...someone stole it."

I was speechless.

"Don't judge me, Kat. Not you. You've had an affair with a married man."

"Is this about Rupert Honeychurch?" I said coldly. Piers had been right all along. "And for the record, my relationship was out in the open, so it was not an affair. Pippa! Have you thought what that would do to Harry if he ever found out?"

A siren and flashing lights ended our conversation and

within moments it pulled up alongside followed by Shawn in his panda car.

"Oh great," I muttered.

The Cruickshank twins—Tony and John—leapt out. "We'll take over from here, Kat," said Tony or John. As they were identical twins, I could never tell one from the other.

Pippa and I and sat on the wall that bordered the stream.

The minute Shawn saw me he stopped in astonishment. I realized I was still wearing my pajamas.

Pippa, who was openly sobbing—although I felt quite certain it had nothing to do with poor Violet—haltingly told Shawn about the runaway car.

"And what were you doing down here at this time of night, Ms. Carmichael?" Shawn demanded, pencil poised above his notepad.

"I often take a late walk," Pippa lied. "It's only twenty minutes from the village. Suddenly Violet's car came out of nowhere. I was upset and that's when I called Kat."

Shawn regarded Pippa with suspicion. "It's no secret that you and Violet Green can't stand each other."

"It's true. I don't take kindly to blackmail—forget I said that. I'm in shock," she said quickly.

"*Blackmail* is a serious accusation," said Shawn.

"I told you!" she exclaimed. "I'm in shock, that's all."

Shawn switched on his flashlight and swept the beam up and down the lane. It was dry as a bone.

"No skid marks," said Shawn thoughtfully. "What on earth was Violet doing out here so late?"

Tony or John strolled over. "She'll survive. Though it's a miracle. Those old cars don't have air bags, but they do offer a lot more protection than some of the modern rubbish we have today."

"We'll talk more in the morning." Shawn closed his note-book with a snap. "I suggest everyone go home and get some sleep."

I drove Pippa back to the village. Neither of us spoke.

As we pulled up outside her cottage, I noticed a flurry of activity in the churchyard. A flashlight suddenly went out.

"Those boys shouldn't be out alone at night," I said.

Pippa got out. "Harry, Max, in. Now!" she yelled without any consideration for those villagers who were asleep. "And I mean *now!*"

The two boys peeped over the low wall. I left them to it and drove back to Jane's Cottage.

I was far too upset to go to bed. Pippa had mentioned black-mail. Had Violet found out about Pippa's affair? I could see Muriel trying to blackmail someone but never Violet. But then again, I had found from personal experience that people were rarely what they seemed. Wasn't that the message Alfred chan-neled from my uninvited guest?

It had been such a strange twenty-four hours I hardly knew what to think. But I couldn't shake this feeling of premonition that something awful was about to happen.

It was four in the morning when I heard a loud crash and the sound of breaking glass. I sat bolt upright in bed with my heart racing until I smelled the overwhelming scent of sweet honey mixed with the salt of the ocean in my bedroom. Once again the room was icy cold, but this time I felt as if cold fingers were creeping over my skin.

The room felt heavy and oppressive. I switched on the lamp and slowly became aware of a dark shadow standing at the top of the spiral staircase. It had no form, no real shape, just gazillions of molecules racing around like an old-fashioned television set that had been set to the wrong channel.

Was this what ghost hunters called an apparition? I couldn't believe it. I didn't want to believe it. All my senses refused to believe it.

But yes—there was the outline of a gown, a face, but whose features I could not see, and long curling ringlets. The specter hovered above the ground just watching me. I sat there, gripping the sheets, terrified beyond anything I had ever experienced before.

I found my voice.

"We know what happened to you, Eleanor," I said aloud. "We're going to reunite you with your husband, I promise."

Suddenly the window blew open with such force that it whipped my hair away from my face. I scrambled out of bed, unsteady on my feet, and tried to close it. When I turned around the specter had gone. But instead of silence, I heard the sound of running water.

Downstairs, every tap was turned on full blast in the kitchen and the bathroom. All my birthday cards had been tossed about the room.

"What do you want from me?" I shouted. "Tell me what you want!"

And then it was over. The torrent of water abruptly ceased.

I knew she had gone. I just *had* to talk to Alfred. He would know what to do.

Chapter Twenty-nine

"Where's Alfred?" I demanded as I walked into the kitchen and went straight to the kettle and flipped the switch. "I need coffee!"

"Good God, what happened to you? You look like something the cat dragged in," said Mum with a knowing wink. "What have you been up to?"

"I'm sorry to disappoint you, but I had a horrible night. I need to talk to Alfred right now."

"You know where to find him." Mum regarded me with curiosity, but she must have seen something in my expression, because she said, "Go and sit down. Let me make you some breakfast."

I allowed her to take care of me. It was one of the many things I loved about my mother. True, she irritated the hell out of me a lot of the time, and vice versa, but when it really mattered she was the best mum in the world. And she was mine.

"Toast would be nice," I said. "Thank you."

Mum got busy. "Did you go out with Piers again? Is that why you feel so tired?"

"Oddly enough, no," I said, and went on to tell her about Violet's car accident and going to rescue Pippa.

"Well, well, well," said Mum.

"You sound like a policeman."

"Pippa was telling the truth about one thing," said Mum. "Rupert's Range Rover was stolen last night. Alfred called and told me."

"Was Alfred following Rupert last night?"

"Unfortunately. No. After the upset with the police yesterday afternoon, he got spooked."

"Where did Rupert say the Range Rover had been stolen from?" I asked.

Mum laughed. "Where do you think? Outside the Hall."

"Pippa told me the car was stolen from Bridge Cottage whilst they were *distracted*—that was the word she used."

"So Rupert must have walked home," Mum mused. "He's got himself in a bit of pickle, hasn't he? It will all come out. It always does."

I had a wild thought that maybe, just *maybe*, Piers had followed Rupert and Pippa and had deliberately stolen the Range Rover just to expose his sordid affair, but I decided to keep that theory to myself.

"What are you doing today?" Mum said.

"I've got that appointment at the Dartmouth Antiques Emporium," I said.

My mother pulled a face. "Opening a stall?"

"Not a stall. A space. I just want to take a look and see if it's worth me having one during the summer months."

Mum frowned. "But you've got the gatehouse."

"I already told you that I hardly get any foot traffic along

Cavalier Lane," I said. "Anyway, the other day you thought it was a good idea!"

"Are you alright for money, dear?"

"Of course," I said. "Why?"

"You should let that flat in Putney go."

"We've had this conversation before," I said. "I want to keep it."

"I can give you some money," said Mum. "You're going to get all of it when I'm dead, so why not have some now? I've got loads."

"Don't be silly," I said. "Anyway, you might need it if you get caught and have to pay all those back taxes whilst you are in prison."

Mum scowled. "Not funny, Katherine."

"You keep telling me to go out more. I'll meet a lot of people in Dartmouth."

"If you're going into Dartmouth, you should change that silver bangle," said Mum. "The shop is on the quay. You can't miss it."

Half an hour later I was stuck in bumper-to-bumper traffic crawling at a snail's pace into the town. I had completely forgotten about the annual music festival.

Finally I crested the brow of the hill where the magnificent building, home to the Britannia Royal Naval College, afforded a spectacular view of the fishing port below. The River Dart was full of all manner of sailing vessels and the entire town was decorated with bunting. Trying to park was always a nightmare, but fortunately, Dartmouth Antique Emporium was not located in the center. The newly converted barn and outbuildings had its own car park for customers.

It was only when I parked that I remembered that my parking mascot, Jazzbo Jenkins, was still missing from his usual place on the dashboard. I double-checked all the footwells. It was most odd and more than a little worrying. In fact, I couldn't remember the last time I had actually seen Jazzbo Jenkins at all.

I met Fiona Reynolds, who managed the Emporium. She was around my age, with a friendly smile. I liked her immediately and, like me, Fiona had relocated from London. She had been living in Dartmouth for the past ten years.

"I must say having you here will definitely boost sales," she said warmly. "Perhaps we could even host a fakes and treasures day once a month to lure in the locals. We do a roaring trade during the summer months, but in the winter it tends to be trade only."

"I love the idea." And I did. I realized just how much I had enjoyed working with the general public. Fiona outlined the terms of renting the space and her commission. "And of course, we all help each other out. You don't have to sit here every day. You'll find we're a friendly bunch."

Fiona showed me to a prime space that was closest to the main entrance. It caught the natural light through a large window that would have originally been a door that opened into the interior courtyard. My predecessor had left some dusty old shelves and a ragged rug, but I could easily replace both.

The Emporium also boasted a coffee shop selling home-made cakes. Everything was classy, with top-notch fixtures and fittings.

"There is another woman who deals in antique dolls, bears and toys," Fiona went on. "She's located at the far end by the coffee shop. You probably know her? Cassandra Bowden-Forbes?"

How could I forget such a name? It was Piers's betrothed. "I haven't met her."

"She's pretty new at the game," Fiona went on. "We do have security cameras, but they don't cover the entire interior. I assume your stock will be valuable, so I urge you to install your own. Unfortunately, we do suffer from the occasional theft or misplaced object. Cassandra had a Jumeau stolen, but then it turned up just yesterday on a shelf in our rather marvelous antiquarian book section. The place gets exceedingly crowded at times, especially when it rains and the tourists all seek refuge in here. And of course, I'm sure you've heard of next weekend's Skirmish? The English Civil War re-enactment?"

"Yes. I live on the Honeychurch Hall estate," I said.

"It attracts a wave of fans from all over the country, and given that we're just a mere ten miles away, it can be a very lucrative time for us."

I began to feel a stir of excitement and realized just how much I had missed being part of this world, interacting with other dealers, talking with the general public and just being surrounded by beautiful things. Of course, I'd still keep the gatehouses as my base, but this would make a huge difference, and besides, I didn't have to be at the Emporium every day.

"I'll take the space," I said happily.

We disappeared into a small office next to a huge armoire. Fiona produced a contract offering a one-year lease. "I'll start moving in tomorrow if that's okay."

I spent the rest of the morning taking measurements and photographs and getting to know the other dealers. I even sought out Cassandra—curious to see Piers's intended—but I was told that she was rarely there.

At lunchtime, I took a walk to the quay to find the jewelry shop. The place was packed. I'd never seen so many different kinds of music on offer—from classical to swing dancing; sea shanties to jazz and choral music to big band. The whole town was buzzing.

The day was beautiful. The sun was shining. Spirits were high. For the first time in ages I felt that things were looking up!

The jewelry store was packed with tourists, too. I soon found my bangle. It was in a locked glass case along with exquisite earrings and matching pendants. The tag said "Made locally by Vivienne." I couldn't see the price.

"Madame would like to see?" said a man in his sixties wearing a red silk cravat. He had to be boiling hot. There was no air-conditioning in the shop and the number of browsers was making the place claustrophobic.

I retrieved the bangle from my tote bag and unwrapped the tissue paper. "I'd like to change this for a larger size please."

The man smiled and took the bangle. He put in a loupe and inspected the inside.

"It was a gift," I said.

The man kept turning the bangle around and around. "Would Madame have the box?"

"No. It was given to me in a gift bag," I said. "But obviously, my friend purchased it here—unless Vivienne sells elsewhere?" I hadn't thought about that possibility.

"No," he said slowly. "This was definitely purchased here. Each bangle carries its own unique stamp. Would you wait here a moment please?"

"Of course." I stood and waited for what seemed like forever. As I hovered about in the shop, a couple in their fifties who were clearly on holiday, judging by the size of his camera, asked if I was Kat Stanford "from off of the Telly." I was in such a good mood that I chatted with them for a little while and agreed to have my photo taken.

Finally, the man returned. "Would you mind following me for a moment?"

I started to get a horrible foreboding that only increased when we stopped outside a door marked: EMPLOYEES ONLY.

"Is there a problem?" I asked.

"This way, please." He opened the door and gestured for me to go first. We stepped into a narrow corridor and stopped outside another door marked: MR. BRYCE. MANAGER.

Behind an oak partner's desk sat a very thin man with the red-veined cheeks of the hearty drinker.

Mr. Bryce got to his feet and pointed to a chair. "Do sit, Ms. Stanford."

"Yes. Is there a problem?" I said again.

"Where did you get this bangle?"

"A friend gave it to me for my birthday."

Mr. Bryce looked uncomfortable. "I'm afraid this is stolen property. Ms. Stanford, I'm going to have to call the police."

Chapter Thirty

"What!" I was horrified. **"Are you certain?"**

"Absolutely," he said. "Each piece is carefully marked. Vivienne only makes a limited number of bangles."

"I would never steal anything!"

"That's what Winona Ryder said when she was caught red-handed in Saks Fifth Avenue," said Mr. Bryce somewhat nastily.

"This is ridiculous!" I was furious and more than a little worried. Jess must have stolen this bangle and given it to me as a gift. But no, I just refused to believe it. I recalled her delight at giving me the present. I just couldn't imagine her stealing it. She wouldn't need to. She'd told me a gazillion times how generous Aubrey was. Aubrey was a magistrate for heaven's sake.

There had to be an explanation. My thoughts flew to Piers and his childish pranks. Was this something he would have done out of spite? He had made it clear that he didn't like her.

"Perhaps my friend purchased this directly from the artist?" I said.

Mr. Bryce shook his head. "No. This was in our inventory."

"Do you have CCTV in here?"

"Yes."

"Then please, at least look at that first."

"Very well. We will turn over the CCTV footage to the police when they get here."

"You're calling them now?" I was stunned.

"Of course." Mr. Bryce opened the top drawer of his desk and pulled out a business card and dialed a number.

"Ah, Detective Inspector?" he said. "I'm sorry to bother you on a Sunday, but you did say that if it was important I should call you immediately." The answer on the other end was short. Mr. Bryce replaced the receiver. "He'll be here in ten minutes."

We sat in an awkward silence. My eyes caught yesterday's *Star Stalkers* with my face splashed across the front page from the humiliating experience at NINE. It was little wonder that Mr. Bryce didn't believe me.

Ten excruciating minutes passed until there came a knock on the door.

To my astonishment, the police officer was none other than Detective Inspector Shawn Cropper. He strolled in wearing jeans and an open-neck shirt. The minute he saw me his jaw dropped.

"Kat!" he exclaimed. "What on earth is going on?"

I had never been so pleased to see him in my life. "Thank God it's you!"

Mr. Bryce regarded us both with surprise.

"I'll take it from here, Tim," said Shawn. "If you don't mind. Would you leave us for a moment?"

Mr. Bryce shot me another filthy look and left the room.

Quickly I filled Shawn in on how I came to acquire the bangle and that I needed a larger size. "I don't know what to think."

"All very interesting," said Shawn thoughtfully.

"But why are *you* here in Dartmouth?" I cried. "This isn't your jurisdiction. And why did the manager have your cell phone number?"

"I was taking the boys to listen to the sea shanties." Shawn gave a heavy sigh. "I'm sorry, but I am not at liberty to tell you. Believe me, I wish I could. But for now I suggest you give all the Carews a wide berth and if you do see any of them you must act completely normally."

"This is to do with Piers, isn't it?" I exclaimed.

Shawn stiffened. "Your personal business is nothing to do with me. But I've known Piers Carew for a very long time and you need to be careful."

"Oh for heaven's sake," I said crossly. "I was only having dinner—"

"A dinner that neither of you paid for—"

"I already told you. We were talking about the skeleton in Cromwell Meadows," I retorted hotly. "Piers thinks she is Lady Eleanor Honeychurch and that she was murdered by her cousin."

"That sounds like a Piers Carew theory," said Shawn. "His imagination is even wilder than your mother's."

"Am I going to be charged?"

"Not yet," he said. "But I want you to continue to wear the bangle. I'm sorry I can't tell you more—and I know this annoys you—but in this instance, I am not the officer in charge of the investigation."

"Oh. I didn't realize—"

"Of course you didn't," said Shawn. "But there is something I am able to tell you. Violet Green will make a full recovery. She has two broken ankles and a nasty bump on her head where it struck the steering wheel."

"I'm glad to hear it."

"So perhaps you can tell me why you asked her to pick the dowager countess up from Totnes railway station in the middle of the night?"

"I have no idea what you are talking about," I said. "Edith isn't due home until tomorrow."

"Apparently, a note was slipped through Violet's letterbox asking her to do you a favor. It was signed by you."

"But I'd never do that!" I exclaimed. "Where is this note?"

"I don't have it with me right this minute," said Shawn sheepishly. "But that's why she raced off to meet the last train from London. There isn't even a train that comes in at that hour."

"You know I'd never ask that of Violet, Shawn," I said.

He hesitated for a moment. "We've since learned that the brakes on her Morris Minor were cut."

"You mean . . . it was deliberate?" I was astonished. "But why would anyone do that? It makes no sense."

"You seem to forget that Violet is a witness. She saw two people in the churchyard on the night that Muriel was killed." He hesitated again. "How well do you know Pippa Carmichael?"

"Why?"

"Well . . . you *were* the person she called for help."

"I don't know what's she's up to," I lied.

"It's a bit of a coincidence that Violet's accident occurred right where Ms. Carmichael was taking a midnight stroll."

He was right. I didn't know what to say, so I said nothing.

"If we find out that Pippa had something to do with cutting Violet's brakes, you could be an accessory after the fact. Do you want to add that to your current rap sheet?"

I was taken aback. "That's hardly fair, and to be honest, even though Violet and Pippa don't like each other, I don't think Pippa would do that. She has Max to think of!"

There was a tap at the door and Mr. Bryce peered inside.

"We need a larger bangle," said Shawn.

Mr. Bryce nodded and withdrew. Moments later he was back with a replacement.

I slipped it on and fastened the catch.

"And remember," said Shawn. "Just act normally."

I left the jewelry shop filled with mixed emotions. There had to be a connection between Muriel's death and Violet's attempted murder. The only connection I could come up with was Pippa. She'd literally just moved to the village and had made no effort to endear herself to either woman. I thought of poor Lavinia and her decision to divorce Rupert if she found him cheating on her again, but would Rupert do such a thing to make sure Lavinia wouldn't find out? And what about the bangle? How did the theft of that fit into the picture? Why did I have to pretend everything was normal?

"Kat!" came a familiar voice. I turned around and found Jess waving from across the street. I immediately panicked.

She darted through the stationary traffic. Jess was carrying a large canvas bag. "Isn't this music festival amazing?" she beamed. "I begged Aubrey to bring me, but he's too caught up in his silly weapons."

"You've been shopping?"

"Just a few knickknacks," she said. "There are so many little boutiques in Dartmouth." She caught sight of my bracelet. "Oh! You're wearing it."

I found myself reddening. I was a hopeless liar. "Yes. It's lovely. Thank you again, but I still feel very uncomfortable accepting such a generous gift."

"It wasn't expensive."

"It *was* expensive, Jess," I said. "I know how much it cost."

"Oh! Alright, I'll tell you." She gave an exaggerated sigh. "I have a confession." She linked her arm through mine and we began to walk together. "I hope you don't think it weird, but... actually, Piers knows the designer—"

My heart sank. "He does?"

"You know what he's like with the ladies," she went on. "He bought a few of her bangles to help her start off. He gave me one for my birthday, but Aubrey had already bought me one. So you see, you don't have to feel bad about it after all—but don't tell him I told you that."

So my instinct was right. For whatever reason, Shawn was looking into Piers Carew. I was bitterly disappointed. Should I tell Shawn what Jess had just told me?

"Do you have time for a cup of tea?" Jess pointed to the Dartmouth Antique Emporium. "They have a little cafe inside."

"I know," I said. "I've just signed a contract to rent some space. Normally I would, but I want to get back and get organized." This was partly true, but really, I felt incredibly uncomfortable.

As I crossed the street I felt Jess was watching me. I turned to find she was. Jess waved and ducked into the National Trust Gift Shop.

It was only when I walked past the front entrance to pick up my car that I saw the notice pinned outside on a wooden board. Fiona had put up the CCTV Surveillance warning but added a flyer. It offered a reward for the safe return of a Jumeau doll that had been stolen last Tuesday from the Emporium.

I stared at the photograph in growing dismay.

Withdrawing my iPhone from my tote bag, I scrolled through the photographs until I found Aubrey Carew's antique doll.

It was a match.

Chapter Thirty-one

I stared at the photograph and wished I knew what I should do. I thought back to Aubrey and how nervous he was at having the Jumeau in his possession. He was a magistrate and a leading figure not just in the West Country but an expert in antique weaponry also. It's hardly the kind of scandal that he would want let out in the open. He had to have known the Jumeau was stolen.

Lavinia had mentioned that Piers was notorious for getting into mischief. The Honeychurch family was renowned for keeping things quiet. Why not the Carews as well? It wouldn't be the first time that families of influence avoided the law.

I made a decision.

I went back inside and sought out Fiona. "I just saw the flyer for the missing Jumeau?"

"Oh, is it still up there?" she said. "I thought we'd taken all the flyers down. That was the doll that Cassandra thought had been stolen but hadn't been stolen at all."

"When did she find it?" I asked.

Fiona thought for a moment, "Yesterday morning, I believe. We'll see you on Monday?"

"Yes, bright and early," I said. "I'm looking forward to it."

I returned to my car thoroughly puzzled. There had even been a reward offered for the doll, but it seemed that whoever had taken it had simply sneaked it back.

As I reached the gatehouse my heart sank again.

Pippa's Vauxhall was parked outside. I really was not in the mood to hear about her broken heart. I wasn't being callous. She was putting me in a terrible position. Lavinia would find out and she would assume that I had known all along.

Where did my loyalties lie?

Pippa gave a pathetic wave and got out of her car. She gestured to all the bunting and banners that framed the main gate and made some comment about everything being in place for the following week's revelries.

"I can't talk right now," I said abruptly. "I've got too much to do this afternoon."

"Kat? Please." Her face was pale and puffy from crying. "I just have to talk to you. Just for five minutes. *Please.*"

"Okay." I let us both into the gatehouse and headed to the small kitchen to put on the kettle. "Tea?"

"I wanted to apologize about last night," she said. "You're my friend and I want to be honest with you."

"I'm not sure I want to know, Pippa," I said somewhat primly.

"Oh come on! Get off your high horse, Katherine," Pippa snapped. "Yes. I am—or was—having a fling with Rupert. Okay? Happy now?"

"I told you I don't want to know."

"But it's over." Tears welled up in her eyes and spilled down her cheeks. "I suppose I thought I was different. I just thought—" She dashed them away angrily. "I know you understand. You have to."

"I'll try to."

"If you'd seen how horrified he was when he realized we were going to get caught—" Sadness turned to disgust. "He couldn't care less about poor Violent!"

"Don't call her that," I snapped.

"Well, you know what I mean," Pippa went on. "And when he realized that his wretched car had been stolen . . . I knew then that he would be a coward. He left me stuck in the middle of the countryside. He didn't care if Violent was dead or alive."

Not surprisingly, my opinion of Rupert sank even lower. "Well, you'll be relieved to know that Violet will make a full recovery. Two broken ankles and a concussion."

"Will I?" Pippa said. "You may as well know everything. Violet was threatening to tell Lavinia about us."

"I don't believe it."

"Really? Take a look at this." She withdrew a pale-lavender-colored envelope from her handbag and handed it to me.

The moment I saw the envelope I knew that Pippa had the wrong person. Muriel's thank-you letter to me had been written on identical notepaper—a bouquet of irises in the top right-hand corner. I also recognized her quavery handwriting.

I know what you are up to with his lordship at Bridge Cottage. Close your tearoom and leave Little Dipperton and her lady-ship will never find out. Signed, A Friend.

"She wanted money," Pippa declared.

"There is no mention of money here," I pointed out. "Just demanding you leave the village."

"Oh." Pippa seemed taken aback. "But why should I?"

"This is not from Violet."

"She wanted me to close my tearoom."

"This letter was written by Muriel. I'm sure of it."

"But why would Muriel care?"

"Violet was Muriel's best friend. It seems that she was looking out for her, after all." I was also certain that it would have been a hollow threat. Muriel may well have been a gossip, but she was not a whistle-blower.

"What are you going to do now?" I said.

"If Muriel did write it, then the letter doesn't matter because she's dead."

"Pippa!" I was appalled at how callous she could be.

"Well, it's true," said Pippa. "So what do you think I should do?"

"I can't make that decision for you," I said.

"Did Muriel really try to commit suicide?" said Pippa.

"What have you heard?" I said carefully.

"Jess Carew told me," said Pippa.

"I honestly don't know," I said. "Did you hear any screams or see anything in the churchyard on Friday night?"

Pippa shook her head. "I was with Rupert, although I doubt if he would ever admit it." She gave a heavy sigh. "Oh, Kat. I can't afford to move again so soon. I have tried to talk to Rupert, but he's not answering his phone. It's such a mess!"

She started to cry, loud noisy tears. I handed her a mug of tea. "Drink up."

"Tea in a crisis," she said. "I wonder why we British always feel consoled by a cup of bloody tea." She gave a weak smile. "You're so lucky, Kat. You can't possibly understand what it's like to be a single mother struggling to make ends meet."

"What about your ex-husband?"

She shook her head. "Getting money from him is like getting blood out of a stone. Rupert was ... generous. And I liked him."

"I think you are better out of it," I said, and meant it. "But what's going to happen next weekend? I thought you were overseeing the Hog Roast, and with Violet out of the picture ..."

Pippa groaned. "Oh God. I had forgotten all about that. Will you help me?"

"Alright," I said grudgingly. "We've still got Mrs. Cropper, remember."

Pippa blew her nose. "I feel a bit of an idiot now. It's all so humiliating."

"At least your humiliations don't end up on the front page of the newspaper," I said ruefully.

"Oh God, no they don't." Pippa grinned. "Did Piers really impersonate a food critic?"

"Yes, he did, and he did it very well."

"What a laugh!"

"It was funny to start with, but then when our meal was on the house it was mortifying." I had a sudden thought. Piers had been determined to catch Rupert out in his affair. In fact, we had both seen his car emerging from the undergrowth near Bridge Cottage on Friday evening. It wouldn't surprise me if Piers had driven the Range Rover somewhere just to teach

Rupert a lesson. "Do you remember seeing a Mercedes last night?"

"No cars. That's why we picked that place—actually, it gave me the creeps," said Pippa.

"I just wondered who would have stolen Rupert's Range Rover. I mean, it had to have been someone who knew it would be there."

"Whoever took it certainly knew how to start it," Pippa said. "It had state-of-the-art technology, so they knew what they were doing." Pippa thought for a minute. "Are you going to see Piers again?"

"I don't think so," I said. "It's like going out with a grenade. You never know when it's going to go off."

"So he's single?"

"Pippa ... seriously?"

"Well—he's attractive, eligible and heir to a fortune."

"You sound like my mother. Apparently he's betrothed to his childhood sweetheart. Lavinia told me."

"The rich really are different, aren't they?" Pippa got to her feet. "I'd better get back," she said. "The boys are still out ghost-busting." She gave me a sad smile. "I'm not a bad mother, Kat."

"I know."

I saw her out of the gatehouse, made myself another cup of tea and got cracking. I needed to separate the stock and decide which items I was going to take and which to leave behind, but I found it hard to concentrate.

Was Piers capable of doing something so petty? Stealing a car? Framing Jess with a doll that he might have taken whilst visiting his betrothed at Dartmouth Antique Emporium? Jess had mentioned that Piers had also dated the jewelry designer, too. Would he really go to such great lengths to incriminate Rupert?

Piers wanted to protect Lavinia, not make her unhappy. His actions would certainly provoke a divorce. Much as I knew Piers disliked his brother-in-law, his major flaw was being a practical joker. I had not seen anything vindictive in his personality at all.

My stomach grumbled and I realized that I hadn't eaten all day. Mum was so inspired by the idea for her new book that she asked if I wouldn't mind us forgoing our usual Sunday night ritual.

I thought of Pippa's comment about Jess buying bacon sandwiches from Violet. Something seemed odd. I remembered the smell of bacon in the church. Jess had said that no workmen had been at the barn this weekend because they were waiting for materials.

I found a piece of cheese and an apple that would have to keep me going until I got home.

It was gone nine by the time I turned out the lights in the gatehouse. I was getting into my Golf when Pippa's Vauxhall turned into the entrance, almost knocking me off my feet.

She slammed on the brakes and reversed, opening the window as she did so. I took one look at her face and knew something bad had happened.

"Pippa? What's wrong?"

"Are the boys here?" she said anxiously. "Max and Harry? Have you seen them?"

"No," I said, "but I've been in the gatehouse all evening. Are you sure they aren't in the churchyard?"

She shook her head. "No. I've been driving around the

countryside looking for them! Max promised they'd only play in the village. He promised me!"

"What about Jess's barn?"

"I told them not to play in there. It's too dangerous with all that scaffolding."

"Did you call the Hall?"

"I got that stupid butler on the phone, so I hung up, and Rupert won't answer his damn phone! That's why I'm here."

"I understand." I tried to keep my voice calm, but her fear was contagious. "Have you called the police yet?"

She shook her head. "No. I don't want... I don't want my ex to find out about this. He's already tried to take Max away from me once."

"Alright. Drive to the Hall and tell them. I'll call my mother and Alfred. Also ask Eric and the Croppers. If the boys did come here, we'll soon find them. Rupert knows all Harry's favorite haunts. I'll go back to the village and check Jess's barn."

Pippa nodded mutely.

As I headed back to the village, I rang my mother, who was predictably irritated. "I'm really in the middle of something," she said. "But I'm sure Alfred will help. You know, I think this new book of mine is going to be the best ever. Do you *really* think *Betrayal* is a good title?"

As I sped back to the village I kept my eyes peeled for Max and Harry. The problem was that there were so many tiny lanes leading off from one another. They could be anywhere.

Much as I tried to reassure Pippa that they were safe, a part of me feared otherwise.

As St. Mary's loomed in the distance, I caught sight of a

light flaring inside the church again. It was just for an instant. Perhaps they'd been hiding in there all the time.

I left a message on Pippa's mobile, parked my car and went to find them.

The village seemed eerily deserted. With Muriel's, Pippa's and Violet's cottages all in darkness and the full moon hidden by heavy dark clouds, the air felt unusually full of menace.

Large spots of rain began to fall faster and faster. I raced across the grass and into the front porch of the church just as the heavens opened. I stepped inside and remembered there was no electricity.

Fortunately, my iPhone flashlight worked just as well.

"Harry?" I called out. "I know you boys are in here."

There was no response. I started to walk slowly up the aisle, flicking the beam up and down the box pews.

Still nothing except the sound of my shoes clicking on the quarry tile and the wind gusting against the stained-glass windows.

"This is not funny!" I said sharply. "Stop messing around and come out right now. You both have to go to school tomorrow and it's getting far too late. Max, your mother is worried about you."

Still there was no answer.

I gave a thorough search of the church, into the vestry, looking under the refectory table and into the cupboards.

Harry's white scarf was lying on the floor by the Parish chest.

To my surprise, the padlock was dangling by the hasp. Curious, I lifted it and discovered a treasure trove of bizarre objects. A china Dalmatian; a tea caddy; Muriel's pink Croc; a Crown Derby teapot; a book on Greenway, Agatha Christie's home; a beautiful leather Chanel purse; a set of makeup brushes still in their original packaging; a leather riding crop that I knew belonged to Lavinia and there—right at the bottom—Jazzbo Jenkins.

My heart sank. So it was true. Max and Harry had been stealing after all and squirreling their loot in the old Parish chest. I was very disappointed.

Hearing footsteps hurrying behind me, I was just about to turn when an arm was thrown around my neck and a hand clamped a damp cloth over my nose and mouth.

I doubled over, trying to escape the suffocating stench. It was cloying, sickly, nauseating—and very familiar.

My head ached. My heart began to race and then . . . I plunged into darkness.

Chapter Thirty-two

My head felt like lead and my eyes so heavy it was hard to open them. There was a disgusting taste in my mouth. I doubled over and threw up into a plastic bucket just as hands grabbed my hair and held it away from my face.

"It's okay, it's okay," said a voice I recognized. "You'll be okay in a minute. Really you will."

Exhausted, I leaned back on the chair. The bucket had gone. I heard the flush of a loo and running water.

I was in my sitting room at Jane's Cottage. As my eyes struggled to focus, a figure returned with the bucket.

It was Jess.

"Are you feeling better?"

I looked to her in confusion. "What are you doing here? What happened? I was in the church." I tried to remember, but my mind couldn't form the thoughts. "Did I pass out?"

Jess nodded. "Are you able to stand up?"

I tried to, but the room began to spin, and again I felt ex-cruciatingly nauseous, reached for the bucket and threw up again. "I feel terrible. Can I have some water? God. Is this what a migraine feels like?"

"Wait there." Jess disappeared into the galley kitchen and returned with a glass of water. "Drink this."

I felt marginally better, and slowly everything began to come back to me and I remembered seeing Jazzbo Jenkins in the Parish chest.

"Was it you who took all those things, Jess?"

She just looked at me with those large eyes in her elfin face and shrugged. "It's no big deal. I was going to put them back. I was only borrowing them. Having a bit of fun."

I regarded her with growing dismay. "So it was you who stole the Jumeau and then put it back?"

Jess's eyes widened. She looked scared. "How do you know about that?"

"Because your husband brought it to me for a valuation."

"Aubrey *knows*?" All the color drained from Jess's face. "I don't believe you! You're lying!"

"How else would I have known?"

"What did you tell him?"

"That's she's very valuable," I said. "You'd never be able to sell her. She's one of a kind."

"Sell? Why would I sell? I told you. I just borrow stuff. I always put it back eventually." Jess raked her fingers through her short hair. "What did Aubrey say when you told him?"

"He told me it belonged to his first wife."

"His first *wife*?" I could see Jess trying to process this bombshell. She suddenly brightened. "That means he doesn't mind," she said firmly. "He knows and he doesn't mind."

I thought it more a case of the local magistrate avoiding a

scandal, but Jess's erratic behavior was alarming. The odd assortment of treasure was peculiar as well.

And then I remembered Muriel's pink Croc. It couldn't be a coincidence. Alfred had commented that she had been wearing only one shoe when he found her. Shawn believed Muriel had been attacked in the churchyard, and that was exactly where Harry and Max had seen her, too.

"What happened in the churchyard, Jess?" I demanded. "Did Muriel find the Parish chest with all your treasures inside?"

"Iris was right. Muriel was a snoop!" Jess said defiantly. "She was opening my letters, but she was the thief."

"What are you talking about?"

"I saw her digging in her old man's grave. She buried that biscuit tin and then pretended to get robbed."

"Did Muriel see you?"

"It was an accident," she whispered. "I swear."

"Look, Jess, I don't know what on earth is going on here, but I think you should come clean with your husband. Tell him everything. It's obvious he loves you."

My mobile rang on the kitchen counter. It rang and went to voicemail and then rang again... and again. Jess glanced over at the caller I.D.

"Shawn? Why is he ringing you?" she exclaimed. "Did you tell him about me?"

My heart skipped a beat. "Believe me, there are more important things than you, Jess," I said as suddenly I remembered the reason I had been in the church in the first place. "Harry and Max didn't come home. They are missing—"

"What do you mean, *missing?*" she said sharply.

"Well, maybe they've been found by now," I said. "But somehow I doubt it. Why else would Shawn be calling me?"

"But it's gone eleven o'clock!" said Jess. "Aren't they with Lavinia or Pippa?"

"Let me call him back. I must know what's going on."

Jess hesitated. "But why do you think they're missing?" she said.

And then I remembered. "Harry's white scarf was in the church."

"When?" she shrieked. "What time? Today?"

"Yes. Why? What aren't you telling me?" Jess's anxiety was contagious. "Call Aubrey," I said. "Please."

"I can't. They're out," said Pippa. "There's a banquet tonight for Cromwell's New Model Army. Men only. They won't be back until gone midnight."

I was confused. "But how did I get back here?"

"In your car," said Jess. "I drove."

"Then I'll drive you home," I said. "I'm feeling so much better now and I must find out what is happening."

"No! Please!" Jess put her hands on my shoulders and sat me back down. She seemed tormented, almost anguished. She kept glancing through the rain-spattered window and checking her watch. "Nothing will happen to Harry and Max. Nothing. I know it won't. They'll be fine."

"You're scaring me, Jess," I said. "You're acting really strange. Give me my phone please and at least let me make a call and find out."

"I can't," she whispered. "I'm sorry."

"If this is your idea of a practical joke it's not funny!" I said. "Did Piers put you up to it?"

And then I heard the sound of an engine in the distance. Even from my chair I could see headlights winding their way up the track to the cottage.

Jess fell into a fever of agitation. She was actually trembling. "You were out for so long," she said. "He gave you far too much."

"Who gave me too much?"

"You have to believe me. This was not my idea."

I heard the throaty roar of a V8 engine. Headlights swept across the windows.

"Stay where you are," she said quickly. "Just stay still and let me do the talking. Understand?"

"Jess—"

"Do you understand?" She seemed hysterical. "Please do as I say and you won't get hurt."

The engine stopped. I heard a car door slam. She jumped, momentarily distracted, but I saw my chance. I lunged for my mobile, but she was too fast and snatched it up and clasped it to her chest.

"This is getting stupid!" I exclaimed.

She darted to the front door and threw it open. Rupert's Range Rover was parked outside.

Thank God! But relief turned to confusion and then horror as I stared at the man in the doorway.

I'd seen him somewhere before. His face was familiar and then, as he joined Jess in the light, I thought I was seeing double—elfin faced, short hair and the same height. They were identical twins with the only difference being that he bore all the signs of sleeping rough—dirty clothes, a tattered rucksack and a scraggly beard. I'd passed him hitchhiking along the main road from Totnes to Little Dipperton on Thursday. I distinctly remembered because the car in front of me had slowed down to give him a lift and he'd waved that car on and then climbed over a five-bar gate and into a field.

"You go home now, Maureen," he said quietly. "I'll take care of this."

Maureen. He called Jess Maureen. The same name that Eric had called Jess on Friday morning. Was it really only two days ago? So much had happened. So much had changed.

I found my voice. "I don't know what the hell—"

"Shut up!" the man shouted, and then began to cough so violently that I thought he would pass out.

I was so surprised at his tone I shrank back. Then, to my dismay, I saw him pull out a small knife.

I looked to Jess or Maureen, whatever she wanted to be called, and tried to keep my voice steady. "What's going on, Jess?"

"She won't betray you, Danny," Jess pleaded. "I know she won't."

"It's too late for that," he said, and started to cough again. "And no thanks to you."

"Don't do anything stupid, please." Jess's voice had shot up an octave.

"What do you care? Go home to your sugar daddy," he said with a sneer.

"I can't," Jess wailed. "Aubrey knows about... about... my hobby."

Danny's eyes flashed with anger. "I knew you'd mess it up! I knew it! You just can't help yourself, can you?"

I took a deep breath and said, "If this is just a case of stealing—"

"Shut up!" Danny yelled again, and again began to cough. I remembered Jess buying Lemsip in the post office. Had it been for this man?

Jess started to cry.

"That's right. Turn on the tears. This is all your fault!"

"No, it's not all my fault," Jess retorted. "Muriel saw you in the church. You were supposed to stay hidden. You gave her too much of that stuff. I told you not to. I told you she was too old."

"Yeah, well, it was a mistake."

"A big mistake," Jess said. "You should never have come here! Why did you come here? *Why?*"

I felt as if they had forgotten I was there. I wondered if I could make a run for the door, but Danny turned on me. "Don't even think about it!"

"You could have been out in two more years," Jess raced on. "I could have found you a job on the estate. You would have had your second chance, just like me."

"But you messed up your second chance, *Jess*." Danny's mood had turned ugly. "You really think your old man is going to stay with you now he knows you are a thief?"

Jess's shoulders slumped.

Danny's mood changed again. "Come with me, Mo," he said gently. "It's always been just the two of us. You know that. You know I'm the only one who will really take care of you."

Jess nodded. She seemed so different from the bright, confident young woman of just a few days ago. Danny was a manipulator and a bully and I felt a rush of compassion for her.

"Jess? The boys?" I said. "Harry is still your stepgrandson." She gave a moan of dismay and looked to her brother.

"Danny? Did you? Have you ... Tell me and I promise I'll come with you."

"They're in the crypt."

I felt a surge of relief. The crypt! Of course, St. Mary's church had an underground crypt.

"Having a great old time, judging by their excitement when they discovered it," he said.

"But they're safe," Jess said eagerly. "They're safe, Kat. It's going to be alright."

Danny turned back to his sister. "I'll meet you at the ferry. Go now. Go straight there. Understand?"

"Yes. Straight there."

"Give *Jess* the keys to your car, Ms. Katherine Stanford," Danny said nastily.

"I've got them already," said Jess, who seemed to have bounced back. "But you promise you won't hurt her? She's been so kind to me."

"I'm not going to, you daft thing," he said. "Just buying some time. That's all."

"I'm sorry, Kat," said Jess, and hurried out of the cottage.

Danny said nothing until the sound of my car had gone and Jane's Cottage was quiet once more.

I forced a smile. "She's right," I said. "I won't say anything."

Danny laughed. "Maureen was always the naive one," he said. "You've got to love her for that. No, you won't be able to say anything because you won't be around to say it."

He dumped his rucksack on the floor and retrieved a roll of duct tape.

Chapter Thirty-three

"I'm not going to scream, you know." I tried to make light of it, but when Danny marched me into the kitchen and sat me down on a wooden chair I began to get seriously scared.

Without saying a word he taped my wrists behind the chair and my legs to the chair legs. It hurt.

"I won't say anything; in fact, I think I can probably get you a fake I.D." Alfred was famous for creating forged papers. I don't know why I said it, but there was a determination to Danny's actions that I didn't like. "You promise that the boys are okay?"

"Don't you ever shut up?" he hissed.

"The boys—"

He grabbed my hair and duct-taped my mouth. I began to panic again. The feeling of suffocation I had in the church hit me afresh. I watched in confusion as Danny shut the small kitchen window and placed a towel on the floor next to the back door. He disappeared for a few minutes, but I could hear him upstairs, closing more windows.

Danny returned with a church candle. I recognized it as one taken from the box in the vestry. Opening the drawer next to the gas stove, he pulled out some matches and lit it. Carefully, he waited until there was enough candle wax to pour off into a pool and leave in a saucer. He set the candle down.

Then he turned on all four gas burners.

"I'm not making the same mistake again," he said. "This time I won't get interrupted."

And then, with a sickening jolt, I knew. Danny must have tried to cover up Muriel's death by faking a suicide.

Alfred must have interrupted him. But who was going to save me?

I began to struggle, but my bindings held me captive. My face felt hot; I couldn't breathe. I couldn't believe this was happening.

The smell of gas began to fill the room. I tried to fight down my rising horror. The whole place would explode. It was as if my life slowed down with every second turning into minutes. Would this be painless? Would it hurt? Poor Mum. My eyes began to smart and I felt tears trickle down my cheeks.

And then Danny gave a cry of sheer terror. He turned ashen and began to back against the wall from something unseen. His hands raised in horror, eyes bulging out. He seemed rooted to the spot, unable to move, and began to shake his head vigorously in disbelief.

And suddenly the smell of gas was overpowered by the fragrance of sweet honey mixed with the salt of the ocean.

The lights began to flicker.

The room grew icy cold and all the hairs on my neck rose up in unison.

Eleanor was here.

Together we saw a swirl of black dots materialize in front of our eyes. Eleanor hovered under the arch just feet from my chair and where Danny stood.

He seemed paralyzed with fear and backed to the wall. She advanced, growing larger, taller, broader—towering over him in a menacing swirl of ectoplasm.

With another cry he darted to the left, but again she blocked his way.

Suddenly he thrust my chair sideways, sending me crashing to the floor.

Screaming at the top of his lungs, Danny bunched his fists and ran straight through the spectral shape and on out of the front door, slamming it behind him.

I heard the car engine burst into life, followed by a rush of gravel that spat at the wheels as he tore away.

The chair had fallen sideways, but my bindings still remained. I couldn't move.

And then . . . a deafening crash as the kitchen window blew open, sending a shelf of long-stemmed wineglasses tumbling to the floor, where they shattered into tiny pieces. The wind swirled around the room, picking up stray papers and anything in its path; books catapulted off shelves and crashed into the wall and anything not nailed down was swept up into the vortex.

Then suddenly it was over. The wind left and all was quiet once more.

The candle had been extinguished.

The gas burners had blown out.

I was safe.

I just lay there in shock until I heard the sound of a car outside and two doors banging shut; a fierce hammering on my front door followed by a jangle of keys.

Mum burst in and found me in the galley kitchen.

"Good heavens!" she exclaimed. "Are you having a party?" Then she promptly burst into tears.

Alfred removed the duct tape and freed my bindings. "You alright, luv?"

"I think so."

"I just had the most extraordinary phone call from Jess Carew," said Mum. "She called from your mobile. She told me to get here as quickly as I could but wouldn't say why. Then she said the boys were safe and playing in the crypt and hung up. Why is there glass everywhere?"

Quickly I told them both about my ordeal and how I was convinced that I would have met the same fate that had been planned for Muriel.

During our conversation, Alfred didn't utter a word but stood quietly in the corner of the sitting room.

"Alfred?" said Mum.

He turned to me and smiled. "Eleanor knows you will help her be reunited with her husband, but she stayed to save you."

"Thank you, Alfred," I said. I had got the proof I had been asking for. I had seen Eleanor with my own eyes and she had saved my life. It didn't matter if no one else believed in the spirit world. I knew that I now did.

And so did Danny Coverdale.

"We'll never stop them," I said. "They could be anywhere."

"I thought I passed Rupert's Range Rover," said Mum. "Wait! Alfred! Didn't you put a tracking device on to that car?"

For the first time ever, Alfred reddened.

"You didn't do it?" Mum demanded.

Alfred shrugged. "I did, but I don't know how to activate it."

"But the police do," I said. "Call Shawn's mobile, Mum."

"I suppose I could light a fire and send smoke signals."

"Maybe when you move into the twenty-first century you'll get a mobile as well as a computer," I said. "There's a payphone in the village. Let's get those boys."

We piled into Mum's MINI. With Alfred driving we screeched to a halt outside the churchyard in eight minutes flat.

Fortunately, Mum had bits of change in her glove box. We left Alfred making the call and hurried into the church. It was deathly quiet inside and black as pitch, but I knew exactly where to find a box of candles.

"Harry! Max!" I shouted, but there was no answering call.

"They'll never hear you underground, dear."

I felt a stab of fear. Mum and I had gone over the church and had never seen the crypt. What if there was no air inside? How long had they been down there? What if we were too late?

My mother marched on ahead to the vestry, but there was no entrance to any crypt in there.

I retreated to the arched doorway beside the pulpit and pulled back the curtain. There, tucked into the wall behind a tapestry, was a tiny door. I dragged it open to reveal a narrow stone staircase.

"Harry! Max!" I yelled.

"It's Kat!" I heard Harry say. We heard shrieks of laughter, and then, after what seemed like forever, a face appeared at the bottom of the stairs.

I had never felt so relieved in all my life.

"It's wicked down here," Harry said excitedly as he emerged from below. "There is a tunnel and a secret room and everything. There's even a camp bed and snacks! And it wasn't dark. We had tons of candles. It's our underground bunker!"

"Well, I think we've solved the ghostly happenings in the churchyard," I said to Mum. "Danny Coverdale was obviously hiding out down here all the time."

Mum wrinkled her nose. "And the mysterious smell of bacon sandwiches."

Suddenly there were flashlights everywhere and shouts of excitement. Rupert, Lavinia, Pippa and Eric poured into the church. There were scoldings and hugs all round, and then Shawn turned up, along with DC Clive Banks.

Shawn promptly declared the crypt a "crime scene" and herded us all outside. Moments later we were sitting in Pippa Carmichael's tiny kitchen drinking gallons of tea.

As Shawn gently questioned Harry and Max about how they came to find the crypt, I looked over at Pippa, who was watching Rupert and Lavinia with acute disappointment. They were sitting together with their arms touching, which I suppose was the closest they would ever get to a public display of affection.

Eric suddenly drew up a chair next to Pippa. He whispered something in her ear. She laughed rather too loudly and ruffled Eric's hair.

Mum leaned in and said in a low voice, "I bet she's trying to make his lordship jealous."

"We'd love to take a look at these ghosts you've been photographing," said Shawn. "Can we borrow your camera, Max?"

Leaving Pippa, Max and Eric together, we all trooped out into the night.

I heard Lavinia say, "I'll be there in a minute, Rupert." She gestured to Mum. "Iris! I must talk to you."

As Alfred and I waited for my mother to join us, Shawn walked over.

"Thanks to Mr. Bushman here, you'll be glad to know that Danny and Maureen Coverdale were apprehended at Plymouth docks," he said. "They were about to take the ferry to Roscoff." Shawn regarded Alfred with amusement. "I won't say how or why you knew there was a LoJack tracking device on the Range Rover—Rupert knew nothing about it—but we're grateful for the information."

Alfred just smiled.

Moments later we were heading home. "That Rupert is a bounder," Mum exclaimed. "You'll never guess what Lavinia said."

"You know I don't like guessing games," I said.

"She told me that she felt very foolish about suspecting Rupert was having an affair. She was relieved it wasn't Jess—especially given the circumstances—and then she was convinced it was Pippa Carmichael, but now she realizes that Eric and Pippa were together all the time."

"So yet again Eric is cleaning up after Rupert," I said with disgust.

"She's not the brightest tool in the shed," said Mum. "Now,

just for tonight I think you should sleep in your old room at the Carriage House," she went on. "You can't possibly sleep at Jane's."

For once I agreed with her.

Chapter Thirty-four

The Little Dipperton Skirmish was finally over and pro-nounced an overwhelming success. Rupert was happy with the number of people who came from all over the country to camp and park on the estate.

A local television crew turned up to film the living history exhibits and capture the various skirmishes for a documentary they were making on the social consequences of the English Civil War in the West Country.

Piers did an impressive job of choreographing numerous fight scenes so that they almost seemed real. Naturally he ignored the Health and Safety ruling and brought cannon from the Carew collection, firing them with panache in the field that would have housed Jess and Aubrey's new home. Sadly, half the barn was destroyed, but neither Piers nor his father seemed to mind.

No real blood was shed, although St. John Ambulance was kept busy with numerous cases of sunstroke from over-zealous zombie soldiers who had passed out from drinking too much Scrumpy on the battlefield.

It wasn't just the villagers and tenants of the Honeychurch Hall estate who donned seventeenth-century costumes, but many visitors were in character, too—myself included. My mother had curled my hair into ringlets and she had run me up a beautiful gown in forest green with the fashionable elegant falling collar edged in lace and loose sleeves—not exactly practical when it came to carrying wooden platters of dripping roast pig, but I didn't care. I was having too much fun even though at the last minute Pippa decided that village life was not for her after all and moved back to London. I knew that Harry would miss Max, but I also knew he'd bounce back.

As for the missing funds, Rupert and Lavinia made a short speech thanking an anonymous benefactor for stepping forward at the last minute to save the day.

I turned to my mother. "Did you have anything to do with that?"

"Let's just say that Alfred had to make a quick trip across the English Channel," she whispered. I just smiled. Today wasn't the day to scold her for the risks she made Alfred take—who, under great duress, agreed to dress up but looked more like a pirate than a musketeer.

Mum told me that Alfred had known all about the notorious Coverdale twins. Tragically, their father had been killed in a mining accident and their mother had gassed herself when they were barely teenagers. I felt sad for Jess—or Maureen—who, if I were to believe her, really did want a new life but could not break away from her brother, or he from her. I suspected that Aubrey Carew must feel a bit foolish, although he seemed to have recovered remarkably quickly. Over the last

"She was caught on camera stealing a pale-blue leather jacket from NINE on the night of her birthday. Detective Inspector Sue Brampton from Plymouth had a photograph of Jess that we wanted identified at the restaurant. That was why we were there that night."

"Why didn't you arrest Jess then?"

"We were after the bigger fish."

"Her brother?"

"Danny Coverdale is a hardened criminal. He engineered a highly successful car theft ring in London. Jess was the honey trap. She targeted wealthy married men on adult dating sights, lured them into a hotel room for"—he reddened—"sex and such. Sometimes she would give them a sleeping pill, but more often than not she waited until they fell asleep and stole their car keys. Danny or one of his crew would be ready to take the stolen vehicle to a safe location where the cars were sprayed a different color and the plates were changed. The vehicles were then shipped off to the Middle East."

I was astonished. "And it worked because Jess never stole money or credit cards." I thought of Rupert being left to walk home. "And the cheating husband would have to admit to his infidelity or make up some other story as to why his car had vanished."

"Exactly," said Shawn. "Poor Eric fell foul of Jess's charms. He lost an Audi Quattro."

"What about his wife, Vera?"

"He and Vera had been going through a rough patch," said Shawn. "One of Danny's team was caught and started talking. He made sure his sister didn't serve any time, but prison was hard for a pretty boy like him. He heard that Maureen had few days he'd asked Mum to repair his leather tunic and she'd eagerly obliged.

In fact, she had been in excellent spirits, having heard from her publisher. Apparently, Clara St. James loved *Ravished* and was very excited about the proposal for the next book in the series, *Betrayed*. All was well once more.

A fanfare of trumpets, followed by cheering crowds, announced the arrival of the king and his entourage.

"I can't see!" Mum exclaimed, and roughly elbowed a couple aside to get a better view.

Harry rode past on Thunder proudly carrying the king's colors and looking adorable in his outfit, but then I started to laugh. Just behind him was none other than Eric Pugsley! Despite the long wig, beard and mustache, it was hard to miss those signature eyebrows.

Mum was bitterly disappointed. "I don't believe it. I've been duped!" She turned away in disgust and bumped straight into the dowager countess. "Begging your pardon, milady, but I thought we'd get a real member of the Royal family."

"Never mind, Iris," said Edith. "I'll introduce you to the Princess Royal next month. She's patron of the Pony Club and we'll be holding a rally here at the Hall."

Edith went on to tell us that Cropper had spent days going through the vast attics and had finally located a portrait of Lady Eleanor Honeychurch. "It was probably put there centuries ago because it was damaged—a nasty slash across her face. I'm sure Katherine will know the right expert to restore it, and then of course she'll go back on the wall next to her sister Frances where she belongs."

"That's wonderful, milady," Mum enthused. "We were able

to locate the Parish registers and confirm that Nicholas Carew and Eleanor Honeychurch were married on May 22, 1646."

"Of course there's a black sheep in every family, but we don't need a daily reminder that Bootstrap Jim did such an unforgivable and evil thing. Aubrey and I have agreed that Eleanor will be buried next to Nicholas in the chapel at Carew Court. It seems the right thing to do. Perhaps they will be reunited in the afterlife."

It was toward the end of the day when Shawn came to the refreshment tent looking very flushed in his costume. On closer inspection, I saw he had his full police uniform on under his cape.

"You look hot," I said.

"You look beautiful," he said, then turned beet red. "Sorry. Can we talk?"

Leaving Mrs. Cropper to man the refreshment tent, I followed Shawn out where he made a beeline for an enormous oak tree.

"I couldn't tell you this before because I didn't want to jeopardize the investigation," he said. "I was working undercover that night I saw you at NINE."

"Oh, I didn't realize," I said.

"Piers had asked me to do a discreet background check on Jess—or should I say Maureen Coverdale—because he didn't trust her motives."

"You could have told me that," I said.

"Once I began to dig, other things came to light," said Shawn. "I do believe Jess . . . did care for Aubrey, but she just couldn't shake off her past—"

"Or her kleptomania," I put in.

changed her name and got married. The moment he was transferred to Ford Open Prison, he bolted. We knew he'd come after her."

"But how did they communicate?"

"Disposable phones," said Shawn. "Harry told me that he found one in the churchyard—"

"And Jess had the other," I said, and told him I'd seen hers in her handbag when she'd accidentally pulled it out by mistake.

"Danny used the mailbox at the barn for Jess to receive the pay-as-you-go phone and also the ferry tickets."

I distinctly remembered Muriel asking Jess about an upcoming trip to Roscoff. "So when Jess realized that Muriel was opening her letters ... she was worried that she would find out the truth."

"When we arrested them at the docks, the twins had two thousand dollars in cash."

"From the re-enactment money?" I asked.

"No. Fred Jarvis had embezzled the lot and more besides," said Shawn.

"The canary-yellow Kia?"

"Repossessed by the dealership," said Shawn. "Muriel faked her own robbery to save face. Violet told us that before they fell out over the roses Muriel had confided in her about Fred's gambling habit. She's devastated about losing her friend."

"Poor Muriel. So she had no plan to blackmail anyone, at all." I wondered if the missing pages of my mother's manuscript had just been accidentally dropped and slipped under the chair. I suspected we would never know.

"We got the report back from the coroner," said Shawn. "Muriel had an acute reaction to bleach cleaning fluid that you found in the vestry in St. Mary's. It brought on an asthma attack."

"And the pink Croc that was found in the Parish chest—?"

"It fell off when they moved the body in Fred's wheelbarrow," Shawn went on. "Using the white surplices from the vestry to cover her up—"

"Which Harry and Max believed were ghosts."

"There is just one thing I can't figure out," said Shawn. "Violet claims she saw two people which we obviously now realize were the twins in the churchyard—and they obviously saw her. Hence why her brakes were cut. Why was Iris's MINI in the Hare & Hounds car park that night?"

I decided to come clean—sort of. "It wasn't my mother," I said. "Lavinia had asked Alfred to follow Rupert. She was convinced he was having an affair. Alfred agreed."

"An affair with Pippa Carmichael?" said Shawn. "Is that what you were doing at Bridge Cottage?"

"Danny Coverdale stole Rupert's Range Rover from their rendezvous at Bridge Cottage. If you cut across the field behind the church where he had been hiding out, it's right there. He must have been watching them."

"There is something I need to show you." Shawn pulled out a note from inside his cape. "The letter you allegedly wrote to Violet asking her to pick up the dowager countess at the railway station. As you see, it was signed by you."

I read it and yes, it was signed by me, but it was definitely not my handwriting. And then I remembered the birthday card from Jess. Above each letter *i* was a heart. "I'd like to show you something that will clear my name," I said. "Do you have time to come back with me this afternoon to Jane's Cottage?"

"No need. I will take your word for it." Suddenly Shawn grew serious. "I don't mention my wife very much, Kat. She was my soul mate and my best friend. Helen gave me two beautiful sons. I can't believe it's been two years since she passed away." He looked deeply into my eyes. "I like you very much; you know that. I just need time."

I nodded. I wasn't sure what else I could say. Of course, I understood that and I was sorry for Shawn and yes, I liked him, too. But I'd heard those words from another man.

"Why don't we just start off as friends," I said.

"Aren't we friends already?"

Later that evening, I heard a car pull up outside Jane's Cottage and opened the door to find Piers standing there holding an envelope.

Still dressed in his leather coat, breastplate and tawny orange sash of Cromwell's New Model Army, he looked particularly dashing.

Maybe it was his shoulder-length blond locks or perhaps it had been the way he'd handled his sword on the battlefield that afternoon, but suddenly I felt incredibly attracted to him. He reminded me of a hero in one of my mother's romance novels. I was still in costume myself and could see by his expression that the feeling was mutual.

Piers gave a sweeping bow. "I thought you'd like to know that Eleanor will be buried tomorrow next to Nicholas in the chapel at Carew Court." He touched the posy ring he was wearing on his pinkie. "I'll be leaving this with Eleanor, too."

"Good. I'm glad."

Piers handed me the envelope. "This is for you."

Inside were two tickets for a weekend in Paris—just as Lavinia had forewarned.

I laughed. "You're so predictable!"

"You don't seem surprised."

"Of course I'm not going to go to Paris with you."

He feigned hurt. "Why ever not? You can have your own room. I can assure you that I will be the perfect gentleman. I give you my solemn word. A Carew never breaks his word."

"What about Cassandra Bowden-Forbes?" I said. "Weren't you betrothed to marry at birth?"

"Yes, my parents had wanted that for us, but this is the twenty-first century and I shall marry whom I please," said Piers. "But I'm inviting you to Paris. Not the altar."

"True."

"You don't need to decide now." He took my hand and gallantly kissed it. "But at some point you've got to let go of the past, Katherine."

I thought of Eleanor and the life she had led so many hundreds of years ago, a life where women had no freedom and when she had the courage to follow her heart it had ended in an unspeakable betrayal and tragedy. I wondered what she would have done if she were me now.

"I'll even bring Mortimer as a chaperone," said Piers. "He's always wanted to visit the Eiffel Tower."

I laughed. "Who can resist being shown around Paris by a teddy bear?"